WHAT'S RIGHT WITH YOU?

'Stars, hide your fires; let not light see my black and deep desires.'

—*William Shakespeare*

WHAT'S RIGHT WITH YOU?

THOMAS ISEBECK

Smoldering ceramic sarcophagi
In the cold moonlight
Their tired eyes
Devoid of direction
Deprived of desire
The two of them yearning
The other two at rest

His build so strong; Her figure immaculate
　　Yet without resolve
　　　　Against its icy breath

Perfect silence–
Still as death
Too sudden; Too soon
This dawn of nightfall

1 SAMUEL

My *eyes shut tight,* twitching from side to side. The sound of rubber tires against tar and rumbling engines saturates the air. I hold my breath, listening, focused on separating the two frequencies: the high-pitched oncoming and low-pitched outgoing traffic. My right heel is raised. The instant the higher reverberation drops below the threshold volume, I dash across the street. My footsteps resonate off the tarmac. The second I get to the other side, the whirring engines doppler shift to a low growl. A hooter blares as if meaning to foul-mouth my reckless behaviour, but my mischievous grin makes it apparent just how much I care. I cough when a veil of warm exhaust fumes passes over my face. I wonder if it will not work out the way I intended one day. But then again, I'm not so sure which outcome *is* my intention.

When my mum had told me that she and I would be moving, I was a little sad, a little scared, but mostly excited. What harm could a change in scenery do?

The city of Xys, however, was not quite what I had in mind when it came into view a couple of days after departing from Pennsylvania. I've heard such good things about Wales. Xys, although in Wales, is nothing like it. It's dull. It's dark. More so, the people who live here are no friendlier than the ominous atmosphere. The sidewalks are filled to capacity by pedestrians, as though everyone is constantly trying to get somewhere other than where they find themselves.

At present, I am on my way home from university. This one, I would find marginally more bearable than my last if it were not for my biology lecturer: his hostile nature irks me terribly. Thankfully, I don't rely on him much. Instead, I study hard and try to be vigilant in carrying out tasks. I used to care little for my studies. Now, however, I treat it as a measurement of my capabilities. Besides, if one can't pass simple tests, how can they be of use later on?

My eyes track the path ahead. The next leg of my journey follows a winding street that is narrower than that of the main road in the city. I walk across the bridge over Caister River, which connects the area, where the university is situated, to the suburb where I reside. The murky echoes of traffic soon fade, and the local park passes me by.

Soon after, I arrive at my house. I put the newspaper under my arm and slide the key into the door.

'Mum!' I call out. 'I'm home.'

I open the door and am immersed in silence. Mum is probably somewhere that she can drink away her sorrows. She has been this way for a long time, ever since Father left at least. Though, she does a fine job of hiding her lack of sobriety. I can't blame her for the most part: living in this decrepit town is easier said than done. And I can't imagine being separated from a person you've loved for so long. I can sense her pain runs deep below the surface.

I toss the keys into a dainty porcelain bowl. My eyes scan the gloomy space. The windows are terribly old-fashioned, with their arch-shaped grids of glass allowing soft, white light to diffuse through the dust on their surface. I walk up the staircase and enter my room, tossing my bag onto my chair. I then slump down onto my bed.

My head flicks sideways when something scurries along my bedside table. My gaze tracks a black and yellow spider making its way up my lamp. Its legs move as if they were mechanical. It then appears to float through the air on its virtually invisible thread. All eight of its shiny, black eyes are unmoving. In fact, spiders do not have the ability to move their eyes inside their sockets, nor do they have eyelashes. Their eyes function similarly to telescopes: they have lenses that remain fixed, and their retinas shift backwards and forwards to focus. A jumping spider has a total of four photoreceptor layers, which they use to gauge distances with unparalleled accuracy.

I admire the creature for its graceful actions. Yet, it does not know it. There is no way for it to know its elegance. It crawls back up the thread and springs onto the chandelier hanging from the roof. It then leaps out of my sight.

My room, like the rest of the house, lacks liveliness and doesn't exactly portray a space that one would deem homely. Mum and I had to settle for this piece of rubble that was sold for next to nothing at an auction. The wallpaper is uninspiring, and although the floor skirtings were once decorative, now their peeling paint gives them a tattered look. We have plans to fix it up at some point, but we don't really know where to start.

I reminisce about all the things that we used to do as a family, back when I still had a healthy relationship with my parents. We used to go camping on the weekends. We'd meander through the forests or find a river to guide us far into the wilderness and back. At that stage, I still needed Father's help to pitch the tent. I wonder how it all managed to change so very quickly. Now, it seems even Mum and I have become somewhat distant.

Footsteps click on the wooden stairs. It must be her right now. I swing my door open and walk over to the top of the staircase, but the stairs are vacant. When I turn back, the door is now shut. I simply shake my head.

It was probably a sign that I need some fresh air. I hurry downstairs, step outside, and walk across the black tiles leading from our front door to the street. I peer over my left shoulder to see two lines of glowing yellow lamps along the pavement. The sun is just about to dip below the horizon. As always, the air is drenched in silence. I walk along the sidewalk for a few blocks. Each picket fence that surrounds their respective properties is washed out from the moisture, and all of the residences on our block, ours included, are painted in dull, pastel colours. Or, perhaps they just became that way over time. It's difficult to tell.

A dense fog rests just above the ground, which makes the buildings levitate on either side of the street. Our property slowly fades as I become entranced by the rhythmic sound of my footsteps. The sidewalks extend before me, two parallel lines diminishing to a single point.

Just as I'm about to go back in the direction from which I came, I recognise the street I'm on. Sure enough, my house comes into view. I shrug, unable to remember the point at which I turned around. I decide that I shouldn't dwell on it. The house is just as peaceful as when I left it.

Mum is still not home, which is somewhat disconcerting. Instead of dwelling over it, I head out the front door and walk over to the garage. I grunt to open its metal door and step inside to find the pile of records, removing one from the shelf. I then go back inside and set it on the turntable. Mum always manages to find peace in a good 1920s jazz album. I think it reminds her of her childhood. All that's left to do now is wait for her to arrive.

HAZE

---

2 LUCINDA

The wind is still bitterly cold** at this hour, and Lucinda's eyes are slits. In her hands, she carries both a notebook and textbook, which she uses to shield a small portion of her body from the elements.

The path ahead of her is barely visible; shadows swallow parts of the sidewalk. Yet, she trudges on through the gust, trying to breathe calmly through her dry throat. The air is terribly thin.

Suddenly her entire body shudders, and, for a moment, she is standing perfectly still. Her knuckles turn pale as her fingers curl around the corners of her books. Her teeth chatter before she forces the breath out of her lungs. 'There's nothing there,' she whispers. 'There isn't anything there.' She begins to run along the street and looks to the sky as she goes over the bridge, stopping when she gets to the opposite side of it. She gazes back toward the road snaking off into the distance. 'They'll go away, I'm certain of it,' she tells herself while strutting forward. 'They never stay for long.'

Just as she says so, the sun appears above the horizon, slashing white streaks in the air that glow in the hazy clouds. She closes her eyes, feeling the warm rays on her skin. It manages to soothe her thoughts. Her fingers burn from the cold, though, to her, it's like having one's hands beside a fire on a winter's night.

She glances at her watch: 07:24. How will she make it before the lecture begins? She leaves the bridge behind her, hobbling along with her head down.

'Can't be late,' she mumbles.

Every so often, she inadvertently turns back to look over her shoulder. After noticing this pattern, she scolds herself. 'Stop being a fool.' At the same time, she implores her inner voice, whether it's fair that she cannot trust the eyes that she's been given.

At this point, she is engulfed by the city. All the movement and oppressive sounds cleanse her state of mind and make them disappear. One by one, they each return to where they came from, as though they were never even there in the first place.

She gets to the glass door outside of the university and leans against it for a second, checking her watch once more: 07:29. She knew she wouldn't be late. She brushes her fingers through her hair, walks into the building, and enters the hall. Keeping her eyes turned to the ground, she makes her way to the front row of seats, as they are seldom occupied.

After sitting down, she opens her notebook and takes out a sharp pencil. The hall is filled with the hum of conversation. Just as the lead touches the page, the lecturer, Mr Diaras, enters. Lucinda's expression is apathetic at best.

'What are you doing over there?' he snaps. This makes Lucinda jolt in her seat. The bustling ceases.

'We aren't children,' she says under her breath and figures he's nothing more than a pathetic soul, masked in a *façade* of smart attire and belittling speech.

He taps his pointer on the board and pauses for a moment before speaking again. 'The circulatory system is arguably the most important system in the body and carries out a wide variety of functions almost constantly.' He paces along the floor. 'It consists of capillaries, veins—' he pauses after scribbling the two points on the board, 'Obviously blood, etcetera,' he says, drawing dots down the length of the board. Lucinda looks tremendously unimpressed by the fact that he forgot about the heart when constructing the list. She rolls her eyes and lies on her arms, wondering why she even bothers to get herself here at this hour.

She looks to the ceiling. The lights flicker ever so slightly. This makes her dig her face into her sleeve, however, she can still see the flashes of white behind her eyelids. Something ricochets off of her shoulder. She doesn't budge, nor does she look back, knowing full well that it is just some idiot who finds it ever so amusing to send hate mail every so often. Whoever coined the phrase "all life has value" clearly wasn't thinking straight. Those bloody cretins can die as far as she's concerned.

Her forehead rests on the desk, and she holds her breath as her gaze fixates on the amorphous ball of garbage. She begins to reach down to retrieve it but hesitates. She shouldn't read it; she knows better than to do that. After some time, however, curiosity gets the better of her. She wonders whether they could even come up with a good insult. It urges her to uncrumple the letter. She skims over it, finding the usual repertoire: loopy... plutocrat... bloody halfwit... stupid dunce. That's rich coming from them. She is certain they are simply jealous, she tells herself, later questioning what exactly there is to be jealous of.

She re-shapes it into a ball once more and places it next to her seat, pretending nothing happened. All they want is to get some sort of reaction out of her; she won't give them the satisfaction. Instead, she hurriedly jots down diagrams from the textbook and begins covering up the labels, attempting to memorise different configurations of coccus bacteria. She figures it would do no harm to be at least somewhat productive, as the curriculum is terribly fast-paced. Directly after a massive assessment, the dates have been sent out for numerous others to follow. It's absurd. But such is the life of a student.

As soon as the lecture comes to an end, Lucinda abruptly stands up and shuffles through the hall. She fetches some books from her locker and leaves the building.

As usual, she returns to an empty mansion with nothing but paintings and statues to keep her company. She meanders along the passage and settles at her desk.

A vast number of snippets and cut-outs are pinned to the board above her desk. It's a collage of newspaper articles, poems, small prints of the paintings done by her favourite artists, and even quotes from plays. Alongside this hangs a photo of her mother, and she gazes at it distantly, wondering whether she'd be proud.

As her mother did, Lucinda holds the belief that knowledge is power. It may be impossible to grasp the influence foresight can have. It has the potential to change one's destiny and alter reality in ways never thought possible.

Sticking out from behind the snippets are glimpses of days in her past life in the form of long trails of papers that have the same phrase written over and over: "Ignorance is evil". She doesn't understand why she thought that way back then, nor does she want to. She has done impulsive, irrational things, which, at the time of doing them, seemed perfectly logical. Though, in hindsight, they make no sense at all. She is left none the wiser, with nothing to look back on other than chaos and deception happening in tandem.

She figures that all her thoughts were like that, at least up until the day when she experienced a transformation so sudden, so abrupt, and so absolute and conclusive, that she, in one defining moment, turned into a completely different person. Surely it was always meant to be that way.

She shakes her head, feeling that she's been caught up in her thoughts for too long. She lays her textbook on her desk, open on the current chapter. Her pen now glides smoothly across the paper of her notebook, capturing concepts previously mentioned in class and making sense of everything she reads.

Every so often, she looks out of her window to the city. It is a vast array of parallel structures, like black thorns rising from the ground and obscuring the colourless sky. She couldn't imagine working there one day, looking out of an office block window, only to see grids of glass on the other side, like prison bars.

Her eyes are drawn to the left, where her gaze traces a dark stream flowing down a valley. It creates a path of rich, green trees that climb up grey and red mountains, which are hardly recognisable behind the hazy sky. They look entirely bleak. It makes her wonder whether there is something beyond this life. If she were to go there one day, would she find something beautiful or just endless, barren land with nothing to offer? And when she looks within herself once she is older, the question lingers whether she'd feel just as desolate.

QUESTIONING

3 SAMUEL

The cool air on my neck draws me from my slumber. I sit up, feeling dazed. My back is aching, and, for some reason, my bed is as hard as a rock. I squint my eyes to see my house materialising before me. I'm outside somehow. I'm sitting on a white bench… outside my house. I scratch my head, entirely confuzzled. I never even noticed this bench yesterday, let alone fell asleep on it.

When I check my watch, I spring to my feet: my lecture started nine minutes ago! I let out a whine, stagger into my house, and grab my books before scooting down the road.

By the time I reach Caister Bridge, my lungs are on fire. I navigate past the pedestrians as best I can and walk like an inmate through the bright white corridors of the science faculty. When I get to the lecture hall, my efforts to sneak in unobtrusively are in vain.

'Ehemm...' pipes Mr Diaras. 'This, my friend, is the second time you have been late this week.' His expression can't hide his satisfaction.

'You don't always have to make it into a scene,' I retort. 'I don't have to be here.'

'Oh, is that so, Mr Onyx? I'll let the state of your grades decide that,' he says with the characteristic coldness I've come to expect from him. The darned test. Our results would have been released today. I grit my teeth at the feeling of disillusionment, tormented by the sound of smirking students. I have no choice but to sit down, defeated.

I usually hate tests, but I thought I managed to pull through on this one. It seems not. His attempts to make me out to be a fool may have been justified after all.

His monotonous voice soon becomes distant. I used to like biology back when I was decent at it. Now, either the tests are getting harder, or I'm getting blunter.

I find myself staring at a diagram of a heart, wondering what the odds of mine failing are. Is there a way to voluntarily induce a heart attack somehow? The thought makes me giggle, which soon becomes a quiet whimper. I take notes on impulse but struggle to engage my mind very much. I've been living in my head far too much lately. Then, just like that, yet another biology class comes to an end. I stack up my notes.

I'm in the corridors once more, unnerved by the clinical mood. I find my locker and curl my fingers over the lock's dial, a tad jarred by the cold steel. I just want to pack my books and get home. I glance to the side, noticing people are shooting me looks and giggling. I pull my locker door open, noticing a small amount of resistance, looking up just in time to see a bucket resting on the top of my locker lean forward before getting showered by icy water. It dangles below the locker now, connected to the door with a string; clearly the work of a tyrant.

Some just look at me with pity in their eyes, but a different group of students behind me are now in stitches. I turn back and glare at them, wondering which one of them is the perpetrator.

'A practical joke,' I say in a matter-of-fact tone, but loud enough for them to hear. 'I can't begin to fathom how one would find this funny, but I am thankful that I seem to have amused your small minds.' Their laughing ceases, and they look at me, seemingly aggravated.

A young lad steps forward. He looks to be in the same year as me, and I find myself wondering whether I've seen him before. 'Well, at least we're not completely unhinged!' he retorts. His grey socks are scrunched over his ankles, and his arms are short but stocky. Two others behind him shift their footing, undoubtedly his associates.

I give them a hostile look. 'I suppose there is some truth to your argument,' I say, approaching slowly, 'Nowadays, it feels as though I am stuck in some sort of nightmare with no beginning or end; no way to tell right from wrong,' I look him dead in the eye, 'and no consequences for your actions.'

The sounds around us have faded. Silent masses stare. I draw near to whisper in his ear, 'And you never know when I might just... crack.'

'You bloody psycho!' he yells and flings himself backwards. He sprints down the hall with flailing arms. I laugh menacingly. Pathetic. The other two brutes vanish into the crowd. A professor enters the hallway upon hearing the commotion. With this, the corridor begins moving again. The professor's perplexed look makes me even happier.

Then I see the notice board, and every bit of bliss is ripped straight out of me in an instant. I obtained forty-two percent. With my previous results, there is now no way I'd ever pass the semester. The numbers mock me, leer at me with total contempt, make me want to sink into the floor. I studied so hard for this exam and *believed* I would get what I deserved.

At the top of the board are the initials of those who did well. Envy consumes me, and the numbers don't lie. I'm simple. Dim-witted. Dull. Whatever you wish to call it.

I pass through the crowds, feeling nothing but shame. What do I have not to be ashamed of? How dare I think lowly of others when I, myself, have nothing to offer.

The students around me all seem so content about something. What is it they value which brings them so much purpose? What is it they are smiling about, laughing out loud for, and how am I so disconnected from it all? It feels as though there's nothing left for me here.

The number flashes in my head again, forty-two. It's the magic number! The answer to the universe, they say, according to some silly pop culture in which I play no part. Though, it's senseless to believe that. Of course, the magic number is zero. It represents nothing. If any other number represents a part of existence, zero represents the lack thereof. Clearly, *that* is the answer to the universe.

This all has to end. It has to stop at some point. Nothing lasts forever, they say, as a means to endure the burden of existence; as an excuse to suffer longer. I think what they fail to understand is that one chooses how long forever is.

My eyes defocus as I scamper over the bridge. I run and run, towards my home, feeling the burn in my legs, the last thing I will ever feel. My rasping lungs heave to keep me going, and I sob, for I will not need them any longer. I won't need these eyes. I won't need these hands. I won't need this beating heart.

I lift the garage door. The place feels as though it has been neglected for years and is entirely still. Thick dust swirls about the floor as I stride into the cavernous space with, for the first time in a while, an actual objective and intent. The weighted door hovers for a second before falling shut behind me. I fumble for the light switch, coating my fingers in dust— a single incandescent bulb burns.

Stacks of crates are lined up against the wall, filled with things that haven't been used in years. Things that are never to be used again. Obsolete things. Just like me.

I set one of them in the centre of the floor and drag myself to the other end of the room where the tool rack lies. My arms move impulsively, brushing against the line of items before stopping at a coil of black rope. I just watch my hands, in a detached sort of way, as they form a loop in the rope, wrapping it around itself a few times. At the other end, I tie it onto a beam in the ceiling with a bowline. I remember the day my father taught me how to tie that knot. It gives me a weird sort of nostalgia tainted with disdain. Who would have thought, he actually ended up helping me with something in the end.

I stand on the crate, which creaks under my feet. The rope hangs before me. Tears are streaming down my face, but it doesn't even feel as though I'm crying. On the inside, I'm calm as ever. Staring through the loop makes me excited. This simple piece of nylon cord is my way out of here. A one-way ticket that will take me far away from anything I have ever known. It will make me disappear.

It's over my neck. I like the way it feels gentle against my skin; it is so utterly reassuring. It's telling me that everything will be ok. I know now that it will be. 'Farewell,' I whisper. My foot kicks the crate from underneath me.

EXODUS

4 LUCINDA

When I'm in the garden, I can't help but smile. My unease is dispersed, but at the same time, I have an alternative source from which I can draw a more positive kind of energy.

I enjoy being able to look after something. I have no pets or siblings, but I feel as though the garden gives me a sense of purpose and pride. Not that the plants would die without my input, as there is plenty of rain, but keeping the plants looking in tip-top condition is most gratifying.

Our garden is spectacularly large but cannot be seen from the road, as it lies at the back of our house. I've divided the garden into six sections, and, if need be, I go about my work on the part of the garden that looks the most unkempt.

My father and I used to collect plants outside of the city. Every time we'd venture there, we find at least one new species, and so our garden is remarkably diverse. Sometimes we brought home plants simply because they attract a certain variety of insects. Though they only make their appearance when the weather is warm enough.

I pick up a garden fork and spike it into the grass before jumping onto it with both my feet so that the prongs sink into the soil. This keeps the roots aerated. My eyes scan the garden's edge, inspecting the row of roses. I walk across the lawn and enter the shed. It's too dark to see anything, but I manage to feel for the pair of gardening scissors.

The garden is semi-circular in shape. The veggie patch, to the left, is sheltered by a translucent cover to prevent the rain from uprooting any new saplings. To the right is the flowerbed. In the centre is the lawn, whose back is enclosed by a thicket of bamboo and various types of trees.

I remove my shoes and slide my foot in an arc across the due-coated grass and watch its blades flick up from under my toes. The fine mist forms miniature rainbows around my feet. I proceed towards the roses, which are due to be pruned. A fair bit of pressure is required to sever the stems.

Once satisfied with the first bush, I move to the right and take on the next. I start to hear it: the crunching sound of my scissors as they cut the stringy lateral shoots. And I watch as a blossom, tainted with black, spirals downwards, shedding some of the dried-out petals that float down beside it. And there it lies, utterly powerless and with no hope of ever returning to how it was before. Not that it could have… I suppose it was only a matter of time before every blossom will eventually fall off on its own. Their only purpose is to ensure the survival of their species. But here, in our garden, they have no purpose. No matter how sublime their petals are, they are equally superfluous: when autumn comes, the flower will swiftly die and disperse seeds, but in Xys, the rain washes away the topsoil too frequently for the seeds to take root. They will never grow.

I wonder if I'm any different. No. I have to be different: I'm a complex life form, able to make my own decisions… but to what end? And what difference do I make in the larger scheme of anything, for that matter? Am I simply a solitary flower that will inevitably crumble into a swirling, perpetual mess; to go to where we are all destined?

'Are you there, mother!' I yell into the sky, 'If you're there, I'd like to see you! I'd like to know who you are!' My eyes squint but see only the bleak clouds idling across the hazy heavens. 'Curse my existence!' I hurl the scissors to my right, which stick into the ground.

I sit down on the cool grass beneath me and hug myself, taking a deep breath. I'm simply being daft: it must be some sort of phase that all people go through. I should just have some faith for a change.

FUTILITY

5 SAMUEL

I*t's not the pain that gets to me;* it's the pure magnitude of it all. I begin to wonder whether I even wanted this. The finality of the situation begins to settle in: there's no turning back from here. I feel even more empty than I've ever been. My unblinking eyes stare forward but see nothing. My ears hear my heartbeat getting louder and louder, reducing in tempo.

The cardiovascular system is swift to react when one's air supply is cut off. I feel the mechanism slowing down to conserve every oxygenated blood cell that remains. Other things begin changing as well, such as the way my mind shifts its perspective. It shows me a holistic view of my life, and it's as though I'm experiencing the entirety of my past in just moments. Long-forgotten times surface. Times I used to visit my friends and laugh with the warm spring breeze on my cheeks. I remember my birthdays and running through the rain without a trace of worry. I see my mum happily married to the love of her life. I realise that I'm not an isolated entity; I will always be tied to others in some way. What will my mum think of me when she eventually finds me here? What will she think of herself? She'd feel lost and confused. She'd feel like a failure... exactly how I feel. That's not what I intended. What have I done?

I grab hold of the rope above me and fling myself around, attempting to, by some miracle, break free. The chord stays put. My entire body longs to escape. It craves life because it sees no alternative. My arms have no strength left to pull myself up onto the beam. I see pliers hanging on the tool rack, merely meters away. I start swinging. My feet attempt to grapple it, but instead, knock the bloody thing off the shelf. It strikes the floor and bounces out of reach.

My muscles feel utterly drained, and the pain in my chest is too acute to ignore. The funny thing is that I know exactly why it's hurting so much: every cavity in my lungs is being flooded with carbon dioxide, which is redistributing into my bloodstream. The body creates agony out of nothing in order to preserve its existence.

My legs spontaneously swing out again, craving to clasp anything off the shelf that may help me. It's unlike anything I've ever experienced: my eyes see my struggling in such clarity, but my ears hear no pining voice to accompany it, almost like a movie with no sound.

I sway yet another time. My bare feet grapple something cold: a tool of sorts. I pinch my legs to keep it locked in place. My hand tentatively reaches down and clutches it. I hold it out, inches from my face, but can't make out what it is as my vision is covered in black spots and pulsating white rings.

I guess this portrayal of reality would appear quite pretty had it not been for the circumstances.

My thumb finds a slider on the oblong object, and I feel a sharp sting across my fingers. It has to be some sort of blade. Reaching over my head, I try to sever the rope, slicing frantically, but can't gauge my progress, and soon I am overcome by exhaustion. My arm, feeling like solid iron, drops to my side. My salvation clatters across the floor.

I feel like I'm falling from this world; escaping from it; going somewhere else. The spots begin drifting downward, falling from a pale sky. Below is nothing but all-consuming darkness. Is this real? Is this what the after-world looks like? How can it be so? I still feel my fiery temples; my icy fingers still sting like frost. Surely the after world wouldn't make me bear the burden of pain.

Then the opaque barrier vanishes completely. I'm breathing. I'm still here in the dust-ridden garage. The rope snapped. Life and death were merely inches apart, and I chose the former. Though, that's not what I chose. I chose to die. I deserved to die. My mind tricked me into seeing it differently; the same mind which caused me to do it in the first place. Yet now, it all seems so hazy, as though it happened years ago.

I scold my arm lying in front of me, producing a trail of deep mahogany liquid that expands across the floor, pooling about a thin piece of metal. My limbs briefly feel separate from my body, but I gradually seem to regain control. I sit up. My neck feels bound by a ring of fire.

I clutch the soaked blade between my fingers. It's a simple utility knife used for precise scoring. I can't quite tell whether it just saved me or simply prolonged my misery. I set it down beside me and took off my shirt to wrap it around my palm. I flinch when I ball my hand into a fist. The cotton quickly turns a rich red, and I like the way it runs across the material fibres as if they were rivers flowing down an escarpment. I stagger to my feet and walk like a lost spirit, fleeing surreptitiously from his grave.

I should've known it wouldn't turn out so simple; nothing in life ever is. I come to realise that what just happened was nothing new. I've merely done what I've always done: I've failed once more. I failed at everything I could have in my life, and I failed, as well, to end it. Even so, an underlying feeling of restlessness remains. I know what it means: today was not the end, but I can feel how near it is. It's standing right beside me in comforting silence, almost like the friend I never had.

FEY

6 LUCINDA

All is dark. All is silent. A mechanical pop echoes through the hall as the spotlight strikes a red curtain. The low bustle of the crowd expresses excitement. As the velvety cloth parts, a beam of light falls onto a solitary dancer, who draws the sweetest melody from the strings of a violin on her shoulder. She strides across centre-stage as the melody progresses, increasing in tempo and pitch. She pauses on the highest note of the scale as the entire stage lights up, revealing an orchestra. One by one, the musicians fall in, enriching the sound.

She places her instrument aside and is joined by a row of men in white socks and black waistcoats. She is carried, like a dove gliding through the air, her hand reaching upwards. Suddenly, five more twirling ballerinas enter on stage, each finding a partner. The sound of the ensemble guides their movements.

I am utterly fixated and can't take my eyes off them, not even for a second. I feel torn between bliss and envy, thinking about what it would be like to inspire hundreds of people with a single act; to have perfected an art that is so technical yet equally effortless. I then feel no detachment: I am them. I am simultaneously the fluid forms, who balance on their toes, and powerful, yet reserved figures who let their partners defy gravity.

I can tell, just by the way the crowd reacts to the closing of their final act, that we've all fallen in love with them. They stand there for a moment, each partner bound by their arms, before bowing their heads as the crowd erupts once more. I feel my hand gripping my seat and sense an astringent desire. A sort of aching that isn't satisfied with merely spectating. At that point, the thing I need most is to *be* them. I need to know what it's like to capture the hearts of hundreds and take them to your place of fulfilment, where you feel whole and free. Even as the curtains close, my father and I just sit there, almost in denial of the performance coming to an end. But when we finally do leave our seats, it's almost as if a part of us remains behind, still spectating in faded reminiscence.

Then, it's swept from our minds as we exit the macrocosm of the theatre and embrace the sharp wind ripping through the streets. We barely say a word, just the odd mumble here and there.

I always find it difficult to let go when I've seen something incredible. My mind holds onto every bit of it, ensuring I don't forget, and this time is no different. I settle down for some studying, but only half of me is present; the other half is craving an experience that is now gone. It needs that moment back to fill a void that it, in itself, created.

After twenty minutes of study, I make little progress, so I decide to take a shower. The water is soothing and makes me less agitated. I then stand in the steam, brushing my hair and taking deep breaths. I didn't think that a ballet performance could have such a profound effect on me. If I'd have known, I... I do not know what I'd have done differently. I can't help but wonder what I could have been had I taken my dancing lessons more seriously. My father gave me ample opportunity to become something great, but I simply did not have the drive for it, and so all the dancing lessons I went to translated into an unsatisfactory level of competence. In hindsight, I realise it was a mistake not to have taken advantage of the opportunity.

I get into bed and stare at the golden outline of my door in the dark. *It's* right there, just outside my room. I can feel its menacing presence rippling through the air. It's scolding me with indifference. I retreat under my duvet but stick my head out just enough to see it under the doorframe: the silhouette of flat-toed ballet shoes.

DEPLORATION

7 SAMUEL

I *lie on the sidewalk*, staring up at the swirling mass above. In Xys, it constantly seems as though a thunderstorm is on the horizon, with electric clouds coating the sky, just itching for a massive bolt of lightning to act as the catalyst for a downpour. I've grown to enjoy the climate. There is a window period just after the rain falls, during which the air is pristine.

A delightful smell passes over me, so I step inside the house to investigate. Bacon sizzles on the stove beside a pot of boiling vegetables. I take out a pan and light a match, after which I crack an egg in the centre. To my disappointment, the yolk bursts open. It's worsened when I try to flip the thing. By the time it's on the plate, one wouldn't be able to tell whether I was attempting a fried or scrambled egg because neither would fit the description.

My mum enters the kitchen in her gown and slippers. 'Oh, thank you, poppet,' she tells me.

I blink. It's embarrassing when she calls me that. 'Morning,' I reply while dicing an onion, scrunching my eyes at the acidic aroma. 'Please, take a seat,' I offer and walk over to the table, pulling one out for my mum. I crack another egg for her, managing to keep this one intact.

She praises me when I plate up the food. I remind her that she did most of the work. Mum never takes credit for things like that.

'I need to be off,' I say, checking my watch.

'Thank you for breakfast,' she says, 'I'll see you later.'

I unlock the front door and slip the key into my pocket. My mind is submerged in thought. I can't help but feel sorry for Mum. In spite of her past, she tries so hard to be happy. I think of how she would react if she were to find out about what happened in the garage but quickly brush aside the thought. I unconsciously pull my sleeve over my hand, ensuring the cut is not visible.

Before entering the university, I pause outside the entrance and look up at the massive building block above me. This monstrosity belongs to the faculty of the sciences. The building is shaped like an 'H' when viewed from above. In front of the entrance lie three silver flag poles, each with a word embroidered on their surface: 'love' and 'hope' on the outer ones; the middle one says 'life'. What are they meant to be, inspiring or something? If anything, they do a better job at getting on my nerves; simply reminding me of that which I have a complete disregard for.

I walk through the centre of the sciences building. The seemingly identical law building now lies ahead of me, though I've never bothered to go into it. I figured it would match the first, only with different room labels.

Now I am in the university garden. It's a square piece of land enclosed between the two buildings. A handful of trees dot the garden. Right in the centre of the garden lies a sundial, acting as some sort of relic. Ironically, there is too little sun to make it worthwhile. I turn right and cut over the grass, then exit the garden where the two buildings form a gap. The faculty of the arts lies ahead. To be perfectly honest, it looks more like a fort than anything else. It has sandstone walls and frosted windows. It is also slightly raised above ground level, with jagged stairs leading up to the entrance.

Despite its appearance, the atmosphere within bustles with excitement. One can hear faint melodies of musicians on instruments. Those walking through the halls are not your average student. There are dancers in ballet costumes and many with paint-ridden clothes, carrying portfolio cases or folders containing artworks. Others lug around their instruments.

I turn left into one of the first classrooms in the corridor and sit down. This is where my literature club is held.

'Good day, class,' says Mrs Miller, the coordinator. 'How are you?' she asks and, without waiting for a response, she adds, 'I'm fine as well, thank you, for today is a particularly good morning. It appears that all of you seem quite cheerful.'

As usual, I am sitting in the back row of seats so as not to draw attention to myself. It was mandatory to be a part of a club during one's first year of studies. I can't tell why I took a liking to this particular class. We could join many interesting clubs at the beginning of the year. I was initially part of the archery club before discovering just how uncoordinated I was and silently leaving.

Even though I like art, I'm no good at it, so any club involving painting or design wasn't an option. I figured that people interested in literature wouldn't likely make my life a nightmare, more like the quiet ones who simply let each other get on with it. Now that I'm in my third year, I'm no longer required to be here, but I suppose I may have grown a little sentimental.

'I assume that all those wide smiles are because each of you is well aware of the fact that today is National Poetry Day.' The students scoff. As if we would have known such a trivial piece of information.

'This day is dedicated to the love of poetry and spreading the joy and inspiration it brings. With that in mind, we shall be hearing a poem today. It is entitled: "When it strikes".'

She removes a little black book from her desk. I notice how chaotic her work is, with books and office supplies strewn all over the desk. Her hair is equally chaotic. There is English terminology scribbled on her whiteboard because, apart from running the club, she is also an English lecturer. She wears a polar neck and jeans. Her elderly features create an aura of wisdom, but her friendly appearance never leaves her. She reads from the book:

Hope is your destiny
It will take your fate and seal it
Sometimes it may seem lost as a drifting leaf,
But when it strikes, you'll feel it

Passion is your friend
A force we cannot forsake
It will show itself when least expected,
But when it strikes, you'll shake

Love is your purpose
Fiercer than the burning desert sun
Yet gentler than the midnight moon glow
It may feel as though it can never be found,
But when it strikes, you'll know.

'This poem shows us how unexpectedly we can stumble across feelings that can change our lives forever. Within an instant, we can be swayed; urged to do things we may had never considered before. They are inevitable. We must not fear them; rather, we should be ready to embrace them when they become real and dare to let them lead us.'

I grin at the overly optimistic piece of writing. Hope, passion, love. Where do they lead us? What is there to be hopeful of? When are we meant to feel passion? And how can someone love another when they cannot love themselves?

'I implore you to remember these words,' she continues, 'Particularly when you embrace the many challenges that you will face from this day forth. If they are not already on your doorsteps, they will arrive.' She shows a hint of sadness. 'It may seem as though I am addressing you with a departing speech. That is because I am.' Some gasp. Others whimper a little. Many just look disappointed.

'Bearing that in mind, I would like to end my time here on a positive note,' she says with composure, but her eyes are hollow. 'Each of you is to write a poem of your own as a culmination of all that you have learnt thus far in my class. It should be a descriptive piece based on your holistic experience of life. Anything from your views to your feelings or attitudes. It may be happy, sad, or even a tad scary, as long as it is true to yourself. I believe that this classroom has exposed you to numerous great works from many great writers. For that reason, you all possess the skills required to carry out such a task.' She looks around the room, 'Questions?' When no one speaks, she adds, 'I wish you all the very best of luck.'

SEVERANCE

8 LUCINDA

Paint *splashes about*. The brush surges across the canvas as Lucinda frantically tries to finish her artwork. She has until the sun goes down.

The Art Faculty has the sort of buzzing atmosphere perfect for allowing the creative juices to flow. Painting is usually a timeless activity and a means of releasing pent-up energy. Except, now she feels the underlying pressure of the exhibition drawing nearer.

She wonders whether it is just to rush an expression of the soul. This, however, does not deter her enthusiasm. Her work maintains fluidity as the sun arcs across the sky until she eventually lays down the very last stroke.

She is approached by her art lecturer, Mr Hopson, who noticed her backing away from the painting. 'That certainly was cutting it fine. Though, by the looks of it, more paint ended up on you than the canvas, Lucinda.' Few students major in painting, so Mr Hopson has become quite familiar with each of them. Despite his spontaneous nature as an art lecturer, his suit and neatly-trimmed moustache are spotless.

She looks to her hair and dress. 'Oh, it seems so,' she says, attempting to wipe her face clean with her fingers, inadvertently making black rings around her eyes.

'I never thought of you as a goth until now, Ms Perdita, but I am aware of the alarming rate at which you teenagers change your sense of "identity".'

'A goth?' asks Lucinda, perplexed. Mr Hopson laughs. 'Sir, do you think it will be dry by the exhibition?'

He eyes out the painting for a moment. 'I'm sure it will, but we'll be extra careful when moving it there.' She nods.

She's the only one left in the class, so she quickly goes to the sink and washes her hands. When she leaves, Mr Hopson stays behind, studying the other paintings.

Few still wander the grounds, but those who do act rather odd to Lucinda. They point at her and make strange faces. She walks up to a window and, upon seeing her reflection, even she can't help but chuckle. She looks ready for warfare, with grey smudges of paint on her face. She scurries to the nearest water fountain to clean it, then crosses the courtyard and enters the science building.

Every time she exits the art class, it serves as a reminder of the synthetic and inorganic feeling of the university environment. Painting surrounds her with colour and chaos, but here, the buildings are perfectly geometric, with white light hanging in the air like a monochrome veil.

She gets home to hear a pin-drop and sits on the leather couch without turning on the lights. In front of her lie various sculptures and ornaments her father has collected over the years. She sees only the outlines of their shapes, dimly illuminated by the moonlight.

One of them is a man in a crouching pose. She always wondered why her father had shown a particular interest in this sculpture. The figure is by no means elegant, made from rusted metal with jagged edges. Even the sizes of its limbs are not quite in proportion. Its hand covers its eyes as if it were trying to hide from something it can't bear the sight of.

'Lucinda,' comes a voice. She shudders. Did she imagine it?

'Lucinda, I'm here,' the voice sounds again, this time clear as day.

Her eyes dart around the room frantically. Could there be someone else here? Her gaze becomes fixed on the sculpture. To her horror, its mouth gradually spreads to a wide grin. It raises its head, and its fingers, like spines, come to rest by its side, revealing lifeless, metal eyes. Suddenly it is flying through the air as it leaps from its pedestal. It strikes the tiled floor, producing a metallic shockwave.

Lucinda yelps and desperately clambers over the back of the couch. Though, it continues pressing forward. Its hunched figure and large limbs are not quite humanoid. She yelps; her entire body is quivering with utter terror. Clank-clank-clank. Its obscure copper exterior moves in sets of abrupt steps. She blocks her ears, trying to drown out the sound, but it rattles her bones. She frantically searches the room. On the opposite wall, she sees her refuge: the light switch. She closes her eyes and dashes towards it. Panic pins her to the wall. Her trembling hand reaches up behind her back. When she flips the switch, the statue instantaneously disintegrates and is once more crouching on its pedestal.

Clank-clank-clank. 'Lucinda, I'm home.' It was just her father knocking at the door. She breathes a shaky breath, walks up to the door, and hesitantly unlocks it.

'Father, thank goodness!' She hugs him. Upon seeing her state, he pats her on the back.

'My word, Lucinda, you look as though you've seen a ghost. I forgot my keys inside the house when I left for work this morning.' She looks to the side to see his set of keys hanging on one of the hooks.

'I-It's… it's all right. All is well,' she says, trying to put on a convincing smile.

'Could've fooled me,' he says, concerned. She carries his briefcase in for him and does not make eye contact. She figures that cooking will help to lighten things up.

'I think I'll go and prepare dinner,' she says.

'Thank you, sweetheart,' he says, loosening his tie, still studying her. He then makes his way upstairs to get changed. She rubs her hand through her hair and scrunches her eyes shut, trying to come up with something to prepare.

She finds her mind is simply too frazzled to think clearly. Instead, decides to take a more pragmatic approach, turning on the stove and setting an oiled frying pan on top.

After sharpening the chopping knife on their set of water-stones, she holds it up, inspecting the blade. One by one, the ingredients seem to present themselves. She mixes lemon juice, parsley, green onion, and melted butter for a garnish. It smells, to her, like a fish dressing, so she opens the fridge, finding a fresh salmon her father must have bought recently. Soon the kitchen is filled with the tantalising aroma of seared fish and spices.

Lucinda enjoys cooking thoroughly. She does not see it as a chore. To her, it is an art form. Just like painting, it requires precision and practice. It took experimentation, but now she can produce several dishes with flavours that work well together. Many of the recipes she uses, she just so happened to stumble upon when reading some of the many cookbooks that her father owns. Others, she derived herself.

Fried vegetables and cream cheese, smeared over the salmon wedges, complete the dish. She dishes up in time for her father's arrival, who helps her lay the table.

'So how was your day?' he asks. Their dining room table is more than five meters long and oval in shape. It has only two chairs accompanying it now— one for Lucinda and the other for her father, both near the head of the table.

'I'd say it was above average,' she replies, 'I even managed to finish my artwork in time.'

'I never doubted you,' he says. After tasting the fish, he remarks, 'If I didn't know better, I would think that I was in an Italian restaurant.' He takes a sip of wine. 'Your mother had the same gift that you have. She could cook an entire stack of recipes straight from her head,' he looks dreamily at the ceiling. 'If only she were here to see the fine young woman you've become.'

She has a winsome smile. 'You give me far too much credit.' She sips her wine, mainly for her shattered nerves.

'No,' he says, assuming an Italian accent, 'I insist, madam. Perfetto!' he declares, raising his glass.

Lucinda struggles to suppress laughter, 'Grazie, signor,' she says, unable to ascertain how she could speak those words. Perhaps she visited Italy at some point.

After dinner, her father does the dishes, and so Lucinda is left to do as she pleases. She goes upstairs and falls backwards into the soft duvet. Her eyes defocus. Although she feels full, a strange sense of hunger is prominent. The wind picks up, and the house creeks. Her eyes turn to the ceiling rafters. Before she realises it, papers are flying about her room. She springs off the bed and begins lowering the window. As it slams shut, the grandfather clock chimes. She glances at her watch, deciding to head off to the exhibition. She goes downstairs, then looks back at the statue, just to make sure— she then walks out into the wind.

FRAGMENTATION

9 SAMUEL

Samuel walks down the street, grinning from ear to ear. The wind flicks his hair about in all directions, and he occasionally stumbles when a particularly large gust passes through. The vast, black storm clouds rumble overhead. His tie flutters over his shoulder, and he can hear the buildings creak. Every so often, a shutter or door slams like the crack of a whip. The streetlamps shake and flicker. None of these things, however, manage to get under his skin. He stretches his arms wide and zips along the sidewalk, inhaling the chaos with somewhat juvenile laughter.

When he enters the display hall, situated around the back of the faculty of the arts, he blinks a few times as his eyes to adjust to the light. He passes his hands through his hair. The hall is filled to the brim with a crowd which moves like liquid. All he sees are waistcoats and headscarves. As always, he makes his way to the left side of the hall to proceed with his methodical inspection of each artwork.

Each year, he is astounded by the level of craftsmanship that is so very evident. Few his age are at the exhibition; it appears to be more popular among parents and lecturers. The paintings seem to be grouped according to their content. There are works depicting old women with defined wrinkles and expressive eyes. There are running boys and country maids. He passes paintings of buildings with crumbling facades and tin roofs, later coming across some still-life: pottery and vases with flowers, along with fruits in ornate porcelain bowls painted in oil or acrylic.

He sees a painting of a coastal scene at night. It looks as though the colours were inverted, showing a single red moon whose reflection scatters across a pale sea. It has a blue-black nightglow in the background, and right in the centre is what looks to be the silhouette of a figure falling from the sky. What an interesting colour palette to use. He reads the initials in the bottom right corner: L. Perdita. He's seen that name before. In fact, he's seen it numerous times.

His mind is taken back to that day. For an instant, he's looking at the notice board once more, gazing at his hopeless grade being shown to the world. But it was at the top of the board where he saw those initials, among the lines reserved for those prestigious few who ranked higher than all the others. He is riddled with envy. They are proof that one can succeed, but at the same time, they taunt him when he isn't able to. How can they achieve top grades on tests he can barely even pass?

He looks away from the painting and moves towards the abstract section, surrounding himself with bright shapes and amorphous curves. Brightly-coloured lanterns hang overhead, along with the paintings, create an arrangement of scattered contours and vivid hues. He looks up towards the hanging, glowing spheres, then back at the paintings. The longer he stares, the more the pigments seem to swell and mix into one another, losing separation and form in the process. A wave of nausea passes over him. Before he knows it, he is pushing past the crowd, desperately trying to escape the kaleidoscope of overwhelming colours.

He sits on the first step outside the display hall and sighs, feeling he should have foreseen this. What is it with bright colours? It's not as though he'd get sick at the sight of a rainbow, so why now? At least he managed to see a fair number of paintings beforehand.

He checks his watch, almost hoping for some time to have passed. It would give him an excuse to leave. Perhaps it wasn't the best idea to come here after all. He looks directly out over the campus. Dark shadows are swaying from side to side: the people leaving the exhibition. Beyond that, he can see next to nothing; this draws him.

The university grounds appear quite welcoming in the evening, especially now that the wind seems to have diminished to a gentle puff. He walks around the back of the art building and crosses a dainty, wooden bridge. The path ahead of him disappears into darkness. Before long, it opens up to reveal a courtyard which the law building overlooks.

Brass statues pass him by. He figures cutting through the law building would shorten his journey. His footsteps echo through the empty halls, and he exits on the other side, expecting to see the main gate. Instead, another courtyard comes into view, looking identical to the first.

Among the statues, he stands, scouring the shadows for the bridge, figuring he must have just gotten muddled up. It is nowhere to be seen among the thick brush. The place gives him a strange sense of déjà vu.

For a second time, he hears his footsteps in the dark hallways of the law building. But, once again, he cannot find the bridge when he gets to the other side.

He collapses onto his knees, burying his hands in his face. His heart throbs in his temples. Why is this happening? How could he be lost? He's been here a million times before but can't seem to find the bridge. He sits at the base of one of the statues and sighs. With their hollow eyes, the brass figures leer at his pathetic existence.

'Howdy,' comes a voice. 'I was wondering whether something was troubling you, Sir.'

'Sir?' he looks up, perplexed, promptly feeling relieved to see another face, although not recognisable due to the lack of light. 'Thank heavens!' he exclaims.

'Whatever seems to be the matter?' she asks.

'I can't seem to find my way back to the faculty of arts.' He tries to mask how flustered he feels.

'I presume you to be a newcomer,' she says with a minor chuckle.

He goes quiet, embarrassed. 'Quite the contrary. I've been attending this university for a couple of years.'

She doesn't seem to know how to respond. 'It is odd that you are lost, then, don't you think?' He cannot see her expression but imagines her suppressing laughter.

'All right, all right. So, what brings you here?' he asks, trying to change the subject.

'Microbiology,' she says.

'I'm… doing the same degree,' he says.

'Yes, I recognise you,' she says and leans forward, emerging from the shadow cast by the statue. Her face looks friendly. She has a petite build and wears a blue Alice band in her light hair.

'As do I, you,' he says, a little awkwardly, 'W-Were you studying just now?' he asks, trying to keep the conversation going. She nods. 'It's quite late,' he adds.

'I'm not a morning person,' she says, crossing her arms. 'And what brings you here?' she asks.

'My course or being *here* particularly?' he asks.

'The former,' she says, a little irritated.

'Biology. Soon to specialise in microbiology if everything goes to plan,' he says, half-heartedly.

'Well, good luck to you then,' she says, trying to stay positive, despite his melancholic tone. 'In any case, would you like me to help you find your way?' she asks.

'I would be lying if I said I didn't need assistance,' he tells her, overcome with embarrassment.

'Follow me,' she says, grinning. They backtrack through the courtyard and under the arch. Then, as if by magic, the bridge appears in front of them.

He looks exasperated, 'I could've sworn—'

'There's nothing to be ashamed of,' she says, 'except for the fact that you got lost in a place that you know very well.' He has a smug grin when she looks back.

'I never caught your name, by the way,' he tells her.

'Charlotte,' she says. He nods, and they continue walking. 'Are you not going to tell me yours?'

'Oh,' he says, 'It's Samuel.' She titters as the exhibition comes into view. 'Thank you very much,' he says, holding out his hand. Charlotte shakes it awkwardly.

'Don't worry about it,' she says, 'Happens to the best of us.' She smiles politely.

'Have you seen the exhibition?' he asks.

'Yes,' she says, 'It's quite extraordinary.'

'Agreed,' he says, nodding, 'So you like art?' he asks.

'Of course,' she says, 'In whatever form it takes.'

'You should join the literature club,' he says, 'We're writing poems of our own for next week.'

'Interesting proposition,' she says, 'I may very well take you up on that offer.'

SCATTERBRAIN

10 LUCINDA

Lucinda *walks down the stairs,* rubbing her eyes. The kitchen smells of sweet syrup and butter. She inhales the aroma, noticing her father standing at the stove. He is cooking pancakes in a cloud of steam, wearing an apron over his usual work attire. 'Good morning, Father,' she says.

'It is, isn't it?' responds Jonathan.

'That smells wonderful,' says Lucinda.

'Let's hope that it tastes that way,' says her father, clearly cheerful. He flips a pancake with the spatula.

Lucinda decides to help out with the preparation and quickly whips up some cream. They have their breakfast topped with maple syrup. Lucinda's father then sets off.

'Have a nice day, Dear,' he says. She waves goodbye as he closes the door behind him. She finds herself wondering where he went, though it is too late to ask now.

Today is Sunday, so she is in no mood to work. She scans the numerous rows of books in her father's library. Most of them have been in her family for over five decades, and so some are quite ancient. She finds the language fascinating. Spoken English has changed so much in mere decades. Sometimes she stumbles across humour written in some of the older books. To be quite honest, she does find it amusing (not the actual jokes, but the fact that people back then found such odd things to be comical). Other really old texts are almost beyond her comprehension.

The library also contains a stack of books on wildlife, which, over the years, she and her father have taken an interest in. Even though his job requires him to be a CEO, Jonathan is a wildlife enthusiast at heart. She looks through a book about the natural world of North America and yearns to go there. There are strange animals, such as armadillos and beavers. She flips through the pages, noticing just how diverse the landscape is, ranging from coniferous forest to snowy tundra. A photo of a grey wolf catches her eye. It is a slender beast with a coat of dark ash on top and splendid white underneath. Its eyes are a captivating, deep-orange hue.

She slams the book shut: no point in hankering over something so out of reach. Perhaps she should simply set out and see what she can find right here, in the neighbourhood. Just as she is about to exit through the front door, it swings open. 'Oh, Father, you're back,' she acknowledges. 'Did you forget something?'

'Yes,' he says, 'My office keys.' He snatches them from the table and dangles them in the air, then places them in his suit pocket.

Lucinda simpers. 'Typical Father,' she says.

'It seems as though you were about to head out as well. To where might I ask?' enquires Jonathan.

'No-where specific,' she says foolishly. 'Just on a walk, I guess.' She has never lost her childlike curiosity.

'That's perfectly fine, as long as you're back before dark,' says Jonathan. Lucinda nods. 'I'm meeting with a few colleagues of mine this morning. I think we'll head over to the pub later on, so you don't have to make me dinner.'

'All right. I was wondering why you presumably had to work on a Sunday,' she teases. 'I'll see you later then.'

After her father leaves, she spends a good few hours wandering the vacant neighbourhood streets. Some foliage to the left draws her. Her footsteps veer off towards the park.

Where there are trees, there has to be life, she figures. She unconsciously stops at the swings and begins rocking back and forth. She likes how it makes her feel dizzy when she tilts her head back far enough. She then goes to the merry-go-round and spins it with her hand, patiently observing how it gradually slows to a stop. There are trees around her whose branches curl and twist. It reminds her of a Van Gough painting or even something Alfred Sisley may have done.

She sits on one end of the seesaw and stares at the other as if her concentration could somehow make it move. Lucinda wants to have friends but finds that she is isolated because of her academic prowess. Whenever she tries to strike up a conversation, it's as though others are intimidated by her. They think that she's a different type of being; that she is gifted. Yet, all she wants is someone to confide in and know that she means well. Doesn't everyone need friends? Is she ever to find someone she'd please?

The thought makes her feel terribly vulnerable, so she jumps off the swing and runs into the forest. She kicks her shoes off and kneels beside a small stream that winds its way through a grove of trees. To her disappointment, she finds nothing of interest. 'Water is meant to bring life,' she mutters.

The moment she has some spare time to think, the same hollow feeling returns. It makes her skin sting and her chest boil. She dunks her head into the crystal-clear stream to try and escape from it. Tiny bubbles rise through quartz pebbles on the streambed. The meniscus looks like liquid mercury swaying back and forth. She flicks her head out of the water and fills her lungs with fresh air. She then lies on her back, feeling the grass on her fingertips. The trees above her creak, swaying from side to side like the bony fingers of an old man. The wind is icy on her cheeks, but she finds a strange sense of comfort in the sensation.

She gazes up at the sky, and her mind begins to project objects onto the outlines of the moving clouds: a flower that seems to melt slowly into the earth, a smiling man whose grin becomes elongated and disfigured. Then a giant hand protrudes from the clouds. It draws ever nearer. Lucinda grimaces as she starts to make out the wrinkled skin and fingernails. She squeezes her eyes shut, hoping she's simply imagining, willing it to go away.

'Are you all right, Miss?' A man is peering over her, waving his hand in front of her face, trying to break her trance. He seems baffled by her dazed state.

She blinks a few times, 'I'm... I'm perfectly fine, thank you,' she responds, recognising him from somewhere she cannot place her finger on.

'Is that so? You look as pale as can be,' he observes.

'That's just my complexion, you see,' she says, laughing it off, 'Do I know you from somewhere, Sir?' She stands up, shivering, when water runs down her spine.

'Well, I own the antique shop down the road,' he says.

'Yes!' she says, snapping her fingers, feeling that she should have remembered. 'I haven't been there in a while. Perhaps I should visit again.'

'You're most welcome any time,' he says, grinning.

'What was your name again?' she asks.

'Graham,' he says.

'I'm Lucinda,' she says, feeling pleased that they have become acquainted. 'I am thankful that we have now properly met, Graham, ' she says and curtsies.

'Likewise.' After a short pause, he adds, 'There is a strong wind. You could catch a cold. Are you not chilled to the bone?' He looks a tad concerned.

'Not at all,' she says and, straight after, realises how odd she must be sounding. 'Well, not exactly,' she says, quieting down a little. 'I quite like the cold, you see.' She faces the trees and closes her eyes.

The man smiles. 'Why would anyone, in their right mind, be fond of the cold?' She considers this, wondering if she is, in fact, in her right mind.

'I suppose it's distracting.' Her fingers curl.

'Distracting? From what, exactly?' asks Graham.

Still with her closed eyes, Lucinda whispers to him, 'Sir, with all due respect, no one deserves to know that.'

The dark branches above them buckle and twist as a strong gust of wind causes them to bow under its breath. He looks up to the swaying trees.

'I'll take your word for it,' he says. Lucinda listens to his footsteps as he continues on his afternoon stroll.

'I'll be sure to come by your store again soon!' she adds as he walks off. He waves graciously. She stares at his white suit and hat, wondering whether she made a positive impression, but later concluding that it doesn't matter all that much in any case.

The sun is resting on the horizon at this point, and so she slips her shoes back on. By the time she gets home, the gale has dried her hair.

Most people who live in Xys think of the wind as an annoyance. Though, she has never seen it as such. On the contrary, she quite appreciates it. To her, it is more like a friend giving one a gentle push.

She enters through the front door of her house, not bothering to switch on any lights. Her fingers run across the surface of a soapstone sculpture. She stares at the paintings hanging on the walls. Without the lights on, the canvases look desaturated, and the sculptures appear ominous too.

She hurries upstairs so as not to give her mind a chance to begin with its nonsense again. Once in her room, she falls onto her bed and sinks into the quilted duvet. The house is silent with her father out. She sighs and hugs herself as though it would bring her comfort somehow, but her thoughts begin to spiral back to where they were. Soon she is overcome with a sense of hopelessness and dread that takes her by surprise, making her arms feel heavy.

She cannot begin to make sense of it: despite her life of abundance, she feels time passing, like her soul is slowly eroding. She realises it will eventually lose all of its integrity and fade into dust. Before that happens, she needs to know what it's like to be truly understood.

She feels the dark ceiling above her weighing down, making her seem small and insignificant. She falls backwards onto the covers, not daring to close her eyes.

DETACHED

11 SAMUEL

The class falls silent at the sound of Mrs Miller tapping the pointer on her black board. My fingers curl around the piece of paper on my desk. It's the poem I am to read. I feel an odd sense of confidence regarding the entire situation. I have not gone over my poem, though am sure that I can wing it.

Mrs Miller arrives, and students part to make way. It's difficult to believe that this is to be the last lesson Mrs Miller will ever present to us. The class immediately falls silent when she taps her pointer on the desk.

'Good day, students,' she says. 'I hope that all of you managed to conjure up a compelling piece of writing.'

As she tells us this, I begin to get tunnel vision. Perhaps I was a little overconfident in thinking that I did not even need to read my piece of writing beforehand. I look out the window and tilt my head up to see the Humanities building cutting out a piece of the sky.

'Well,' she says, 'who would like to begin?' She removes her arm warmers. I raise my hand, funnily enough. 'Would you?' she asks, looking at me, though I can't quite figure out why I happened to do that.

'N-No,' I stutter but begin to feel like an utter fool.

'Ok then,' she says, not quite knowing what to make of my response.

'I have a question,' I say, trying to rectify the situation.

'Go on,' she says.

'Is it all right if one's piece of writing is about something that's not entirely normal?' I wonder if my question pertained to my poem alone or if it also included my identity as a whole. Gosh, I'm overthinking this.

'Anything is acceptable in this class,' she reassures me. This is followed by a moment of silence.

I can't tell why I care for normality. Why do I let these thoughts wreak havoc? No one cares, so why should I? I find myself wishing that Mrs Miller would continue so as to take the attention off of me.

'I'll be happy to go first,' says a quiet voice that I instantly recognise. Her face confirms my assumption; it's Charlotte. She's in a spotless white dress with a green ribbon tied around her wrist. Her blonde hair is cut to shoulder length, different from when I first saw her. Her face is a little pale, and I can't help but feel sorry that she is going first. I would never have expected it since she seemed quite timid when I met her.

Perhaps she just did it for my sake. Did she feel obliged to divert the attention from me? It makes me feel uneasy.

She clears her throat, trying to conceal her nerves, to little avail. I hold my breath, hoping for her to find strength. Though she then begins:

All around me, nothingness
The night, the darkness, the abyss
But where I am is my refuge, my bliss
It is my garden of happiness

When my thoughts are bleak
And nothing seems to be going well
I go there, to my garden
So, on these thoughts, I do not dwell

It is wind-still and serene
In there, of my troubles, I am naïve
If I had it my way, the garden of happiness,
I would never leave

We applaud, though Charlotte appears shy from all the praise. Perhaps I should have written something more along those lines. Was I too honest in the swing of writing it? As the following poems are read, my stress levels intensify.

'Lucinda,' says Mrs Miller. 'Would you be so kind?' She skips to the front of the class, wearing an entirely black dress. Her skin is naturally pale. 'Thank you, Ms Perdita.'

I stare in disbelief: Ms Perdita? Lucinda Perdita! My eyes narrow. I now envy both her grades and confidence.

She turns to Mrs Miller. 'Would it be acceptable to sing my poem?' she asks.

'Certainly, that would be lovely.'

Sing? Now I have no doubt: she's utterly mad. The class tracks her movements. She holds her breath for a second, then begins:

If my soul were a letter,
Would you want to read it?
If my heart were an amethyst,
Would you string it around your neck?
If I were a single black rose,
Would you pick me from a field of white ones?

The stars shine brighter than the sun ever could
The winter wind is the warmth on my cheeks
I cross the bridge in my soul
With my head to the sky, for I know
I'd stumble at the sight of what lies below

But it is too grim, too dismal, too depraved
And so, the black rose may never be saved

We all applaud, and Lucinda curtseys. I watch in awe. That must have taken tremendous courage, courage that certainly paid off. She does have a sweet singing voice, so I suppose that her self-assurance is appropriate. I catch myself gazing for too long and quickly turn away.

I tell myself that I envy her, but now it feels as if it is in a different sort of way because I get the sense that she's somehow not as happy as I thought she was. What more do you need in life other than success? Why would *she*, of all people, speak of being saved? Saved from what? I rest my chin on my arms. It'd sure be interesting to know her. I think about talking to her after the class, but soon after, curse myself for it. She's the very reason I feel so incompetent.

As the next few names get called out, the tension is on a steady incline. At this point, I can't even listen to the poems. It is imperative that I execute this flawlessly. I hold out my hand and study how it trembles slightly. I then hold my breath, trying to calm down.

My name is called. I stand up and look around the classroom, noticing that I am the last one to read my poem—just my luck. Now, if I mess up, no one will be able to shrug it off; everyone will remember. I gulp and move to the front of the class, feeling like I am walking up to plead guilty before a court. I can't figure out why I am so nervous. It's not as though I have a reputation that could somehow be tarnished. My eyes scan the rows of heads. Lucinda is in the second row, showing me a thumbs-up. Why would she... When I blink, she is looking out the window with a slight smile on her face. Did I just imagine that? I cannot let petty things distract me at this point. I must put all my focus and attention on the task at hand. Everyone waits in anticipation. With that, I take a deep breath and begin:

Memories swirling, distorted, twisted
Merged to a fusion of disarray
Stepping on cracks between verity and fabrication
No line to tell night from day

Fearing your own actions
Running from your own dreams
Can't trust your own heart
Nothing is what it seems

Pleasure, happiness, sorrow, pain
Are they not one and the same?
All the things I knew to be true, forsaken
Does my mind speak the truth, or am I yet to awaken?

The class is filled with deathly silence. Everyone is staring at me with blank faces. Nobody blinks. Nobody breaths. It seems as though they want to make me feel uncomfortable. It sure is working. What in the world was I thinking? Why would I read something like that? People think I am strange as it is. Now, I have given them a reason to stray even further away. I could have lied or faked it, made myself out to be a completely different person— a likeable person, at the very least. But then again, would that have stood right with me? I do not know.

I look over to the brass clock hanging on the wall with its second-hand crawling over the face. My eyes dart around the class, desperate to find some sort of refuge. Will I just have to walk away in silence while everyone stares me down like this?

The coo of a dove abruptly breaks the stillness. With that, the students applaud. I breathe a sigh of relief and can feel the colour return to my cheeks. As per custom, I bow. I walk back to my chair and am thankful for the way that things to turned out. I would have regretted not being true to myself.

Mrs Miller stands up. 'Thank you, everyone! Your poems were fantastic!' she says, looking fulfilled. Though, after a few moments, a tear trickles down her cheek. 'These few months have, without a doubt, been a highlight of my career. You are all incredibly talented individuals. Use your skills,' she says, raising her fist. 'The world is a good place, but great literature makes it just that much better. It has been my honour to have worked with you.'

We exit the classroom as she waves goodbye to each of us. I can sense the nostalgia weighing down on us, almost like when you reach the end of a good piece of literature.

PARTING

12 SAMUEL

I *decide to go for a short walk* as the day draws to a close. Strolling through the neighbourhood lightens my mood and lets my mind wander. For the most part, I just look forward, allowing my surroundings to leave me behind.

I pass the local park, which isn't what it used to be in its prime. The apparatuses are coated with peeling paint that reveals their rusted metal structures. I struggle to imagine what they must have looked like the day they were built. Even the trees have managed to lose their leaves, and their branches cast jagged shadows that sway with the wind.

The road narrows slightly. I stop when I reach the centre of the bridge that overlooks Caister River. There are shallow, red mountains in the distance and vast, white grasslands in the foreground. I peer down over the railing.

The water originates at the horizon and flows from distant valleys until, eventually, trickling around the feet of the bridge about ten meters below me.

I put my legs over the railing and stare downward, imagining what it'd be like to fall off. Would I feel nothing; be peacefully swept away by the river? I guess that would depend on exactly how I were to fall— Though I don't let my impulses get the better of me. I just close my eyes and listen to the flowing water. It's calming. When I open my eyes again, I stare at the setting sun and track the snaking river, which makes a silvery trail, leading off into nowhere. When I peer from side to side, there couldn't be a more contrasting effect: to the left, minimal houses with oblique lines and picket fences, calm as a lake; to the right, towering business blocks with sharp, square corners; as restless as crashing waves. These two completely different worlds form a part of each passing day that I decide to put up with.

The sun is showing its very last golden sliver over the mountains, illuminating the ever-present clouds. I figure it is time to head home, feeling as though, for the past half-hour, I have been watching an insignificant time-lapse of my life passing me by. I wonder if that's a bad thing: boredom far beats excessive stress or, even worse, sadness.

On my way back, the wind begins to pick up significantly, almost pushing me in the opposite direction to where I'm going. I try my very best simply to ignore it. The white bench starts coming into view, with the gusts surging along the street, becoming increasingly loud and blocking out all other sounds. I sit down for a moment. When I do so, the wind immediately dies down. I take a deep breath and close my eyes to let my mind rest. I love the feeling of being isolated from the busy world and all the stresses that come with it. The street on either side of me curls away into blackness. There is no sound but the constant, light breeze that passes through the neighbourhood, moaning like spirits. I kind of like this place. There is nothing here of significance. I almost feel like I belong here.

Clack... clack... clack. Footsteps echo down the street. A lady in a black dress is drawing nearer. The streetlamps diffuse around the sharp edges of her silhouette like a lunar eclipse. Her hands are behind her back. I almost jolt when I recognise her. It's Lucinda. Why would she be in a place like this? Could it be that she wants to see me? It can't be, can it? She stops and tilts her head, studying me. The streetlamps reflect a ring of scarlet in her eye. For a split second, she is a surreal painting that I cannot take my eyes off. She takes a seat on the bench next to me, and my gaze quickly snaps downward. She *is* here to see me, but why?

I am filled with envy and confusion. Surely, she has no interest in a person like me: she is something great. I'm... nothing. 'Umm...' I mumble, not knowing whether I should speak or simply continue to wait in silence.

She is swift to reply. 'Nice evening, isn't it?'

A lump forms in my throat. 'Yes... it's quite calm at present,' I say, unable to elaborate. She stares forward and breathes in deeply.

'I wondered why you come here so often,' she says. 'I now know.' She closes her eyes, feeling the energy of the open space. Her sculpted nose and cheeks are pale, like silky linen, against her obsidian hair.

'Is that so?' I ask and begin to wonder, with unease, whether she had been observing me.

'Well, I know why I like it,' she says.

My eyes are turned the other way. It feels strange for her to be so near.

When I say nothing, she elaborates. 'It seems as though there is a void inside of me... and when I'm here, sitting on this bench, it's like I'm looking inside my soul.' I gaze at her for some time, trying to figure out what she is; all the while, she stares back at me. I can't establish what her intentions are.

'So, what's missing?' I ask.

'I can't quite tell,' she says, distantly. We both look across the neighbourhood, sensing each other's presence. This is the first time that I have been alone with a girl of my age. I thought I'd be nervous, but it seems not to be so. Even though no one speaks, it's the kind of pleasant silence that one gets when they're sitting beside a fire.

She places something on the bench. 'I want you to have this,' she says and presses the side of what looks to be a glass box. Something pops out, and she rotates it like a dial. When she releases her hand, a sweet melody plays. We both listen intently. The more we are absorbed by the tune, the more we begin to hear a haunting undertone that tinges the notes. I couldn't have asked for a more intriguing gift. Though, I don't know what she's getting at.

'How can I accept this?' I ask. 'I don't even know you.'

'Samuel,' she says, and I shudder when I hear her speak my name. 'I chose you.' Her voice is like a serpent. With a giggle, she scooches closer. Her hair casts a silvery shadow across her face. 'I know I don't know you so well,' she says and moves even closer. 'So, why don't we—' She takes my hand leans in. '—get to know each other.'

My eyes widen as she presses her lips onto mine, and I shiver as her icy hands move up my back. My entire body feels lighter than air; my hairs stand on end. In that moment, my mind is both serene and stirring with thousands of convoluted thoughts I cannot begin to comprehend. An intense buzzing runs through my bones. I feel a tinge of pain, and our kiss assumes a salty flavour, a taste I know all too well. She retracts abruptly, licking a crimson blemish from her lips.

'I'm sorry,' she whispers, her head low. 'I didn't mean—' The music box becomes quiet once more. She gets to her feet and begins to walk back along the street. Did she just bite my lip? I'm entirely dazed, struggling to make sense of any of it. Her footsteps echo in my head. I look at the glass box on the bench. She wants me to have it.

Am I just going to let her leave like that? I jump up and dart towards her. She stops, though she doesn't turn around. I take her chilled hand in mine. Her breath quickens.

'Lucinda,' I whisper, a little shakily. 'It's ok. I don't mind. I like you.' I can't comprehend where those words came from or whether they are even true. She squeezes my hand and pivots around to face me. She takes hold of me, and again, she giggles. Her slim fingers run up my torso and draw my neck closer. Her eyes jitter from side to side as they gaze into mine, as though she could somehow see what lies within me. Now, there's not even a trace of uncertainty in her face.

'Then I'll see you around, Samuel,' she says, and the intensity of her voice is frightening. Her hand brushes over my arm as she leaves. She looks like the embodiment of darkness as a flash of lightning reduces the neighbourhood to simple, monochrome polygons against a white sky. The heavens open, and another lightning bolt cracks, but she does not fear it; nor does she run. Instead, she stretches out her arms and feels the drops against her palms.

I watch until her figure fades against the dusky sky. My head is ringing with an energy of a different kind, one which I previously never knew. I stand up from the bench and walk along the path leading to my house. All the while, I cradle the box in my arms, cherishing it more than I ever would have known. I decide she must mean well; that I don't know her yet, but I will. And so, I cherish too, the greatest gift of all: someone who has chosen to care about me.

ACCEPTANCE

13 LUCINDA

My eyes are still open when the sun peaks through my window. Overnight, the storm has transitioned to complete stillness. I sigh. There's just no way I could have slept. My mind was far too busy. I wonder if what I did was rash. I mean, obviously, it wasn't. It was deliberate, calculated. But what if it appeared sporadic?

I switch on my bedside light, throw the duvet off, and walk over to the window. I breathe onto the glass and paint a squiggle in the layer of condensation, then sit at my dressing table. It's quite bland, apart from my mirror and necklaces. Makeup has never interested me; I've never felt obliged to make myself look different for others.

Much on impulse, I decide to wear a white dress to class. I usually choose darker colours, but perhaps I should challenge my patterns. My first lecture is only in four hours. I switch off the light and then creep along the passage so as not to wake my father. He doesn't usually wake up early.

When I open the door, the chilled air rushes past my face and is astringent in my throat. The faintest, orange glow on the horizon emanates from dimly lit cirrus clouds.

It takes only a short walk to reach my destination: the park. The icy ground crunches with each step I take. I slip off my shoes, and the turf creates a tingling sensation underfoot. My hand runs along the truck of a willow tree.

As soon as the sun peaks over the mountains, the frosted grass looks like glistening shards, entirely still in the wind. I hear the train passing just behind the tree line and walk forward, drawn to the sound. My bare feet jump from rock to rock to cross the stream, which is partially frozen over at this time of year. I haven't ventured this far before.

Dotting the area are small, half-circle objects. To my surprise, they turn out to be gravestones. Well, I suppose it is quite a fitting environment for a graveyard: it's peaceful in a way. I kneel and take a closer look at the tombs, using the back of my fingers to brush away a thin layer of frost from the granite surface. "Dan Stark, 1871-1934." I shuffle to the side a bit. "Lara Crayton, 1919-1971." She died only three years ago. I look past the trees for a brief moment, wondering whether my father might have known her.

I don't have a faith per se; I don't know whether I like the idea of an afterlife. Do we go somewhere after death? I don't think I'd want to. I hope to decompose into the earth; simply cease to exist if I had it my way.

Just then, a white marble stone captures my attention: "Emily Adler, 1927-1968." I stare at the grave, dusted with pale frost. My body feels rooted to the ground. This… is my mother's grave. At that moment, I can hear the wind but feel entirely numb. It's as though I wasn't even there, like the floating, forest haze was passing right through my chest, and the trees no longer cared for my existence. The streaks of light passing through the branches above are blurry trails.

Father told me that she'd been cremated. The person I so desperately wanted to know, who I *did* know just a few years back, is resting right here beneath the very ground on which I stand. It almost feels like betrayal, though I know better than to trust my judgement.

All the stories Father told me make me wonder what could have been. He said that she and I got along well; that she loved me with all her heart. Seeing photos of us three makes me wish for her return. She was the bravest person Father knew, the most determined person he had ever met; at least, that's what he tells me. Yet, on that fateful day, she could not find the strength to pull through.

If only I could recall just one thing, one moment with her. I close my eyes. Perhaps, then, I'd just be worse off because I'd fully comprehend what I've lost.

ETERNITY

14 SAMUEL

I jump out from under the covers the moment the first light enters my room, promptly hopping over to my desk. I expect to see the music box, but it isn't there anymore. How is it so? I search my entire room and even go downstairs to try and find it. I want to ask Mum if she knows where it is, but she doesn't appear to be here at the moment.

I can't say I'm not at least a tad disappointed by it all, and begin to wonder whether I'm delusional. What if none of it even happened in the first place? Something that I so desperately wanted to happen that it *did* happen— in my mind alone. Who was I kidding? How could Lucinda fancy a freak like me? It simply can't be the case; it never was.

A glance at my watch kicks me into gear. At this rate, I'll be late for class. I throw my books into my bag and scramble to put on my clothes. As I'm running down the stairs, I decide not to bother with breakfast today.

When I set foot on Caister bridge, I hear footsteps behind me. I immediately assume it's Lucinda; however, when I look back, I see I stand to be corrected. It is a girl, though. I'm frightened when I recognise her, though I should at least be friendly: she helped me find my way to the exhibition after all. She was the unlucky candidate who had to say her poem first. I can't ignore the way in which she approaches, skipping as though it were her birthday or something. I wrack my brain, trying to remember her name. How could I have forgotten? The teacher even called it out. 'Hello, Samuel,' she says. Just as she does, the sound of her voice makes me remember.

'Charlotte,' I respond. 'Fancy seeing you here.' She is wearing a plain white dress and doesn't seem to have a care in the world.

My head instinctively turns a little downward. 'Whatever happened to you?' I ask. 'You were quite shy before.'

'Well, the two of us *have* become acquainted. Second time's never as bad as the first.' I nod. 'Also, I wanted to know what's up with your hair.' she says, but then gasps at her forwardness. 'I mean… you know what I mean—'

'Sure do,' I say, not even marginally offended. 'I was born like this. It's genetic. My hair is just dark with a blonde streak. I'm sorry if it weirded you out.'

She chuckles. 'No need to apologise,' she says. 'In fact, you remind me of a Pink Floyd song.'

'What… are you talking about "Brain Damage"?' I ask.

'No…' she says, a little shocked by how I jumped to that conclusion. 'I mean "Eclipse". That's the song I'm thinking of,' she says. 'Your hair at least reminds me of it.' I'm a little flattered.

'Well, you remind me of a Stevie Wonder song,' I say.

'Nervous Breakdown?' she suggests and titters.

'She's a rainbow,' I say. She has a skew smile.

'Hardly accurate,' she says. She thinks for a moment. 'I think the look suits you, though.' I feel as though I want to say something, but she speaks first. 'You know, I think some people have the tendency to think worse of themselves than what they are in reality. Our feelings often do not project truth.' I don't say anything. 'Though on that note,' she says, 'I was wondering if you really feel that way. I mean what you described in your poem. I guess it was—' she trails off, then turns away. 'I'm sorry, you don't have to answer something that personal.'

I'm marginally amused by her taking an interest. She stares at her feet. I figure I might as well explain myself.

'I guess it was quite an accurate description, yes. It's alluding to when one has the sorts of feelings they have no control over. A feeling that you're lost, if you know what I mean. I don't know where I'm headed in life a lot of the time.' I laugh apprehensively. Perhaps I'm being too revealing.

'Oh,' she says, a little flustered. 'It must be difficult to live a life like that.' Her voice is timid.

'No—' I begin. 'I don't know,' I say, wondering whether others have those kinds of thoughts as well. I decide to leave out the part about sometimes intensely craving a way out. 'You know, it's great to have told someone. Still, no matter what, I am guaranteed an interesting life in a way,' I say, trying to lighten things up.

She laughs. 'Yes, that is so. Well, shine on you crazy diamond, I guess.' I almost find myself wanting to smile. The two of us arrive at the lecture hall a tad early. Mr Diaras looks at the both of us with disdain as if to tell Charlotte: 'Don't let this fool influence you.' She goes to sit down near the front and looks my way, expecting me to sit next to her. I look down, ashamed of who I am. Perhaps Mr Diaras is right. When I see Charlotte's smiling eyes, I can't help but feel sad for her, wondering if it's even possible for someone to value my company. I don't think she *wanted* to talk to me. She was simply trying to comfort me.

I shake my head and walk up the stairs to go and sit near the top row. It hurts me to do so, but it's for the best. She probably just doesn't know me well enough; thinks I'm a different person.

As I climb the first steps, I see Lucinda sitting in the middle of a row. She is staring forward, taking no notice of me. Now, I am entirely convinced that yesterday's incident never happened. I sit on one of the long, wooden benches, and after a few minutes, the students that were sitting close to me seem more spread out, as though I produce some sort of repulsion field. Perhaps my mind conjured it all up to escape for a while, to get away from my identity for just enough time to feel real again. My name starts echoing in my head. I get pulled from my thoughts as the sound becomes clearer: 'Samuel!' I look forward, startled. It's Mr Diaras. He has his hand in a fist, and his plump face is scrunched up.

'Huh?' I respond.

'Mr Onyx,' he says, 'your parents are working tirelessly to fund your studies at an institution like this, so you'd better think long and hard about which path you wish to take from this point onwards.' He looks infuriated. 'Please stand up for me,' he says. A wave of mutters passes through the hall. I heed his request, trying not to look at the rows of students, all eyeing me out.

'Mr Diaras,' I remark, 'I don't exactly see the point in this exercise.' His face is cold.

'Could you be so kind as to explain to everyone how arteries and veins only allow blood to flow in a single direction, seeing as you have been listening so *intently*?' he says, practically spitting.

I stare for a few seconds, wondering if what I'm witnessing is even legal. Either way, I've had enough of it.

'Oh, I'd be delighted to!' I say sarcastically. 'Would you mind if I do so using a demonstration?' I ask, feeling crazed. He looks puzzled. Without waiting for his response, I proceed with the explanation. 'You see...' I roll up my sleeve. 'Obviously, I would die if I were to cut the Radial Artery, so, for this demonstration, the Ulnar Artery and Basilic vein will suffice.' I reach into my pocket and take out the utility knife. The silver blade extends from its sheath: click-click-click-click-click. I take a quick breath and make two incisions in my left forearm, clamping them down with my right hand. I then hold my arm up for the students to observe and remove my fingers from the Ulnar Artery. Blood starts to trickle down my arm. 'As we can see, when I release the artery, the blood can flow.' I clamp down the artery once more and take my fingers off of the vein. 'However, this is not the case with the Basilic vein.' The blood ceases to flow, but it looks pretty on my white shirt, like red vines sprouting down my side. 'This is due to Venous valves that prohibit backward blood flow.' I look around the hall, but their faces seem blurry, and I can't make out their expressions.

I hear a commotion outside in the corridors; people yelling, the kind of subdued sound of a crowd. There seems to be a sea of light moving over the seats.

'Was that explanation to your liking?' I ask, virtually falling over. 'The only question now is: "Will all great Neptune's Ocean wash this blood clean from my hand?"' I implore, and I find myself finding the entire situation quite hilarious.

When I sway back and forth, I feel dizzy and ecstatic. I begin laughing unconsciously. Perhaps I was too hard on the poor guy. He's just going about doing his job as a lecturer. Now he has to put up with this hysterical situation. I hear someone yell, but it sounds muffled, as though it were underwater. I feel very weak, so I sit down and let my face rest on the table. It's completely numb but in a good way.

Then a giggle, clear as can be, fills the hall. My surroundings are blurred beyond recognition. Finally, I think, someone on my wavelength. I begin laughing along with whoever it is. I find myself staring at something moving in front of me.

'I can't see the board,' I say. My arms are moving all on their own, with white stripes starting to cover them. It looks pretty, I think, and all I see is red and white, and it feels like I'm dying again, but it doesn't matter because it looks so pretty, and the only place I want to be is here, and I like the feeling— I want to feel like this, it's warm and fluffy and cold and calm, all at once.

'How did you know I was fond of Macbeth?' I hear someone tell me in a hushed voice, which I, for some reason, recognise. I then begin to wonder why they are speaking to me because it's nighttime, and everyone should be asleep. There shouldn't be people talking in the nighttime, but I figure that I can go to sleep on my own and I don't need someone to say goodnight, and I let myself rest and wish them a good night as well, and I know that when I fall asleep, everything is going to be ok.

VENGEANCE

15 SAMUEL

My *mind is wrenched into consciousness.* I find myself lying in a hospital bed, covered by a thin sheet. The bright lights hanging over me don't help my feeling of faintness. All the walls are immaculate and a scent of disinfectant hangs in the air. My eyes focus on a woman's hand, holding a syringe containing a clear liquid.

'How are you feeling?' she asks, looming over the hospital bed. 'Want to tell me what happened?' she asks, just marginally irritated. I figure she's simply concerned.

I remain silent. Even I don't know quite what happened. I guess I felt possessed or something like that.

Her gaze pins me to the mattress while each beep of the heart rate monitor increases the intensity of her stare. I realise that I'm holding my breath.

Finally, she speaks. 'You are fortunate that your friend brought you in when she did. A severed artery can very easily be fatal. You underwent Haemorrhagic shock.'

The monitor shows fewer than fifty beats a minute. A tube is connected to my arm, through which my blood supply is being replenished. Funnily enough, the utility knife is still in my pocket— or was it perhaps replaced?

'Would you by any chance know who it was?' I ask.

'It was a girl,' she says.

'M-may you describe her?' I ask.

'White dress. Wasn't that tall,' she says, choppily. 'Don't ask me how she got you up the stairs. Must have sprouted wings for all I know.'

'Did she have blonde or black hair?'

'I don't recall her hair colour, nor do I think it's very relevant at this point in time. Blood loss is known to cause memory gaps.'

'That's comforting to hear,' I say unconvincingly. I look down at my other arm. The lacerations are now neatly stitched up. The medic appears to be quite capable. Unfortunately, my shirt is stained red. When I wiggle my fingers, pain shoots to my neck. I wince.

'Don't try to move yet,' she says. 'Your muscles need time to fuse properly.'

'Understood,' I reply.

I try to think clearly and ignore a migraine that is becoming increasingly prominent. It must have been Charlotte: she sure has been unusually friendly towards me.

I should probably thank her for taking the initiative. At least Mr Diaras might think twice before picking on me again.

'I'm concerned about you, Mr Onyx,' she says with a stern look. 'Your friend refused to disclose exactly what happened, and your lecturer hasn't spoken either; however, because of the positions and accuracy of the lacerations, I can only deduce that they were self-inflicted.'

I remain silent and unconsciously break eye contact. I can hear my heart rate go up on the cursed monitor, which immediately makes it apparent that I am intentionally withholding information from her.

'I am contacting the psychiatrist. It would also be beneficial for you to consider therapy as a means to treat your condition.' She walks to the other side of the bed. I look back to see her pick up the telephone and listen for the dialling tone, after which she begins spinning the rotary dial.

'Condition?' I frown. 'Please don't contact anyone,' I plead. 'I promise to be responsible from here on out.'

'I am legally obligated to report this. Whether or not it's reported as an accident is another story.'

'Please say it was an accident. It's just—' I frantically try to think of an excuse to avoid all of this. 'Well, think about what it'd be like for me if this were to get out. People must think I'm strange as it is; imagine if they knew I went to a psychiatrist. Please have mercy,' I beg, though I don't expect anything to come from it: she seems unsympathetic at best. I can't make out her expression under the mask.

'Very well,' she says. 'I'll let you off the hook just this one time, but in the event that something like this happens again, I won't hesitate.' I'm stunned.

'Th-thank you,' I manage. She removes the needle from my arm, and I tentatively watch her place it among her assortment of hospital supplies scattered about a silver tray.

'You are free to go–' she says. I begin stirring. 'After you have recovered,' she adds sternly. I sink back into the pillow. 'And don't overdo anything for the next few days.'

Nevertheless, as soon as she disappears around the corner, I hop off the bed and fumble my way through the curtains of the cubicle. I remember to roll down my sleeves and cross my arms to cover the stains. In spite of this, when I walk down the corridor, it seems as though many have caught news of the incident. Many of them leer at me and whisper to one another. I hear their mutters as I pass them by: '...Weirdo...Freak...' I don't let it get to me. In fact, it almost sounds right.

It's already four o'clock. I realise that my notes are probably still in the lecture hall, ruined without a doubt. I toss my bag inside my locker, take out my genetics book, and walk out the university's front door.

I guess it could have ended up far worse. Perhaps the best thing I can do is simply to pretend it never even happened at all.

EVASION

16 LUCINDA

I've studied to the point where it seems the returns are diminishing. My eyes are reading the words on the page, but my mind is elsewhere. I can't stop staring at the stopwatch hanging on my necklace stand. I place it face down on my desk and leave my room.

Standing at the end of the passage, I momentarily feel a slight breeze. It must have been the front door opening. I tiptoe forward and peer around the wall to see Father entering the house, closing the door with his shoulder. In his hands, he holds a stack of shopping bags, so I scuttle over.

'Good evening,' I say, dividing the load evenly.

'Evening,' he says. 'I decided to stock up for the week.'

I peer into the bags, allowing my mind to begin forming groups of ingredients which ought to go well together.

'I know what we're going to have tonight,' I tell Father.

'I see that you're eager, but I'll help you this time.'

'Alright. Will chicken kebabs be fitting?'

'Sounds great,' he says, also keen. 'I'll light the fire.'

He places the bags on the kitchen counter and walks out to the porch. I unload the items of food, arranging them neatly beside one another. I then dice the chicken and slice the peppers, onions, and pineapple into chunks. I make the marinade from lemon juice, soy sauce, ginger, and salt, after which I peel and chop the sweet potato. I begin stacking the ingredients onto the kebab sticks.

Father walks through the door. 'The fire should be ready in no time,' he says. When he sees I've already prepared a fair number of kebabs, he says. 'Slow down there a little. Leave some for me.'

I smile apologetically. The two of us stand side-by-side and continue to skewer the various ingredients.

'This is nice,' he tells me. 'You are just as fun a cooking partner as your mother was.'

My mind flashes back to the grave, which makes my eyes watery. 'That's great to hear,' I say, trying to keep it together. My chopping hand suddenly feels weak.

'I remember the time when she and I—' Father stops chopping. 'Lucinda, are you alright?' he asks. 'What's the matter?' I turn my head the other way.

'Must be these onions,' I say quickly. 'I think I may need to go and shower.' I disappear into the passage before he can protest.

'Sure thing,' he calls out. 'I can take it from here.'

I turn open the shower nozzle and flinch; the falling droplets feel like needles against my back. Before, my mother was merely a faint trace of remembrance, but now, she feels like someone who lived and breathed and, most of all, loved me with all her heart. What am I to tell Father? Will I pretend as though I saw nothing— just let it go?

It seems like I just untied the first thread in the tapestry of my conscience that will eventually unravel, no matter how hard I try to keep it together. Suppressing a secret on this scale surely isn't viable. I need to know why he never told me that Mother was buried here. It's sure to consume me otherwise.

I turn the shower off and watch the steam rising from my fingertips. What if it makes Father sad? Perhaps he didn't tell me because he wanted to forget about everything. Is it too painful for him to remember her?

I twist open the cold faucet completely. The freezing water burns. I then hop out and sit on the floor, shivering. I can't breathe a word of what happened. I promptly wrap myself in my robe and scamper along the hallway to my room. After getting dressed, my gaze drifts towards the circular mirror hanging beside my wardrobe. I wonder what Mother would have thought of me as a daughter. Sitting cross-legged on my bedroom floor, I inhale deeply, not knowing whether it's water or tears running down my cheeks. I wipe my face and study the wavering mass of liquid hanging from my fingertips. It gradually becomes opaque as streaks of red swirl within its centre, but as it falls and strikes the tiles below, it's clear as glass once more. I stand up and walk down the stairs, feeling morbid over her absence but equally restless, unable to decide whether I've managed to live up to my potential.

Outside, the scent of kebabs is thick, but it provides no refuge from the raging anxiety within. The dimly lit patio mirrors my inner sullenness. I tell myself these thoughts will surely diminish after enough time has passed. My father stands in front of the fire, tending to the meat.

'How are the kebabs coming along?' I ask.

'Just fine. It's nice to relax a bit after such a long day,' he says, nudging my shoulder. I smile and nod. After all these years, he can immediately sense that something isn't quite right. 'Lucinda,' he says, 'did something happen today?' He pats my back.

The last thing I want is for Father to feel sad. It's one thing losing a mother, but quite another to have the love of your life slip through your fingertips. I don't think I'd have coped with it at all. I'd have perished with grief. Deep orange flames are the source of embers that rise into the black sky; beyond them, I see faint writing etched into the fireback: "Emily Perdita, 1927-1968."

'I found Mother's grave today,' I hear myself say, and it takes me by surprise.

When I glance sideways, I feel my heart sink at the sight of Father's eyes, which glint in the firelight. How could I be so insensitive? A feeling of vulnerability and shame forms within my chest. I feel like a fiend, that I have no empathy, yet I don't know if there was another way out of this. I would have lost my sanity eventually.

'I meant you no harm,' he says. 'I never meant to hide the truth.' He sounds distracted in a way, and the flames dance in his eyes. 'You loved your mother with all your heart, and she loved you just the same. We three were remarkably close when you were a little girl.' He pauses for a moment, and the crackling of the fire feels like my heart disintegrating. 'So, when she— when she died, you had a difficult time letting go, as did I, but to witness the effect that it was having on you—' he trails off. 'It felt like a part of you had faded away, though, after you lost your memory, you had returned to your good old self: my passionate and content daughter. It seemed like the peace you once had was there again. I wanted that for you.' He pauses. 'But it was wrong of me to hide this from you.'

I, too, gaze at the fire, tracking the rising embers. 'Father, I'm glad,' I say after some time. 'I see now that you did the right thing. And—' I sigh, 'I promise not to lose heart. I'll have faith.'

He hugs me. 'I know you will, Dear. Though, you don't have to force yourself to do anything or be anyone you aren't. Whichever path you choose to take, I will love you nonetheless.'

CONFESSION

17 SAMUEL

As **I near my house,** the sight of the bench looks inviting. I sit down and stare at the faded, white grain of the wood. This place now imparts the strangest feeling. It's bewilderment and longing and warmth, in and amongst a fair number of other sensations. I decide that each is equally irrational. One thing I've come to know about myself, is that I have the tendency to focus more on ideals than reality. Though, what do I consider ideal in any case?

I scrunch my eyes, looking into the dark haze which engulfs the properties around me. Soon after, I become aware of the silence; it makes me a little uneasy. I think about the question more deeply this time, and the more I do, the more I begin to feel something verging on desire.

I stand up and move briskly down the narrow path leading to my home. After entering through the front door, the gloomy living room greets me. It's usually like this at sundown. 'Mum,' I call out. 'I'm back.' I massage my shoulder, realising how tense I am.

'Always nice to see you, dear.' I jump a little. She's in this very room, sitting at the dining table.

'How was your day?' I ask, turning on a light.

'It was superb, thank you,' she says. 'Look what I got myself.' She stands up and spins around, showing off an emerald, quilted bolero.

'Looks fantastic on you,' I say. 'I love the patterns.'

'Thank you,' she tells me. She then reaches under the table. 'I also got something that I thought you'd like.'

My eyes light up. 'Really?'

She slides a gift bag across the table. 'To add something a little different to your wardrobe,' she says. I open the bag and take out a maroon, long-sleeved shirt.

'I love it,' I say.

'Thank goodness. I know what you are like with bright colours.' We laugh.

'You know me too well, I think. Should I try it on?' I ask, excited to have something new to wear.

'Yes, definitely.'

'Super,' I say. 'I'll just get supper on the go before I do so.' I stand up and walk towards the counter. 'Putinesque?'

'Just what I'm in the mood for,' says Mum. I peer back to see a careless grin on her face for the first time in a while. Getting out to the shops must have done her a world of good.

I give my hands a quick rinse before preparing dinner. After dicing the tomatoes, I mix in anchovies and olives and then heat the sauce in a pot. I also get some pasta on the boil.

Afterwards, I dash upstairs and change shirts. Thank goodness it's long-sleeved. The last thing I want is Mum needlessly worrying. While walking back down the stairs, the sound of the music box rings in my head. How can I remember it so clearly when it was just a dream? I can't keep giving in to these delusions. As soon as I enter the living room, however, I see Mum staring at the contraption.

'What in the world—' I mutter, then blurt out, 'Thank goodness, I thought it was lost!'

'Is it yours?' asks Mum.

'Yes,' I say. She waits for me to elaborate. 'A... friend of mine gave it to me as a gift.'

'A friend?' she asks. 'What sort of friend?'

'A good friend,' I say quickly. I can't wipe the grin off my face. 'It means quite a lot to me,' I add, trying not to give away too much.

Now I'm certain of it. If Lucinda truly gave me that gift, then all these crazy occurrences have to be real. Whether I like it or not, all of it is undeniably real.

'A girl gave this to you, isn't that right?' she asks. I almost choke on my words when scrambling for a reply.

'How could you possibly have known?' I manage.

'I can see it on your face. You look love-struck.'

'You could tell from my expression?' I ask, aghast.

'Yes.'

'Am I *that* predictable?'

'Yes.'

'Dammit,' I say under my breath.

'Don't curse it,' she says. 'I think she ought to find it cute. It'd possibly make her like you even more than she already does.' Her smile is slightly irking.

'Well, I don't think it's *cute*. I think it's a darned nuisance.' She chuckles. 'Mum!' I exclaim. 'I'm serious.'

'I know you're serious,' she says, 'and she is too.'

'Not in that sense!' I say, exasperated.

'So, tell me if you like her. I want to hear about it,' she says. I can feel my cheeks turning red.

'All right!' I say. 'I think that's quite enough prodding for one day.'

'I'm just badgering you,' she says. 'I've gathered you like her already. I just wanted you to admit it.'

'You're too embarrassing for words,' I say.

'And such is a mother's duty,' she replies, and without hesitation, asks, 'So, when shall I meet her?'

'Until now, I wasn't even certain whether or not she even likes me... or whether I like her! Lay off a little,' I say, though find myself grinning.

'Hmmm?' She locks her eyes into a stare. 'It had better be soon,' she says hastily. 'Meeting her, I mean. Aww, my little boy's growing up. I'm so happy for you.'

'Mum, if you say things like that in front of her, it won't—'

'Take a chill pill. I'll keep it groovy,' she says.

'Good Lord,' I say. 'Slang is even worse!'

She winks, then looks down at the box. 'I've got to say, she must fancy you an awful lot to give you such a lovely gift. Oh, do tell me about her,' she says. 'What's she like?'

'Hmm. I don't know all that much at this stage, though she is remarkably clever.' I pause. 'Now that I give it some thought, perhaps she only spoke to me out of pity—'

'Oh, nonsense!' interrupts Mum. 'You're a handsome young man with numerous likeable qualities.'

I shake my head. A lull in the conversation follows, and I hear a bubbling sound coming from the stove.

'Gosh!' I exclaim, running over to the pot. 'The sauce!' I take it off just in time. I then strain the pasta, dish up and garnish each dish with basil leaves. After both plates are on the table, I fill our glasses with water.

'I love the shirt, by the way,' I say.

'I knew the colour would suit you,' she says, looking me up and down.

'It sure does.'

We dine in relative silence, which is mostly a reflection of us simply enjoying the hearty meal.

After dinner, Mother goes and reads the newspaper, and I begin delaying the table. While rinsing the dishes, Mother calls to me from the living room, 'You looking after yourself, Samuel? Out near the city, I mean.'

'I think so. Why do you ask, Mother?'

'They say the crime rate has doubled in the last couple of years,' she says. 'Probably the wealth of the city that's incited this nonsense.'

After placing the last dish on the rack, I walk over to Mother. 'Let me see.' She hands me the newspaper.

'It seems there are gangs on the loose. You had better watch yourself out there.'

'Alright, Mother,' I say, glancing over the article, 'I'll keep an eye out.' I'm usually sceptical about those sorts of statistics. Technically, two incidents is double one, but both are negligible. I tear out the top corner and use it to light the fire, then curl up on the sofa. Mum decides to read a book.

Before long, I wake with a creak in my neck and realise that I'm lying on a long desk. I go from a dazed state to virtually jumping out of my seat when I find myself in the biology lecture hall with the mid-morning sun shining through the window. My mind must be splitting at the seams.

Mr Diaras is strolling up and down in the front of the hall. His voice carries through the space. '… to make you all aware of the upcoming practical assessment that will take place tomorrow afternoon in the laboratory on floor five. You will need to know chapters four through seven in order to have the necessary knowledge to complete the required tasks. Also, check the list on the notice board to see which slot each of you is required to attend.'

The murmurs that follow express agitation among the students. Hmm, a science practical. I struggle to consider the implication of this, as my mind is still pretty clouded. Though, I figure it should be bearable— perhaps.

The clock strikes eight, and we all exit. Upon departing, the students swarm around the notice board outside the hall. I sigh. This will surely take longer than I had initially planned.

I find myself wondering why I don't see Charlotte or Lucinda among the diminishing group of students. At that point, however, I get a chance to take a look at the notice board. I ascertain that I happen to be in the same group as Charlotte, along with someone called Mathew. I give a half-pleased, half-dissatisfied look. She is sweet, and I'm fortunate to be in the same group as her; on the other hand, I have yet to experience a group activity going according to plan. I'm often ostracized, with good reason, no doubt. I wonder whether she's even still my friend, considering how rashly I acted. She may very well have chosen to avoid me.

I take note of the timeslot. I'd better begin preparing for it. I haven't had the chance to study further than chapter six. I guess I've been preoccupied with my thoughts lately. I unconsciously rub my arm; though covered by my sleeve, I can feel the stitches in my skin. Whatever transpired that day, I need to know the truth.

RUMINATION

18 LUCINDA

Lucinda sings a melody muffled by the wind. 'Oh, do not shun the look in my eyes that shows you are my own.' She holds her shoes in her hand and balances on the guardrail that encompasses the bridge. 'Be, for me, the path of liberty I never would have known.' The sound of metal moaning under her feet passes through her skin in waves of excitement. Treading this fine line makes her feel ethereal, rebellious even, as though anything of this world may do her no harm.

She hops off the rail on the other side, and her feet touch the ground with grace beyond measure. 'I plea to be the flower that grows from the seed which you had sewn.' Her body forms a pirouette, and she leaps into a jeté with such confidence in her movement that she could have sworn she had done it before. 'Would you care to be my dancer when I'd have danced alone?'

Just then, she hears a peculiar sound: a whisper in the shadows; recurring clicks of— of claws striking the ground. It circles her, its shoulders becoming white and grey waves, moving along its wiry fur like the spines of a sea urchin. Oh, and its eyes, she decides, are blood moons suspended in darkness. It seems like a prophecy to her, one which arrived in the form of a wolf.

Lucinda's skin grows cold in anticipation. It can't be real, she tells herself. Oh, do the heavens deceive her? She stares at it intently, waiting for it to disintegrate into dust. Though, at the same time, she is entranced by its splendour.

It's the teeth that eventually sets her into motion: the set of incisors, far too large to even fit inside its jaw. A snapshot in her mind materialises: her body torn in two, reduced to nothing more than a ragdoll. Her shoes slip from her fingers as her hands become jelly and her legs spring into action. Instinct guides her away from the bridge and into the forest, where it is less exposed. She navigates patches of sunlight, striking the forest floor in blinding, white bands. She cannot suppress the crunching sound of dry ground beneath her feet. Dark stripes mask the terrain; she inevitably treads on a dozen thorns.

She soon realises that wolves are at home in the forest and are far more agile than she. On top of this, her scent would promptly give her away, should she try and hide. Before she's made it very far into the brush, the beast leaps forward and slashes her arm, though she doesn't dare look back. Her teeth clench, but no sound leaves her lips.

A dark-brown fence comes into view. Her palms touch the wooden slats. She has already made the decision to scale it. Her arms, which aren't all that strong, somehow manage to pull her body over the top of the planks. She briefly sees the façade of the property on the other side. Upon landing, her ankle buckles, and she topples onto the grass. She breathes out shakily. The fence is a little under three meters high, surely no match for the wolf. She closes her eyes and balls her twitching hands into fists, waiting for the beast to leap over it and be her demise. Yet, it stays on the other side, scratching at the wooden slats.

What she just experienced is by no means congruent with her previous knowledge of wolves. She can't fathom why it would make its way into the city. They're supposed to live in remote areas, far from any human activity. She gets to her feet and takes in a shaky breath, figuring it must simply be in dire need of food.

Moments later, the beast lets out a series of barks and whines for a little while longer. Though, it soon gives up, leaving her be. It sounds far less aggressive and intimidating to her than how it appeared. 'For goodness' sake,' she whispers. 'A barking wolf?' She never knew of such.

PHANTOM

19 SAMUEL

A *pair of swings hang vacant*, oscillating in the breeze. I've walked past this park almost every day since moving here, yet have never given them a second thought until now.

I make my way over to examine the integrity of the ropes and wooden seats before sitting down. These apparatuses haven't been serviced in years, though I figure the chances of breaking something are low enough. I cannot help but feel for the unfortunate soul that is one day destined to bring forth the demise of this rickety structure.

I begin to move my legs forward and back. Soon, I am swinging through the full range of motion. At the zenith of each arc, I feel light and dizzy. I close my eyes and enjoy the carefree feeling of freedom. I never knew that something as simple as a swing would have me smiling like a child.

Before I realise it, the swing next to me also begins to sway; unlike mine, it does so in a way that's eerily quiet.

'I thought I'd find you here.' I recognise the voice, like that of a spirit's, smooth and calm. 'You wouldn't believe what just happened to me.'

'L-Lucinda,' I stutter. I stare at her rocking figure, the ground and the sky blurring behind her.

'You'd think me mad if I were to tell you,' she says, as though we already knew each other well. 'Instead, answer me this: do you know the reason one feels times of weightlessness when swinging?'

'Please, enlighten me,' I say, listening to the sounds of the swings, the way the creak in the chains becomes higher when you're going forward and lower on the return.

'At the top of the arc, the downward acceleration of your body is equal to gravitational acceleration. You are essentially in free-fall for a split second and, therefore, experience no force. Interesting, is it not?'

'It would have been had I not already known it.' I grin.

'Then why ask me to elaborate?' she asks.

'I just wanted to hear your voice,' I say, startling myself a little. She giggles at this. 'Though there is something else as well—'

'Anything, Dear,' she says, cutting me off. At this point, I wonder if it'd be just to get mad, yet, at the same time, I find her to be so enchanting that I don't think I could bring myself to do so.

'Did you kiss me?' I ask her. She looks marginally shocked.

'Did you not want me to?' she asks.

I hesitate for a moment, wondering what in the world she's thinking at that point. 'That's irrelevant,' I say.

'I don't think that's the case,' she says, completely calm once more.

'You don't kiss someone you just met,' I say. This makes her think for a while.

'Sorry?' she says and shrugs.

'Don't apologize for the greatest moment of my life,' I say, which makes her burst out in laughter.

'It may have seemed rash,' she says, 'though I do admit to it being quite calculated. I wanted to capture your interest, though I didn't know how to go about it.'

'Believe me, you did more than capture my interest,' I say. I look her way again. She appears pleased but also a little withdrawn, perhaps pondering her actions.

I decide to jump off the swing. I land with surprising precision, after which I stoop down in an overstated bow.

'Bravo!' she exclaims. 'You know Newton said that Tact is the art of making a point without making an enemy.' I notice the look of mischief in her eye as she continues rocking back and forth on the swing. 'How about we do a little experiment to test my previous notion?' she suggests. 'I want to feel it entirely.'

I give her a perplexed look but do not have time to dwell on it: a split second later, she is flying through the air. Her eyes are closed, and her long hair trails behind her like black smoke. I jolt forward, just managing to catch her in my arms, surprised by how light she is. I laugh nervously.

'I did indeed feel weightless,' she says, reminiscing.

'You seem to put an awful lot of trust in others,' I say.

'Not just anyone,' she says. 'I trust *you* specifically.'

'And why is that?' I ask.

'I figured you would be obliged to return the favour,' she says. She hops back onto her feet and sashays toward the roundabout. I hobble along to catch up.

'What do you mean *return the favour*? What favour?'

She takes the railing in her hand and pushes the roundabout into motion. 'Saving your life, of course.'

Saving my life? I begin to figure out what she is alluding to. 'Do you have a scar on your collar bone?' I ask.

'Yes,' she says and looks over her shoulder, marginally amused. She runs her fingertips across it. 'It's very faint. I'm surprised you noticed.' She steps onto the roundabout. As it spins around, she rotates her head to keep facing me, clearly finding my look of befuddlement rather comical.

'Why would you ever—' I hesitate. 'Now everyone knows you are associated with a total moonling. Some things are just not worth saving.'

'What if I told you that I care for your health?' she says, stopping the roundabout with her foot. 'And why call yourself that in any case? *I* didn't say something like that.'

'Others have,' I say. 'I think it's because I can take things a bit too far sometimes.'

'A bit?' she says sarcastically.

I look down. 'Alright... way too far.'

She lifts my chin with her index finger. 'Where's the fun in knowing when to quit?' she says and carries on walking. 'Besides, what makes you the weird one? Maybe they're all weird, and you're normal.'

I gleam, though I struggle to understand the notion of someone showing concern for me. I experience a burning warmth in my chest. She takes my hand, and I try not to gasp at its icy touch. It's as though she isn't even living.

'We all have some meaning to someone,' she says, 'and Mr Diara's reaction was priceless. He collapsed with the most hilarious expression. Serves him right for acting so cold towards you.' I chuckle nervously. Do I deserve to be treated any different in any case? 'Speaking of weird things,' she says, 'I could have sworn I saw you scampering out of the hall on the night of the exhibition. You looked frightened for some reason.'

I'm a little stunned. 'It was me indeed,' I say, putting my hand on my shoulder. 'How do I put this? I'm a bit of a chromophobe, you see,' I tell her, having to express it in words for the first time. It sounds off.

'A chromophobe?' Lucinda looks pleasantly amused. 'As in, you're scared of colours...'

'Yes,' I say, 'bright colours in particular. It's sort of strange, I know.' She seems delighted by this.

'I'll be sure not to point out a rainbow the next time I see one,' she says.

'It's not like that!' I say, exasperated.

She laughs. 'Can't take a teasing?'

I frown, but after a brief pause, I push her teasingly and laugh along. 'So, now you have to tell me about your fears,' I say. 'It'd only be fair.'

'Is that so?' she says. 'I'm afraid I wouldn't have anything to say.'

'You're not scared of anything?'

'No, that's not true,' she says. It only takes a moment for her to come up with something. 'Wolves.'

'Why wolves?' I ask. 'Have you encountered one?'

'Just now, actually,' she says. 'I was being chased down, hunted more like. You should have seen it! It was most horrifying, pale as ever, and its fangs were drawn swords! And—' she hesitates. 'You know I made a mental note not to tell you this, and, well—'

'Are you utterly convinced that you were being chased by a wolf? Are you crazy?' I ask and titter.

'Yes, and maybe,' she responds without hesitation. 'It was a Tundra Wolf, I think. It had grey and white patches on its fur and cobalt eyes.' She shows me her arm. 'Look,' she says, 'it even made this gash.'

'Seems more like you brushed against a thorny shrub, quite frankly,' I say, hoping I'm not sounding rude. 'We aren't in North America or Eurasia,' I say. 'Even if there was a wolf in this area, it wouldn't consider entering the vicinity of the neighbourhood.'

'Hmm,' she says, 'in that case, I have no idea what it was.' She looks down. 'Perhaps I may be a little deranged.'

'As are all the greats,' I reply. I can feel the logic in my head waning.

She beams. 'I'm glad you think of me that way.'

'If anything, I'm no better,' I say.

'Are you alluding to that far-out poem you wrote?' she asks, running her hand through her hair. 'I quite liked it, actually.'

'How so?' I ask hesitantly.

'You're unafraid to embrace who you are,' she says. 'Even though you may not be perfect, you're certainly genuine. In actuality, no one is perfect, but few admit it.'

'Well, I certainly received scorn for it,' I say. 'From the others, I mean. If their glares were anything to go by.'

She looks perplexed. 'Where did you get that impression?' she asks. Before I can respond, she says, 'Time probably felt as though it were dilating since you were feeling nervous.' My brow furrows. 'Because of your raised heart rate and increased adrenalin in your system, your brain captured a greater number of memories per unit time,' she clarifies, 'so when you think back on the situation, it seems to have happened in slow-motion.'

'Oh, sort of like observers only agreeing on the causality of events and not the time interval between them.'

'Yes,' she says, surprised by the analogy. She looks forward for a few moments and then back at me. 'I was wondering if you'd like to meet my father?' she asks, biting her lip as though immediately regretting the question.

I'm caught a little off guard, unable to figure out what it means. 'I'd love to,' I say in the swing of the moment.

'Positive?' she asks. 'You seem a tad startled.'

I then think about what ought to happen if I were to introduce her to my mum. What will she make of that?

'No, well… yes. It just took me by surprise, that's all,' I manage.

'Oh, alright,' she says. She takes out a miniature notebook and pen, seemingly prepared for the situation. 'Here's our address,' she says, jotting down the information. 'You could come for dinner if you like,' she suggests.

'Dinner? You mean tonight?' I ask.

'Yes,' she says, grinning, her eyes like half-moons.

'Sure. I'll be there,' I say, unable to resist the look on her face. It's strange to be the reason why someone smiles. 'Thank you,' I say.

'It's a pleasure,' she says and chuckles. 'See you later in that case.' She waves.

As she departs, she seems to flicker a little, like the wind is attempting to blow her away. Although I know now that I ought to find out who she truly is.

AMBIVALENCE

20 SAMUEL

I *open my cupboard* and eye out the clothing items hanging in a row of no more than a dozen. My closet has a total of seven white shirts. The odd one out is maroon, the one Mum got me the other day. I wonder whether Lucinda would fancy it. I've never quite grasped the concept of fashion, so I figure I should stick to convention for this particular occasion since she hasn't seen me in colour yet. A white shirt will do, with a black tie to go with it.

When I take out my only pair of formal pants, I notice something in its pocket: a stone with a glittering surface. I'm quite taken aback when it strikes me that its origin is, in fact, Pennsylvania. It's got to be the only thing in existence that connects me to my former place of living. Pennsylvania has an abundance of this mineral, blue sandstone. I remember hoarding these rocks as a young boy when I went on trips with my parents. They still used to live together back then. Sometimes, I wish things could return to those days.

I set off down the road. It doesn't take long for the restlessness to settle in: if I don't get into her father's good books, it will have a knock-on effect for worse.

I look at the address written on the note she gave me and then at the number on the wall. At first glance, the house, with its light grey colour, seems similar to the others in the neighbourhood. It has simplistic architecture and a single floor, which gives it a pleasantly minimalistic façade. What isn't at all minimal, however, is the sheer size of it. The towering walls encompass a dozen glass panels framed with brushed steel. The way Lucinda dresses hinted that she was wealthy, but I never imagined it to be on this scale. Dear Lord, I do hope her father never lays eyes on our house.

I step onto the porch and use the brass door knocker. A metallic clang echoes throughout the mansion. I gulp, brushing my hands on my pants. The large, mahogany door swings open almost immediately, and the first thing I see is Lucinda's face with a small flower pinned in her hair. Its silky petals are as white as her cheeks and stand out against her black locks. She gleams, then purses her lips. Her eyes are closed as well, probably because I'd been staring. 'Please, do come in,' she says and tiptoes to one side. 'Father should be ready in just a moment.'

I walk inside, thinking it quite strange that she refers to her dad as 'father'. The moment I look up, I can't shake my sense of bewilderment. The interior is exquisite, with dozens of elaborate ornaments, but laid out in a way that makes it feel spacious. Above my head are naked bulbs hanging from fine chains, which illuminate the halls with pale light, showing off the expanse of the passages.

The walls each hold dozens of artworks, most of which seem to have a prominent form, often a silhouette, with finer details in the background. Some of them have pastel stripes that line the edges of monochrome, swirling streaks, while others look to be desaturated landscapes. In fact, all of them are rather dull and pleasant to look at; this makes them fit together in an odd sort of way.

The room to my left is home to a variety of statues, with a couch in front of a large, glass door. I follow her down a hallway, walking on a carpet with a recurring pattern of overlapping charcoal and pear-coloured rings. I almost feel guilty having to put my feet on such an exquisite rug. Every few meters, hangs a new painting. We pass around five doors to separate rooms along the passage. I wonder if they usually have many guests over at a time.

'Your father has good taste,' I say. 'I love these paintings. They all seem to have the same sort of brushstrokes, funnily enough.'

'That would be because they are each painted by the same individual,' she says.

'All of them!' I exclaim. 'Your father must be quite fond of the artist.'

'Yes, I'd say they are exceptionally good friends,' she says, almost teasingly.

A sudden sense of déjà vu occurs when I realise that I've seen the initials before… at the exhibition. They're *her* initials: L. Perdita. Though, this time, it feels different. It feels lovely. I stop and stare at one of the paintings. My face is glowing when I look at her with pure adoration. The instant she notices, she blushes and traces a half circle on the carpet with her foot.

'You're such a tease! I should have guessed they were yours. They're incredible,' I tell her. She huffs and puts her arms behind her back. I place my hands on her shoulders. 'I could kiss you!' I laud.

'Well, why don't you?' she says immediately, as though anticipating the question. 'At least *I'd* kiss you back,' she says, simpering.

All of a sudden, the door beside us bursts open and I lurch backwards. Now I'm the one who's flushed.

'Oh, father,' she says, unfazed. 'This is Samuel.'

Her father is tall in stature and has a rugged face with grey-black hair. He wears a formal shirt with a green polka-dot tie. When he reaches out for a handshake, I am astounded by the size of his forearms. 'Good evening,' he says with a sure tone of voice.

'It's a pleasure to meet you, Mr Perdita,' I say.

'Likewise,' he replies, 'but please, call me Jonathan.'

'Noted,' I say.

'I see my daughter invited you to dinner,' he says. 'I cannot wait to hear everything about you.' At that point, I smile nervously, unable to ascertain whether he means to be sarcastic. His one brow is slightly bent, and his shuttered eyes give nothing away as to what his intentions are.

'Oh yes,' I say, faking another smile. At the same time, I wonder whether Jonathan was even aware of Lucinda's invitation. 'I am grateful for your hospitality.' He nods, and the three of us begin back-tracking along the hallway.

Gesturing to the walls, he says, 'All of these works are the product of my daughter's talent.'

'Yes,' I say. 'I just so happened to find out. They are truly astounding.'

'Aren't they such?' he asks rhetorically. 'Her art has proved world-class, so much so, that—'

'Father!' whispers Lucinda, clearly exasperated. 'You're embarrassing me.' I smile apologetically. Her father just laughs.

'Lucinda, why don't you prepare dinner for us?'

'I may be of help as well,' I offer.

'Nonsense, you're our guest,' says Jonathan.

'What if he'd like to?' asks Lucinda, almost teasingly.

'Would you?' asks Jonathan, peering over his shoulder.

'Why, of course,' I say.

'All right,' he says, nodding. 'I suppose one can at least *try* to keep up with my daughter's exceptional cooking.' Lucinda exhales and scrunches her eyes.

'Give yourself some credit,' I tell her.

'Ay, this sort of thing is typical of father,' she whispers. The two of us enter the kitchen, and Jonathan turns into the dining room. 'Well, what do you wish to make?' she asks.

The place looks as though it were straight out of a science-fiction film. All of the appliances have a brushed metal finish, and the counters are made of grey granite. The cupboards don't even have handles!

She and I wash our hands together. She nudges me on the shoulder. 'It depends on which sort of food you fancy.'

I'm quite stumped, to be honest. 'I mostly like Venetian-style dishes,' I say, dearly hoping she doesn't question further. I have no idea where that response came from, nor do I know any sort of food from Vianna.

'We could make goulash!' she says excitedly. 'The Viennese love it!'

'Ah, yes!' I say, mirroring her enthusiasm. 'Goulash sounds perfect.' I haven't a clue what it is.

'It ought to be fun!' Her eyes sparkle. 'Could you get the vegetables from that cupboard?' she asks, pointing.

'Alrighty,' I say, noticing that the cupboard lacks a handle. I peer sideways and observe how Lucinda presses against a different cupboard with her shoulder to open it. When I push the cupboard door with my hand, I hear a soft click before it glides open on dampened hinges. There is a wide variety of vegetables to choose from.

'We'll need tomatoes, onions and potatoes from there,' she says. 'The sauce will be made from ginger, soy, garlic, and honey, along with lemon juice.'

'Yes-yes,' I say, a little overwhelmed. 'Do you cook this often? You seem to know the recipe quite well.'

'Hmmm,' she begins, 'I haven't actually cooked it as of yet, though I did happen to read the recipe in one of the cooking books at the university's library.'

'And what about the quantities?' I ask, a little sceptical.

'Mix the soy sauce, honey and lemon juice three to one to six, and grate a touch of ginger over the top,' she says.

How in the world is she able to remember an entire recipe from a book she doesn't even own? She turns on the stove and drizzles olive oil in a pan. I hold the vegetables in my arms, hoping I remembered everything. She takes out a chopping board from a narrow cupboard and places it on the counter. She then grabs two large knives from a magnetic strip on the wall.

'Ready for Armageddon, are you?' I ask. 'You sure we need such massiv—'

'Catch,' she says, tossing one of them my way with the handle facing me. I flinch but manage to grasp it properly.

Within seconds, she has already diced an entire pumpkin and made easy work of some spring onions.

'Do you know how I chopped those vegetables so quickly?' she asks.

'Because you're an incredible chef,' I reply.

'No... well— I meant that it's easier to chop with something with a little heft.'

'Inertia?' I suggest.

'Precisely,' she says. 'The weight does the work for you.' With that, she slices through the beetroot. Thunder booms, and the lights flicker a little. Lucinda looks excited.

'I'm glad you arrived when you did,' she says, 'though you don't seem like the type who'd be bothered by rain.' I nod in agreement.

She slides the ingredients off of the chopping board and into a pan; a cloud of steam erupts around her. She emerges from it with one hand on her hip. In her other hand is the knife, dripping red with beetroot juice.

'We'll whip the cream in just a moment,' she says. I jump when another bolt of lightning strikes, scattering white light from the blade in her hand.

'Wouldn't want to come across *you* in the dead of night,' I tell her.

'Why, thank you,' she says and chuckles. After a pause, she says, 'It sure is nice to cook with someone new for a change.' I break into a smile just as the front door slams shut, though it was just the wind. 'I'd better close the shutters,' she says. 'It appears a storm is on its way.'

'All right,' I say. 'I'll watch over the vegetables in the meantime.'

When her footsteps disappear up the stairs, all I hear is sizzling pans and rain on the roof. I wonder if mum is doing fine. I sure hope she isn't out in the storm.

BREW

21 LUCINDA

Lucinda tiptoes along the carpet. The wind murmurs through the passages like the sound of having a seashell on one's ear. After closing the shutters in her father's room, she backtracks towards her own room. She huffs at the sight of the floor, already wet, and battles to pull down the shutters this time. A gust picks up momentarily, slamming another door shut with a bang, and the paintings on the wall rattle, making her spin around and gaze down the hallway. When she turns back, a motionless silhouette stands in front of the window. She jolts before realising it's merely Samuel who has come to be of assistance.

He shrugs. 'Did you see something strange?'

'H-Help me out with the other rooms, will you?' Samuel nods.

The two of them seal off the remainder of the house and return to the kitchen once more. By that stage, the meat is just about medium-rare. Lucinda takes it off the pan and serves it alongside the vegetables while Samuel finishes making the salad. The two of them enter the dining room.

The lights above the table glow orange and reflect off its polished surface, just like the flickering fire which Jonathan lit earlier on.

'The two of you make quite the duo, it seems,' says Jonathan. Samuel rubs his neck and nods. 'May I offer you some wine?' Jonathan asks him. 'We have Merlot, Chardonnay, Sauvignon Blanc...' Lucinda's eyes light up at the thought.

'I don't drink, actually, but thank you for the offer,' says Samuel.

'Hear that, Lucinda?' says Jonathan. 'Not everyone your age drinks.'

'I didn't mean *everyone*, Father,' says Lucinda, desperately trying to conceal her disappointment. 'I was merely alluding to the *vast majority* of people my age.' Though, she finds the thought of wine tantalising.

'Hmmm,' pipes Samuel, leaning a little closer. 'Most interesting.' Lucinda looks smug. He then decides to change the topic. 'Jonathan, is Mrs Perdita home?'

'My wife?' Jonathan asks. There is a brief pause. Samuel turns to Lucinda, who breaks eye contact. 'Emily... passed away,' he says. 'Been close to four years now.'

Samuel is at a loss for words for a moment. 'I'm truly sorry,' he says softly. 'It was very insensitive of me.'

Jonathan laughs it off. 'It's not as though you could have known.' Lucinda looks at Samuel apologetically, though he can clearly see that she is trying to conceal hurt as well. 'In any case,' says Jonathan, 'why don't you tell us a bit about yourself, Samuel?'

Samuel blinks. 'Well, where should I start—'

There's a moment of silence, during which Lucinda also finds herself blanking out a little. She looks past Samuel, noticing it's stopped raining. 'I know,' she then says, inquisitively. 'You ought to tell us about your interests.'

'Well, alright,' he says. 'I do find astrophysics quite fascinating.' Lucinda nods as though making a mental note.

'As in the birth and death of stars, and so forth?' enquires Jonathan.

'Precisely,' says Samuel.

'He has proved to have a broad understanding of various scientific concepts,' says Lucinda.

Samuel smiles. 'I wouldn't call it broad per se… I've just dabbled in things relating to outer space, I guess.'

'Why did you not pursue it as a career, Samuel?' asks Jonathan. Lucinda shoots her father a look, but he shrugs, thinking it to be a legitimate question.

'My father would never have funded that sort of thing,' says Samuel. 'He sees no value in the non-tangible, or that which one cannot experience concretely.'

'I see,' says Jonathan. 'Although, by this time next year, you will have a qualification behind your name. Once you can support yourself financially, there's no stopping you from pursuing further studies.'

'Undeniably,' says Samuel.

The three of them go on to talk about several seemingly unrelated topics, and the food goes down well.

'May I show Samuel the vegetable patch?' asks Lucinda, quite out of the blue.

'Sure,' says Jonathan. 'I shall wash up.' Lucinda tugs Samuel's hand, and they exit through a glass door. She takes him around a corner, casting shadows on the both of them.

'So, where is this veggie garden of yours?' he asks.

'Does it matter?' she says to him.

He initially looks a tad confused but quickly catches on when he finds her gazing into his eyes. One can say that by the time the two of them had finished "looking at the vegetable patch", they felt entirely intoxicated by each other. Lucinda wraps her arms around him for a while. They feel such a warmth that they never want to move from there; that they belong right where they are.

Eventually, her sensible instincts kick in, and they head back inside. The fire opposite the dining-room table looks inviting. They sit cross-legged beside it. She then places her head on his lap and closes her eyes.

TENDERNESS

22 LUCINDA

When I wake up the next day, a strong feeling lingers from the night before, and it's as though it's still running from my fingertips to my toes. I find a note on my bedside table informing me that Father had to head off to work earlier than usual; most probably why he went to bed so punctually.

I head over to my dresser and pick up my watch. In doing so, I realise we'll soon have to partake in the science practicals. If I am not mistaken, Samuel's group will conduct their experiments this morning, and I plan to take advantage of this fact.

Not long after I head out of the house, I am once more under the powerful, white lights within the science building.

I climb the stairs to reach the upper floors, counting each level as I go. Three… Four…

'Samuel!' I cry out in a sort of rasping whisper. He takes no notice of me and stares at one of the laboratory doors as though expecting them to open at any moment. I scamper up to him. 'What on earth are you waiting for?'

'The practical,' he says. 'Mr. Diaras told us to meet on floor four for the session.'

'No,' I reply, 'he said we should meet on floor five, Samuel!' My voice is hushed but equally frantic. 'Five,' I repeat, holding up the fingers of my hand. Samuel blinks. I tug his arm, leading him up the next flight of stairs. We scurry along the passage and enter the lab just before the door closes. 'Where on earth are you living?' I ask.

'I— don't really know,' he says and looks down, seemingly hurt by the comment.

'Luckily, I found you then,' I say, trying to be comforting.

Most of the students are shuffling around and mucking about at their stations. The laboratories are far from modern. There are long, wooden desks to work on, with Voltameters placed at each station. The incandescent lights that line the ceiling flicker every so often.

'Divide yourselves into your prescribed groups,' says Mr Diaras. 'Each group is to find a station and carry out the experiment.' The students scurry about, looking for their group members. 'And do so promptly!' adds Mr Diaras. 'I don't have all day.'

I notice Mr Diaras and Samuel making eye contact, but the two of them immediately turn away from each other. I guess it's awkward for the two of them, though I wonder how things eventually panned out in the end.

I quickly find Charlotte, but the three of us don't manage to find Mathew. I shrug. 'Wouldn't be surprised if he decided to split on us entirely.'

Charlotte laughs and looks terribly shy. Her eyes are turned to the floor, and she swings her arms about. It makes me wonder whether she was home-schooled before enrolling at university.

'Do you think it matters that you weren't scheduled for today?' Samuel asks me, later adding, 'Not that I'm complaining or anything…'

'No one's going to check.' I grin.

'I assume we have all found a station by now,' says Mr Diaras, sounding annoyed. 'Each should have a Hoffman's Voltammeter, Styrofoam balls and a rod.' The three of us huddle behind the station.

Samuel seems to want to say something but hesitates, though neither of us say anything. He then stutters, 'Ahh, Charlotte, this is Lucinda.'

'We're all in the same English class,' says Charlotte.

'That managed to slip my mind,' he says, scrunching his eyes shut.

'Nonetheless, I'm pleased to meet you formally,' I say. Charlotte titters and nods in agreement.

'Well then,' continues Mr Diaras in his usual, commanding tone, 'today's practical is about electrostatics. Follow the instructions on the sheet and record your findings.' He claps. 'Well, don't look at me, get cracking!'

I switch on the Voltammeter, and immediately, a spark jumps onto Samuel's finger. 'Ouch!' he yelps. 'Curse my luck. What mockery is this?'

'Don't be so negative,' I say.

'I was just a little shocked, that's all,' says Samuel.

'Well, witnessing that made me ecstatic,' I say. Samuel looks sheepish.

Charlotte shakes her head; this makes me notice the tiny, silver earrings she's wearing. I decide they suite her.

We scan over the instructions in turn, after which Samuel holds the electric field meter at regular distances from the voltammeter while Charlotte records the values.

'Now, all we need to do is find the work required to move a unit charge thirty centimetres,' I say. 'The relationship between electric field strength and distance follows a hyperbolic curve. Therefore, the work should be ninety joules,' I say.

Afterwards, I write down the equation in order to work it out formally by substituting in values. We do increasingly complex questions involving kinetic and potential energy of charged particles under the influence of forces.

Samuel leans on the desk as soon as we are finished. 'I knew all of that,' he says.

'Oh, so you did,' I say. 'Then I take it you obviously wouldn't mind working out the rate at which the electric field attenuates for us...'

'Certainly,' he says and mutters something. 'What?' he says a moment later, grabbing the page. 'Is that even possible?'

I laugh. 'To calculate? Of course not! It was frivolous talk.' I then take hold of his waist. 'Though, I'm sure you can determine the probability of us canoodling later on.'

He lets out a hic. 'You're ragging,' he says.

'He's getting smarter,' I say. 'Time to up my game.' This makes Charlotte chuckle, though she tries to act nonchalant. 'Well, at least you can now say that you know as many females your age as there are digits,' I tell him.

'What are you suggesting? There are ten digits...'

'I was talking about binary,' I say.

'Oh,' says Samuel. Charlotte laughs at him. He rolls his eyes. 'So, Charlotte,' he says, redirecting the conversation. 'you told me you'd like to specialise in microbiology.'

'Yes,' she says. 'I'm surprised you remembered.'

'That's exactly my plan as well,' I tell her. 'I never asked what you'd like to become, Samuel.'

'What I'd like to become?' he repeats. He becomes introspective, staring out of the window to the right of the laboratory. 'I'm not entirely certain yet,' he says. Perhaps he is simply out to see what captures his interests in the workplace. Samuel taps his finger on the desk. 'In any case, what will you do one day, Lucinda?'

'I can imagine her becoming a paediatrician,' says Charlotte.

I raise an eyebrow. 'Working with children? I can hardly see myself doing that. Those little critters definitely have their way of getting on my nerves.' I give it some thought. 'I suppose becoming a neurosurgeon or ophthalmologist appeals to me for the most part, although I haven't made any decisions as of yet.'

'An ophthalmologist,' pipes Samuel. 'I, too, have acquired an interest in eyes recently.' He gazes at me. 'More specifically, when I first saw yours.'

'I'm afraid corny compliments aren't the way to my heart. Besides, I have grey eyes, hardly flattering.' I brush my hair behind my ear and smirk, a little sassy.

'Grey?' asks Charlotte, intrigued.

'Yes,' I say. 'One's eye colour ranges from colourless to light blue, to green, to brown depending on the amount of melanin in your pupils. So, technically speaking, it's a lack of melanin that causes them to come across as grey.'

'That's strange, to say the least,' says Samuel, leaning in closer. 'I always knew there was something different about their appearance.' I blink.

'You're welcome to stop staring any time from now,' I say, feeling my cheeks getting hot. He's acting more forward than usual.

'I mean,' says Samuel, 'strange in a good way, obviously.' I simper, appreciating the compliment.

'I any case,' I say, 'don't you think we should get back to the task at hand?'

'Sure thing,' says Samuel.

There are numerous other questions in need of answering. Thankfully, they prove no match for our combined efforts.

As we are finishing off the exercise, Mr Diaras walks among the stations, assisting students. He avoids our station, unsurprisingly. Charlotte, who seems to take notice of this, asks, 'Whatever happened that day, Samuel? You know, the day when—' she trails off. 'Don't feel obligated to tell, though I am rather curious.'

'Oh, that,' he says. 'I suppose an explanation wouldn't be out of place.' I'm interested in hearing it from his point of view. 'Mr Diaras and myself were called in to have a discussion with the dean. It was pretty much a blur and seemed pretty grim for the most part, but at some point, the medic was requested for her opinion on the matter.' He giggles. 'I don't know quite what she said, but after that, the dean concluded that neither party was at fault,' he smirks, 'But don't ask me for the details. I'm just lucky I can still be here, all things considered.'

'Oh gosh,' says Charlotte, 'it seems you got off easy.'

'I may have the luck of the devil,' says Samuel.

'I genuinely think you *are* the devil sometimes,' I say.

AFFINITY

---

23 SAMUEL

When I pass the park later in the afternoon, the sky is still as can be. I can hear birds among the trees and insects in the grass. It sure helped to have Lucinda and Charlotte during the practical. I think we outdid ourselves.

I look to my left and see something quite rare indeed: a woman throwing a ball for her dog. Few people in Xys own pets, and I don't recall seeing anyone resembling her around here before. She is middle-aged and statuesque, and wears a striking, blue blouse over her shirt. Her warm smile makes me oddly compelled to say hello.

'Good afternoon,' I say, waving as she passes me. She returns my gesture with a grin.

I admire how obediently the dog darts past the swings, even jumping over the seesaw at times, to return the ball. Its fur is black and white, so I figure it to be a collie of sorts. I'm just about to set foot on the pavement next to my street when I hear the poor pooch whining.

I look back to see the woman staring up at the branches of a tree, with the dog circling below. What could be the problem? I make my way over to be of assistance.

'Ma'am,' I begin, 'what seems to be the matter?' On this windless day, my voice carries far and seems to whisper through the forest. She looks a tad startled when she notices that I'm standing right beside her.

'Oh, I seem to have managed to get my dog's ball stuck in this tree.' She gestures upwards. It proves easy to spot among the bare branches due to its bright orange coating.

'I thought as much,' I say. 'Not to worry, I'll have it down in a jiffy.'

I clamber up the branches. From this greater height, I can now see the entire row of trees growing along the riverbank. I hear a train as well, which passes along the rails behind the park; it sounds oddly close.

'Oh, *do* be careful,' she says, speaking over the click-clack of the train. She has a hand on her brow.

'Fortunately, I happen to be an expert in this field,' I say, grabbing hold of a long branch. 'I've been climbing trees since—' At that moment, I could have sworn the train was coming straight towards me from within the forest. I can see the trail of steam exit the treetops, drawing nearer.

Before I even have a chance to give it a second thought, a branch gives way under my foot. In the blink of an eye, I am plummeting towards the ground. I land flat on my back and am instantly gasping for breath. Straight afterwards, as if it were rehearsed, the ball falls from the tree and is caught by the woman. I scrunch my eyes. What was I thinking? There isn't even a rail here. My heart thuds in my chest.

'Perhaps I was a little over-confident,' I say, wheezing.

She sighs with relief and then laughs. 'I would certainly agree. Are you all right?' she asks.

'Yes,' I manage. 'Just a little out of breath.'

She removes a handkerchief from her pocket and dabs my forehead as though it would stabilize my breathing. Her dog waits patiently beside her. I manage to prop myself up against the trunk. 'I... haven't happened to notice you around here before now,' I tell her.

'I guess you wouldn't have, no,' she says. 'My husband and I only just moved here two days ago, as I was offered a job at the University of Xys.'

'Only two days ago?'

'Yes,' she says. 'Though, we've been planning the move for quite some time.'

'That must certainly prove stressful.'

'Indeed, it has been, but everything seems to be going according to plan.'

'Does your husband work here as well?'

'No. Well, he's a civil engineer. Houston is at the forefront of major engineering projects at the moment, so he thought it suitable to work there. We both have family in

Wales, so it was logical for us to stay here so that we can accommodate his work but see our families as well.'

'That's fortunate,' I say.

'Apart from the three-hour flight.'

'Right,' I say. There is a moment of silence, and I realise I can no longer hear the train. 'Well, I'm currently studying at the University of Xys.'

'Is that so?' she says, looking quite pleased. 'In that case, I may see you again sometime.'

'Yes, so it seems.'

'I'm Tracy, by the way.' She runs her hands through her dog's fur. 'Though I suppose at the university, I'd be called *Mrs Clark*.' she says in a mocking, English accent.

I huff. 'And I'm Samuel,' I say. 'It's lovely meeting you… and, of course, your dog.'

'Charlie,' she says to the dog, 'shake.' It holds out its paw and offers me a formal greeting.

'How clever,' I say, amused. 'I consider myself lucky to have crossed paths with the two of you.'

'Hmm,' says Tracy, pondering the notion. 'I don't believe in luck, per se, or accidents for that matter. Rather, that every encounter we have with others will prove to have some significance later on in our lives.'

'I quite like that philosophy. If only I were more outgoing.'

She laughs. 'Give it some time. You'll learn soon enough.'

I pick up the ball and throw it for Charlie, who runs off, zigzagging past the swings and zipping around the perimeter of the field.

'May I ask you a peculiar question, Tracy?' I enquire.

She looks sceptical. 'Go on,' she says.

'What is your purpose?'

'Purpose?' she repeats. 'Well, I guess that's an easy question for me to answer. My family, my work, my friends, and even my dog... They all encompass my purpose.'

'I see.'

'Do you not have someone or something that you find extremely valuable, irreplaceable at that?' she asks.

'Of course,' I say. 'I just never knew it was that simple, I guess.' I grin.

'The older you get, the clearer it becomes,' she says. 'It's quite normal to feel a little lost when one is young. I guess it's part of growing up.' She pauses. 'It's almost like I know you somehow,' she says, 'as though you were a student I used to teach.'

'I'm glad it seems that way.' I find myself feeling genuinely proud for being able to converse with a stranger.

Unfortunately, reality strikes the minute I get home. I've hardly found time to study during the last week. What makes matters worse, is the series of biology tests coming up within the next couple of days, covering the immune system as well as some content on molecular genetics. I can't fathom how Lucinda manages to ace her classes. After attempting to go over the gene expression process in my head, I get a little frustrated when I can't remember all of the pieces.

My room smells musky, and the sun is about to set. The conversation I had earlier makes me wonder why Lucinda chose me of all people. I look down at my skinny arms and hit my fist against my palm. All I ever do is complain and be complacent, I think. Now I have a reason not to be: if Lucinda chose to love me, then I'd better become someone that she can love fully.

I then attempt twenty push-ups, but barely manage the set before burning out. I curse myself, then get up and scribble something on a piece of paper before sticking it above my desk: "push-ups!". I daren't keep up this laziness.

The moonlight seeps through the dust-covered glass. I hear Mum shuffling around on the bottom floor, so I go down and walk around the corner; the dining room table comes into view.

Mum speaks from the kitchen, 'Evening, Samuel. How was your day?'

'Uneventful.' I sigh.

She peers around the kitchen wall, clearly suspicious. 'Hmmm?'

I shrug. 'In any case, how was it around here?'

She goes and sits down at the table. 'We received a letter from your father. Well, specifically, you did.'

'Isaac? Why would he want to contact me?' I ask, also taking a seat.

'Who knows?' she says. She seems a little concerned but, at the same time, nostalgic.

My parents thought highly of one another before they separated. Towards the end of their time together, my father began to think that their compatibility was lacking. That's what Mum tells me anyway. Mum still loved him long after that, and I feel, to this day, she's having a difficult time moving on. Though, I guess that's how it is with divorce: one person always feels more pain than the other.

I wonder whether Father just didn't have what it takes to give one's life to someone else. Was fear the main driver behind his actions? It makes me think of him as somewhat selfish, and it's why I chose my mother's surname instead of his. He doesn't play an all too big role in my life either. Not that it bothers me. I have never felt obliged to get to know him further. I tear the letter open.

Dear Samuel
I regret to inform you of some news I have recently become aware of. My company has gone bankrupt, and so, this will, unfortunately, be the last year I will have the means to fund your studies. You will need to look elsewhere to acquire financial support to further your education. I apologise for the inconvenience and wish you well.
I. Sanders.

I look over the top of the letter and stare at the table. 'Dammit!' I say and throw it down. I close my eyes.

'What does it say?' asks Mum. 'What's the matter?'

'Isaac won't be able to pay for my final year at university. His business went bankrupt.' I think about the irony of the situation: the first time I've heard from my father in years, and this is what he has to say.

My mum looks a little taken aback. 'What are we to do now?' she asks.

'I don't know,' I sigh. My stomach feels like it's about to implode.

'I can't say for certain what is to happen, Dear,' she says. 'But we'll work something out.'

'We can't even get financial aid from the university anymore,' I say coldly. 'It's far too late into the year for them to accept an application for it; nor are we in any sort of financial state to be approved for a student loan.' My expression is grim.

Mum sighs. 'Have faith,' she says. Faith? Faith in what? I trudge upstairs to my desk, pick up the blue sandstone and stare into the glittering shards. If only it could tell me what to do now. 'What would you have done back then?' I ask myself. The chances of getting a job without a degree behind one's name— I do not even wish to think that far. I find myself craving to be in Lucinda's company: she'd know what to say, but it's too late to see her now, and I wonder if she deserves to know in any case.

CALAMITY

24 LUCINDA

'**N**o,' *implores Lucinda,* laughing. 'I don't think my dishes can even begin to compare to this.'

'Well, *I* can't taste the difference,' insists Jonathan. Lucinda shakes her head. 'Although, this was your mother's favourite restaurant. She loved everything about it: the food, the atmosphere… oh and the wine too.' He studies his glass of Chardonnay. 'That's why we come here so often.'

'Father, I know,' says Lucinda, with an endearing look. 'You tell me every time.'

'I'm just making sure,' he says and pierces another piece of ham with his fork. 'Even though we come here often, it's still special to me.' He takes a sip of his wine. 'You should have seen what it was like thirty years ago. It was ever so cosy. The entire place was made from nothing but wood and stone. We used to come here to hide out from the cold sometimes. They would always have a fire going, you see; why, they still do. It was just this single building in the middle of vast greenery.'

Lucinda looks out of the window, trying to paint the image in her mind's eye.

'Must have been quite something,' she says and sighs. Her eyes defocus; the candle-lit tables become hazy circles. A middle-aged man stands up from an adjacent table, but immediately slumps over onto the carpeted floor. He is helped up by his partner but looks around the room and blinks as though he doesn't know where he is.

Lucinda titters. 'He must have fainted from standing up in such a hurry,' she whispers to her father.

'For sure,' he says. 'Try not to laugh about it, will you?'

'I can't help it,' says Lucinda. 'The way it happened was ever so comical.'

'That's rude!' says Jonathan, though his slanted smile gives him away. 'Anyhow.' He clears his throat. 'I think we may as well be on our way.' He gestures for the waiter.

As the two of them step outside, Jonathan takes Lucinda's hand. She realises just how much time has passed since arriving. Now, the streetlamps are shining, and the restaurant signs are all lit up.

They pass a large man leaning against the wall of a shadowy passage. Half of his face and massive biceps are illuminated from above. His eye sockets seem hollow, like a skull. He mutters something inaudible as they pass. While holding Jonathan's hand, Lucinda notices him tense up.

After the two of them are out of earshot, Jonathan says, 'Sweetie, this town isn't as safe as it used to be. I don't want you alone on these streets when it's nighttime. You should always have someone with you.'

'As you wish, Father' says Lucinda. Jonathan says nothing more, but Lucinda hears his shallow breathing. What's the worst that could happen, she wonders.

As they retreat from the city centre, the whining traffic becomes distant, and he seems to relax. Soon afterwards, the two of them arrive home.

Lucinda walks down the passage and enters the study, where she usually paints. Her brushes and pencils are scattered about the table, and an empty canvas rests on the easel. She sketches the outline of a landscape and, once satisfied, she picks up one of the brushes, inspecting the bristles. Just as she's about to dip her paintbrush into the water, there's a soft knock on the door. Who could possibly be visiting at this hour, and why not use the knocker?

She scampers along the passage in the dark and hesitantly slides the key into the door. When she opens it, however, there's no one in sight. This leaves her rather unsettled. She scans her surroundings and spots someone running down the sidewalk.

'Hey!' she calls out. When he looks back, she sees Samuel's face, and he seems troubled. 'Wait!' she says and dashes after him.

He slows to a stop. She draws nearer, cautiously this time. He remains still, but his shoulders tremor as though he's struggling to breathe. She takes hold of his hand.

'This wasn't meant to happen,' he says. 'I didn't mean to bother you. I don't know why I did.'

'Samuel,' she says quietly, 'tell me what's the matter.'

He wiggles out of her grip. His hair is flicked around in all directions by the wind. 'Please let it be. I'm sorry, but there's nothing that can be done.'

'You can tell me,' she says. 'I'm worried.'

He sighs. 'You don't deserve this. I daren't be so selfish.' He retreats farther and doesn't look back. He gets to the bench and slumps down, fooling himself by thinking that he's in the clear. Out of the darkness, hands reach out and cover his eyes. He sighs. 'Lucinda,' he says softly. 'This isn't your fight.'

She hops onto the bench, sitting next to him. 'I realise that I can't fix your problem.' She looks him in the eye. 'Though, I don't want you to feel this way.'

He shakes his head. 'Sometimes you just need to—' he trails off. She leans her head against his neck.

'I know that you didn't want to get me involved, so I won't ask, but may I stay here a bit?'

He closes his eyes. She hopes that she can help him clear his thoughts.

DISSONANCE

25 SAMUEL

There **is something so alluring** about heights. I've been here many times, on the top of the sciences building, but each occasion sparks the same sort of strange excitement. The grey clouds above have the consistency of lead. A dove perches next to me and begins strutting about in a staccato motion. I sometimes envy them since they lack intelligence to the point where they feel nothing entirely.

The traffic below paints a stream of red taillights, which trail around the buildings. The longer I stare over the edge, the calmer I feel; the more transfixed I become. The gridlines of windows disappear into the black sidewalk, though I see more than that: it feels like I'm looking into another dimension of reality, a more peaceful one. If only I could just get a glimpse of what it's like to be there.

In this world, even if I were the cleverest person alive, there's no funding to finish my degree. Yet I know what people will think. They will tell themselves that I'm selfish for wanting to leave this place, but they are sorely mistaken. They don't know what it's like to feel unworthy; that your absence is a favour to those who you love.

At that moment, the evening sun catches a window on the opposite building, and a golden glow bleeds into the haziness below. I lean over the edge, drawn to the light and yearning for finality, enamoured by the warmth of death's embrace. But something churns and buzzes within me, a pang of isolation so incredibly harsh and biting that it makes me freeze in place, but it's not the height that bothers me: all I can think of is not having Lucinda around anymore. Does she feel the same way about me? Does she deserve to be abandoned?

How is it that she can find even the faintest trace of worth in me? She's impulsive, no doubt, but she'll figure it out eventually. She's not *that* delusional.

I slump back onto the roof, from which a hint of warmth emanates. More tests are just around the corner. I seem to be at the final stage of it all. There's little that can be done now. Indeed, my fate is sealed. I try so hard to grasp the concepts and memorise the complicated diagrams and processes, but it often just doesn't stick.

Part of me feels like I don't belong in this world. That the systems which govern humanity were made for a different type of person, another part of me scolds my arrogance. It only makes sense that things should cater to the vast majority. Then again, we are not made to see reality as it truly is. I'm painfully aware of our tendency to distort things out of proportion yet, at the same time, fail to see a different perspective.

When descending the stairs, my body feels heavy. I'd better head home before I get myself worked up again.

The meandering road takes me across the bridge, and the river below has become a silvery trail originating from jagged, black slopes on the horizon.

When I get to the park, I slump down under the trees, staring up at the dark branches which resemble the spines of a sea-urchin. Sometimes, I have visions of them collapsing on top of me, their branches impaling my body like knives through a sponge.

I hear the train approaching and meander past the grove of trees, feeling my feet brush against small flowers.

The railway line appears before me, and I step onto it. As the locomotive nears, I imagine myself being torn to pieces by the metal beast. It would surely be glorious.

Instead, I simply step off of the track and put my hand out as it passes, feeling its smooth metal skin slide against my palm. It's sort of ticklish but warm at the same time. The friction begins to burn my hand, yet something urges me to keep it there longer, almost like I'm daring myself. The pain surging through my veins gives me a momentary high, and

I fall back onto the grass and clench my quivering wrist. Studying my palm makes me almost certain that pain and peace are just different forms of the same thing.

Suddenly, it clicks: I should not have been on my way home. In fact, it's almost time for an English lecture.

I get up and stagger out of the woods. Soon, I'm hobbling past the flags, after which I bust through the doors of the university, clearly in a muddle. Some of the students in the hallway stop and stare at me; others seem to take no notice. Some tosser juts his foot out in an attempt to trip me, but I grab hold of his shoulder just as I am going to fall. I step back and smile at him, noticing the bloody handprint on his shirt. 'Excuse me,' I say courteously.

'Watch where you're going,' he says, oblivious to the stain.

'Have a nice day,' I remark.

I pause outside the classroom and take a deep breath, feeling queasy from all the emotions swimming around in my head.

'Great to see that you made it,' says the lecturer in a voice that I recognise.

I'm stunned for a moment, then suddenly feel very exposed. 'I would have thought this to be a major coincidence, Mrs Clark, but I know you don't believe in those.'

RELAPSE

26 LUCINDA

T*oday I am awfully restless* and feel the need to clear my head. The past week has been quite the ride, even by my standard; yesterday just topped it off. I decide to visit Graham's shop for a change of pace.

Looking at the open road before me, it doesn't come to mind where the store is located, as I haven't visited for quite some time. Perhaps I'll just wander the neighbourhood until I stumble upon it.

A gust sings over the street, and a shutter slams closed with a jarring clang. For a split second, I am filled with the dreaded fear that was so evident just the other night. I inspect the row of houses, seeing nothing out of the ordinary, but take a second to catch my breath.

Though it takes only a moment for me to get on with it, and, before long, the flickering sign comes into view: 'Old South Antiques', the store Graham owns. I've been here a couple of times before. It should get my mind off things for the time being. Although I do love minimalism, I feel that an aged ornament has character. One can only imagine how much work was put into producing a good piece in times before the entire process was mechanized.

As I walk through the door onto the wooden floorboards, it feels like I have just been transported to the past. The dim lights give the interior a cavernous feel, and there are hundreds of objects scattered throughout the store.

'Lucinda! How truly wonderful to see you again!' Graham appears from behind the counter. He is wearing the most ridiculous purple tuxedo with brown leather shoes and a silver tie. I shake his hand, determined not to laugh.

'I am glad to see you as well, Graham,' I say.

'So, what do you think?' he asks, gesturing to our surroundings. 'Changed quite a bit since last you were here, hasn't it?' My eyes adjust to the light, and I begin to make out the plethora of shapes lying on dusty shelves.

'There are certainly more things to choose from,' I remark. He looks pleased.

Nothing seems to be categorized or grouped according to any logical system. Funnily enough, it's quite comforting in a way; utter chaos is a system in itself, I guess.

'I don't have anything specific in mind,' I tell him, 'but anything will do as long as it is out of the ordinary.'

'I'm sure there'd be something around here that ought to pique your interest.' I find it oddly satisfying to hear the creaking sound of our feet on the wooden floor. I pick up a bronze pocket watch. It has a small dial at the top, embossed with some sort of text, now faded beyond recognition. Although a little frosted, the glass on the front still shows its slightly iridescent, pearly face.

'That,' says Graham, leaning over the specimen, 'is a pocket watch which belonged to a combatant in the military. Most probably a World War Two soldier or fighter pilot.' He pauses. 'It's not working anymore, though.'

'I... don't mind, actually. I like it, nonetheless,' I say, staring at the still, brass hands which will never turn again. I figure it would serve as a reminder that we are only destined to live for a finite number of days, and eventually, each one of our clocks will stop as well.

'All right,' he says, intrigued by my decision. 'You can hold onto it for the time being.' We continue down the aisle. 'We have swords of every calibre,' he says, gesturing to a row of blades neatly stacked beside one another. He unsheathes a massive, steel rapier. 'The craftsmanship of this piece is astounding,' he says as he runs his finger along the fuller. From far, the finish appears to be a smooth, polished surface, but as I look more closely, I start to make out the engravings, almost as though cup-and-saucer vines are growing along the steel in finely cut grooves. He hands me the blade, and I almost sink to my knees under its weight.

'How do you expect a lady of my stature even to carry this piece of lead?' We both laugh. He takes the sword and sheathes it for me.

'Fair enough,' he says. He then opens another cabinet beside it. 'Is this more to your liking?' he asks, retrieving a small dagger. 'It was crafted in the same manner as the sword.' He lays it across my palms. The handle has a matte finish, and the blade is no longer than my forearm. It's rather striking. 'This looks interesting,' I say. 'I'll think about it.'

We continue walking down the dim passage. He opens a cupboard and removes a necklace from one of the shelves.

'How about this?' he asks, dropping it in my hand. I inspect the glistening stone encircled by a thin, golden brace. It has tints of green, red, and blue that seem to jump about as I tilt it in the light.

'This must be opal,' I say.

'Yes,' he says. 'That's... quite right.' He brushes his hand on his chin. 'How did you come to know of this type of stone? Do you already own something made with opal?'

'No,' I say. 'but my father has been all over Australia. He told me that opal was an abundant stone in the jewellery stores across the country and described something like this.' I pause for a brief moment. 'Though it's far too flashy for my liking,' I say and drop it back into his hand. He seems a little taken aback by my audacity, though he then nods.

'How about these pieces?' he says, gesturing to a small, glass cabinet. Before I can reply, he darts off along the carpeted floor. 'I'll just get the keys.'

'All right.' I say and chuckle at his enthusiasm. I look into the cabinet and see a few rolled-up posters, a globe, and also what looks to be a telescope of sorts. His coattail disappears through the doorway behind the shop counter. I peer to the left of the door and see another row of cabinets against the wall.

He doesn't emerge for the next minute, and I begin to get a little suspicious. I walk up to the counter, but the doorway he went in is far too dark to see into. When inspecting the contents of the cabinets, I notice a dainty wooden box with see-through panels on its sides, with what looks to be a sort of clock mechanism within it. The sound of keys rattling makes me look towards the door once more.

'Found them,' he says, scrolling through a set of keys on a large metal ring.

'You know what,' I say, 'could you perhaps show me that little box?' I point into the cabinet.

'Oh, yes,' he says. 'It is one of my favourite pieces.' He shuffles through the keys again before unlocking the panel. As he does so, I hear the faint sound of raindrops. Within moments, the streaky greys line the street.

'Raining again?' he asks.

'It seems so,' I reply.

'Lucky that we're both in the store. It's quite easy to get caught in the rain in these parts. One minute you're strolling along a sunlit street; the next, you're soaked from head to toe. It's ludicrous if you ask me.'

'Yes,' I say, giggling. 'I've experienced it on more than one occasion.'

He places the box on the counter. It is more or less the length of my hand, and its frame seems to be crafted from a type of hardwood, sanded down to a matte but even finish. 'So, what's special about the box?' I ask.

'Just you wait,' he says, gleaming. On every face of the box, apart from the bottom, there is a small, glass panel so that one is able to look within it to see various cogs, ratchets and springs. It rests on a base of engraved wood, a couple of centimetres thick. The larger cogs have a sand-blasted finish, while the rest of the mechanism is polished to a mirror sheen.

He presses a round indentation on the side of the base, and a brass cylinder with grooved edges pops out. He then inserts it into the other side and twists it a few times to wind up the springs. The cogs begin to rotate slowly. An escapement oscillates. Briefly afterwards, a tune emanates from the contraption.

'A music box!' I say, enthralled. 'I'd never have guessed. I can't say I've come across one quite so intricate.'

'That's right,' he says. 'Most music boxes have a coil that is wound up, which simply unwinds afterwards to drive the mechanism. In those sorts of music boxes, however, the tune inevitably deviates from its original tempo as the song progresses. The creator of this piece was obviously determined to get around this, so he implemented a timing mechanism. It's also made with sapphire cog bearings.'

'Fascinating,' I say, leaning a little closer to get a better look. Sure enough, the bearings glint with a rosy hue. It seems to be in cherry condition as well. It'd be a shame if I were to keep it for myself. I wonder whether I could—

'Do you fancy it?' he asks, interrupting my train of thought.

'I think I just might,' I say. 'How much is it going for?'

'Let's see,' he says, removing a book from under the counter. He runs his finger down the page, stopping halfway. 'The seller wanted three hundred and fifteen pounds for it, but since this is your the first time you've visited in a while, three hundred seems reasonable,' he says. 'And the stopwatch, I'd say you can have free of charge.

I'm quite taken aback by the proposal. 'That would cut your profit,' I say. 'I don't mind paying the extra fifteen dollars, not to mention the stopwatch. It has to be worth something, at least.'

'Nonsense,' he says. 'Think of it as a token of our friendship. Rekindling the old flame, as one might say.'

'Why, thank you,' I tell him. He rings up the transaction, and I place the corresponding cash on the counter. 'Oh, the rain has stopped. I never even noticed.'

'So it has,' he says, looking out the window cheerfully.

'Well,' I say, 'hopefully, I'll see you again shortly.'

'I'm sure you will.' He waves to me as I leave the store.

SERENDIPITY

27 SAMUEL

I *sit on the white bench* outside my house, paging through my biology textbook. Mrs Clark's address has been on my mind; the fact that each end leads to some sort of new beginning, and when something leaves, something else comes along. I wonder whether she was referring to things she's personally experienced or if it extends further than life itself. I guess there's no way of knowing whether—

Someone pops out from behind the bench and takes hold of my shoulders. I don't even have to look back to know who it is; the coolness of her hands seeps into my skin.

'Were you watching me?' I ask. She seems disappointed that I appear unstartled by her scheme.

'Perhaps,' she admits. 'I may have even followed you home.'

'You do live quite near.' I glance upwards, and she stares back, leaning over me. My thoughts drift back to a few months ago. I considered complete isolation normality. Now, I'm almost too used to having company.

'What's the matter?' she asks. I can't tell whether I like the fact that she can practically read my mind. I brush it off and simper. 'I won't distract you,' she reassures me.

A few moments later, she rests her head on my lap and looks up at me. I think about how she'd feel, had I really leapt from that building. She sits up with an endearing yet troubled expression. 'Something is the matter. Is it not?'

'It's nothing,' I say. 'I'm just glad that you're here. That's all.' She has a look of satisfaction as she takes my hand beside me but soon frowns as her fingers brush over my scuffed palm. She presses it gently with her thumb while studying me sceptically.

'I fell— down the stairs,' I say, gritting my teeth.

Her eyes narrow. 'Not buying it,' she says and folds her arms. 'I mean, look what you did here.' She traces her fingertips over the marks on my arm.

'My scars? Not that they even matter.'

She stares at me with an intensity that kind of scares me, then sighs and looks away. 'Except, to me, they do. I worry for you sometimes.' She lies down on my lap once more. I laugh nervously, though I can't stop the tears from welling up at the sight of her serene face. I don't understand how someone like her, with all the intellect and beauty anyone could ask for, would waste her precious time on someone like me. With the next out-breath, I squeeze my eyes shut and shiver a bit.

'I don't know why this comes to mind, but I think you're wrong about me.' My blood goes cold in that moment. I hear the words from earlier in my head… pathetic creep. Are they true? 'Whatever it is you see in me simply can't be so. It's my responsibility to bring positivity into your life, and I don't think I'm up for it.'

She sits upright, but I don't look her in the eye. I stand, wanting to leave her be, but she grabs hold of my hand. I wince. 'Nice try, but I reject your self-fulfilling prophecy of nonsense. I know you, Samuel, and I see you more for who you are than you, yourself, do.' Her voice is firm. 'The only thing I want from you is to be by my side, nothing more to it, and there are certainly no conditions involved.'

'I don't feel like I deserve you.' I sigh. 'You've changed my entire life for the better, but why would you?'

'You and I are far more alike than you think. Before I came to Xys, there wasn't anyone who'd accept me for who I was,' she speaks hurriedly, 'because, well— I wasn't who I was anymore.'

'I don't understand. What do you mean by that?'

'It's— it's masking, right?' She has an awkward smile. 'Pretty obvious when you think about it.' I stare at her blankly. 'I changed, Samuel. In a way that people couldn't process. Though, you didn't seem to mind having me around. That's what makes you so incredibly special.'

I'm a bit stunned. 'Even so, how could I live up to someone like you?'

'What on earth are you talking about? You have absolutely nothing to prove.' She leans in close. 'I've already fallen in love with you, the person you are now.' The book falls out of my hand. In spite of who I fundamentally am, she cares an awful lot about me.

'I love you too,' I say clumsily.

'Oh, you're terrible at this.'

I have a sheepish grin. 'Some of it has to do with you putting me on the spot all the time.'

'It's good fun,' she says, tracing my jawline with her finger. She picks up the book and hands it to me. 'Get on with it then,' she says perkily.

While in a state of such tranquillity with her around, I manage to get through most of the book. I wonder why Lucinda doesn't need to study this time, though I figure she may be ahead in the syllabus. She notices when I close the book. 'Would you like to go?' she asks.

'May we walk?' I take her hand, lifting her to her feet. She nods. 'So,' I begin, thinking of something to ask, 'what have been your recent artistic endeavours?'

'Currently, a project based on the realism era, around the 1850s.' We move off the road and onto the grass.

'Making any progress?' I ask.

'Slowly. She sighs. 'Realism isn't exactly my cup of tea. It's a drag to get a good result, and you end up with something that resembles a coloured photo in any case.'

'It can be very technical,' I remind her. She looks a little unimpressed. 'At the very least, it's strengthening some or other artistic skill.'

'It's true, I guess.'

After about a minute, she says, 'The other day, you were going to tell me something, and you said that it would be selfish, should you do so.' We continue in silence. 'Though, that isn't the way it ought to be dealt with. One should talk about these things.'

I stare blankly ahead. 'I haven't changed my mind.'

'You're mistaken,' she says. 'What's selfish is *not* to share and keep me worried.' Her dark eyebrows are furrowed like silvery streams.

'That makes no sense at all.'

Within moments, I'm flat on my belly with my arms pulled up behind me. Lucinda presses her knee on my back.

'You *will* tell me!' she says firmly. I grit my teeth, my cheek pressed against the tarmac. It's all secretly very amusing.

'I submit,' I splutter. 'I'll tell you.' She gets up and looks away from me. '*Now*, what could be the matter?' I ask, rolling onto my back, grinning.

'I'm sorry,' she says softly. 'I don't know what got into me. You need not feel obliged. I just get paranoid when I can't figure out these sorts of things.'

I study her for a second, then sigh. 'I've thought about it in the meantime, and I don't mind sharing.' I get up, and she dusts off my shirt. 'It has to do with our... financial problems. My father was paying for my degree, but his business recently went bankrupt.'

She puts her fingers over her eyelids. 'That's heavy. Your mother doesn't work, does she?'

'No, Mum hasn't worked for quite some time. My best option would have been a loan, but the applications have ended already. I didn't want you to share this burden.'

She gives my shoulder a squeeze. 'You've come too far to lose hope. We'll put our minds together and work something out.'

'Hmmm? People are hard-wired to be illogically optimistic about the long-term future. It's a genetic trait that has led to the success of our species. More optimistic individuals are more likely motivated to overcome challenges, but it often leads to groupthink and delusion. It's why most tend to think that bringing children into this ghastly world is anything less than undeniably worth it.'

'Is that so?' she asks as she draws nearer. 'Do you think it would be worth it for us?' I choke and go rigid. 'I was jesting,' she says. 'I hate the little whippersnappers.'

'You tease me to no end. Why are you averse to them?'

She pauses, then says, 'The start of a child's life is the end of a woman's ambitions, in the current state of society anyway. And I haven't a clue how to behave around a baby. Do I pinch its cheeks, or do I pet it, as I would a dog? Each action you could think of has a chance of triggering its crying state.'

'Women are supposed to be maternal!' I bellow.

'Don't even get me started on the stereotypes,' she says bitterly. 'Yes, generally, it is advantageous for our species to care for its… offspring, though random mutations can cause discrepancies.' She laughs a bit. 'I guess my heritable traits ensure the end of my bloodline. It's the reason why people such as myself constitute the minority.'

I take some time to process this. 'Interesting...'

'Though, children aside,' she says, 'I'm certain that things will work themselves out.' Her walking slows. 'Besides, your heart is beating, is it not?' she asks, tracing a circle on my chest.

'What are you getting at?' I ask, simpering.

'It means you're alive and well.' She stares as though seeing my heart through my skin. 'Things could be worse, that's all,' she says. 'I can see things that you simply dismiss in yourself. Things that make you valuable to me. And not just to me: they make you inherently valuable. You are blinded by your inner critic.' She then exhales.

I try so hard to see what she sees, to know that there are aspects of oneself to be grateful for. I've believed the contrary for so long.

She envelopes me in a hug, and a sense of peacefulness flows through my entire body. I realise then that as dire as things may get, I can't help but feel like I'm worth something when I'm in her arms.

CHERISH

28 LUCINDA

My *clenched fists and tense shoulders* burn from fatigue. I can't take it any longer: being so powerless in this situation. The uncertainty of Samuel's future is truly taking its toll.

It's incredibly frustrating that I'm unable to do much about it. We'll have to get help elsewhere.

I squint, finding the bright lights rather bothersome, but what aches more is the possibility that Samuel might not be here next year. Life would have to go on, but how could it?

My hand jots down notes mechanically, but my mind is fixated on the words Samuel spoke: that we're simply hard-wired to think positively in the long run, even though there may be little truth to it. The concept taunts me. No matter what I try to tell myself, a quiet yet unmistakable voice remains in the back of my mind, assuring me that everything will eventually collapse.

I grit my teeth. This is not like me. I should do what I've always done: keep my head down and take each step as it comes. But is such a mindset worth it when I am aware that my time is finite— and in short supply?

I am the last to leave the hall, hobbling along like a nun. A lump forms in my chest, which makes it difficult to take a full breath. 'Leave me alone,' I whisper. 'Get out of my head. Just let me be.' I've heard so often of the seed of doubt; how it can so quickly spiral out of control. I hug my textbooks, my fingers running over their corners spontaneously.

As I leave the building, the sound of my rasping breath further feeds into the detachment I feel, and my heart is jumping about in my chest.

I jolt when a sedan zips past my face, and am aggravated by the thundering engine and fumes. Upon hearing footsteps on the other side of the street, my eyes leer sideways to see a group of young men walking along the sidewalk, mucking about and teasing one another. They each wear similar-looking clothes and exchange careless grins as well. 'Naïve bastards,' I whisper in envy.

One of them points at me, and I drop my head to the floor. Dammit, they could've heard that. I dearly hope that it's just a coincidence. When they simultaneously crackle at something and cut diagonally into the road, I sense malicious intent. My footsteps escalate in tempo. Though, the instant I pass the middle of the bridge, my wrist is seized. I freeze. My hand twitches ever so slightly.

'You aren't going to split that easy,' he says satirically.

'Kiss off,' I splutter, not looking back. 'I am in no state to contend with fools.'

He glances at his friends and smiles sadistically before wrenching my arm to the floor, pinning it there. The pair of textbooks tumble onto the tarmac; the one lies splayed with its pages rippling in the wind. My shoulder joint crackles as the brute applies more pressure. On a different day, I would have tried to resist it, put up some sort of fight at least. But I feel too drained right now, too downtrodden to do a thing.

'You rich scum look down on us. I can see it— the way you people act around us.' His one hand contorts my wrist, but I try to keep a straight face.

'I can't tell where you got that impression,' I splutter. 'I would never look down on someone based on wealth,' I crane my neck up towards him. 'Though—' I take a shaky breath. 'I can't say I'm fond of those who take out their nonsensical resentment by physically abusing others.'

He stares at me, seemingly more infuriated, though he doesn't move. He then snaps the fingers of his free hand and points at the books.

'They're not even mine,' I protest. 'We don't own those books. I am to return them after the semester.'

'Well, maybe I would have let this slide if you hadn't opened your mouth, you spineless munter.'

My crooked posture causes the air to rasp in my throat. One of his friends picks up the genetics book and dangles it over the bridge. I realise I've seen him before… somewhere. His fringe sticks up and curls back in the most ridiculous way. I figure it'd be unwise to point it out at this point.

He examines the book for a few seconds before grabbing hold of a group of pages. He then rips them out slowly, knowing how torturous it sounds to me, all the while grinning like a sadist. The pages are stolen by the wind and fly skyward. Afterwards, he holds both books over the bridge and lets them drop. My arm is released. They all stare as I stagger to the edge of the bridge, looking over to see the books wedged among the river stones, now waterlogged.

'You will regret this. I swear,' I say, with painful futility.

One of them sniggers and the gang leaves, deciding I've had enough for one day. At that point, it begins to drizzle. My hands clench my hair as a pit of darkness swells up inside of me, tearing up my thoughts.

I walk around the side of the bridge and step down to the water's edge. I pick up the books in turn, knowing that there is little hope for them at this point. The pages have turned to mush, and the ink has become fuzzy. I start to hear my own breathing again, riddled with agitation.

I begin scampering along the street towards my house. Luckily, the gang has since gone the other way. At that point, I see Samuel on the sidewalk and instinctively turn on my heel to head back over the bridge. He shouldn't see me in this state. I hobble along, looking over my shoulder. The moment I think I've lost him, I jolt at the sight of his face right in front of me. He probably thinks it's some sort of game. I just wave and try to smile, now standing in place. Perhaps he doesn't even notice.

But inevitably, he does.

'What on earth happened?' he asks. 'Your books are soaked from the rain. How are you going to study genetics or physiology?'

I keep quiet for a moment. 'It's not the rain that did it,' I say. 'Some things are just out of my control, I guess.'

'So, it was a person,' says Samuel. His eyes are swirling voids, and his expression is dead straight. I can't read him.

'It doesn't matter,' I say, wondering if I managed to set him off. I immediately regret not just agreeing with him—that it was just the rain. I turn away and begin walking towards my house.

'You had better tell me who it was,' says Samuel.

'Not a chance,' I say. 'I know what you're like. You'd stop at nothing just to prove a point.'

'You think that's what I'm after. Oh, you have no idea.' His voice is clear in the dismal air. 'Some things you just can't forgive.'

The two of us are now standing outside my house. Samuel walks away without saying another word. His figure fades into the mizzly haze. I hope he manages to let it go.

What he said makes me wonder what would have happened had I tried to stand up for myself. Perhaps I am, as they say, a spineless— I wince.

Lightning flashes, and I briefly see the outline of houses along the street. Now, the rain begins bucketing down. The hairs on my neck stand on end, but I just stand there. An icy stream tickles my spine, and I cradle the books in my arms. I stare at the wavering droplets, which fall from my hair and soon vanish. The sky is now streaky black.

I fumble for the keys to unlock the door, then go inside and set my books next to the fireplace to dry. I disappear along the passage to fix my dishevelled state. After drying off my hair, I change my clothes and go back to the dining room. The fire seems welcoming, and so I sit there briefly.

Afterwards, I walk, a little disheartened, through the lonely passages, seeing a blank canvas propped up against a wall in the study. It's almost beckoning to be brought to life. A new painting ought to cheer me up.

I put my realism project aside and place the clean canvas on the easel. I start to paint, figuring that I'm just going to have to see where my brush leads me.

My hands are shaking too much to make smooth strokes with the paintbrush, and I just can't seem to focus at all. The canvas glistens with thick oil paint, which sculpts miniature mountains and crevasses of white and grey across its textured surface. I begin to blend the colours to transition between the light and shadow in the scene.

After some time, I observe my emotions changing. It's as though the nervous energy is flowing from my fingertips and leaving me through the bristles of my brush. It draws out some of my anguish and solidifies it as shape and colour, in the form of mountains and trees. I stare intently. The one side of my mind is absorbed by the atmosphere of the alpine scene evolving with each stroke. The other side, my more conscious thoughts, are spinning into a blur that I can't begin to make sense of. I try my very best to ignore the lot.

I'll just have to keep my head down. I can manage things like this. I've done it all my life, I'm sure. Though, it's difficult to believe with nothing to look back on.

My smiling eyes try to hold back the tears. Soon, the canvas is dripping with blotches of black and red, snaking downwards. I'm strong. I have to be strong, but how can I be after what just happened?

I set the paintbrush down and curl up on the floor. The room around me swirls, and it feels as though it's going to swallow me whole. My father always said that it takes a stronger person to forgive than to seek revenge. I will try my absolute best to forget about all of this. Though, something feels different: a puzzle piece that snapped into place, a bitter-sweet sensation buried deep down in my conscience. I feel that I am no longer the same person I was before. Next time, it will be different.

EMERGENCE

29 SAMUEL

Samuel's eyes feel worn out from staring at his books all day. Push-ups, he decides, would be a good change of pace. By this stage, he manages to do fifteen, mostly because of his consistent efforts.

He then walks outside, book in hand. While pacing along the road, staring at the writing, he veers onto the sidewalk as a car flies past, feeling a sense of gratification. I care now, he thinks. It seems like a long time since he felt that: caring about being alive.

He hears a giggle beside him that makes his heart flutter. 'Oh, thank you for finding me,' he says.

'It's my pleasure,' says Lucinda, skipping along in a navy blue dress with a white lining. 'Guess where we're going,' she says.

'We're going somewhere?' asks Samuel.

'Yes,' she says. 'The art gallery, of course. You're dressed nicely for it as well.' He's wearing a deep maroon shirt, which she rather fancies.

Samuel looks a bit flushed at the thought of an art gallery, unable to decide whether or not he approves.

'I realise that you're scared of colours,' she says playfully, 'and that's why we're heading there.'

'It's no joke,' says Samuel, soon blushing. Lucinda just keeps walking as though captivated by something. And to him, she begins to become captivating herself.

'In any case,' she says, 'the both of us like art, and I've decided that we don't see enough of it.'

'Oh, but I'm looking at art right now,' says Samuel.

Lucinda frowns, trying to make sense of what he said. She realises what he means the moment she looks back and sees him gazing at her.

'Oh, *do* shut up,' she says and quickly looks forward, hiding a grin.

When the two of them walk through the glass doors, an old man with thick spectacles looks them up and down. Samuel takes in his surroundings, unable to shake the feeling of isolation. The sort of people that visit places like this seem so foreign to him: dressed to the nines and waddling about in corduroy jackets and navy suits.

Their actions appear unnervingly mechanical. They follow the same pattern of walking up to a particular painting, gazing at it for a few moments, and then calmly continuing along to the next one. Occasionally, they would nod in approval of what they saw. An old man hobbles towards them, so they move to make way for him. Samuel wonders how his flat-cap manages to stay on top of his head, considering his acute shaking.

When he's out of earshot, Lucinda leans in close and whispers, 'Kill me before I get to that point, please.' He gasps. 'You were thinking it, were you not?'

'Quite frankly, I wasn't,' he retorts.

'Well, I'd eat my hat if I had one,' she says. 'Though I demand it of you. "If it were done when 'tis done, then 'twere well. It were done quickly."'

'Gosh, Lucinda, that's one questionable set of morals you have.'

She chuckles under her breath. He takes notice of their surroundings, and it reminds him of the previous exhibition. He shivers a little. Lucinda, noticing this, takes the book from him and grasps his hand a little tighter.

'Oh, I love that one,' she says and takes him to a painting of pale pink flowers. 'They're proteas. And this one's superb as well.' She gestures to an abstract portrait with white tiles in the background. 'It reminds me of something Klimt would have done.' He nods, not knowing who Klimt is, though admiring the work, nonetheless. 'Oh, and this one looks like a Kandinsky,' she says and shows him an array of bright green and red shapes. It doesn't have the same effect that it would have before. Her fingers envelop his hand like the rivulets of a cool stream.

'It does,' he says. 'It's marvellous.' At least Samuel knows how to tell apart a Kandinsky.

'It's always fun to imagine what the artist must have been going through when they paint particular works,' she says. 'The best ones are either utterly dire or entirely out there.' She stops at something resembling a strange sort of cat made out of simple triangles with a spiral in its eye.

'What do you think was going through the head of this artist?' he asks.

She chortles. 'My guess is that he was on the downward spiral of a week-long bender.'

He giggles. 'I think so, too.'

'The two of us ought to travel Europe together. It'd be awe-inspiring to see the works of the greats,' she says. He smiles affectionately, loving the way she becomes radiant when speaking of things she admires. 'I've never had someone with which to do this sort of thing. Thank you.'

'Anything for you,' he says.

Lucinda considers this. 'Anything?'

'Yes,' he says, a tad suspicious. She smiles grimly.

'What are you conjuring up?' he asks, alarmed.

'Oh, nothing,' she says. He glares. 'Nothing yet...'

'What have I gotten myself into?'

She has a hint of mischief in her eyes. 'The possibilities...' she whispers. 'Simply endless.'

COLOUR

30 LUCINDA

*I **look through the antique store's window.*** Graham is sitting with his back facing the door, twiddling his thumbs. I suppose it must have been a quiet day for him. I open the door slowly to ensure that the bell does not ring before sneaking up behind him and giving him a tap on the shoulder. Immediately, I duck down behind what seems to be a medieval set of armour.

'Who's there?' he says. I jump out from my hiding place, and he springs off the chair. 'Jeepers creepers!' he exclaims. 'My God! That probably took a few years off.'

'Am I *that* scary?' I ask.

'*You're* not scary,' he says, 'It's what you *do* that's scary.'

'I'll take that as a compliment.'

'Goodness gracious.' He exhales. 'So, what are you after today?'

'I was thinking something at least a little bit old, and it has to be artistic.' I purse my lips, wondering if that was perhaps a little too specific.

'Old and artistic,' he says, looking sideways. 'You do have strange requests.'

'Naturally,' I say. 'Strange is novel, novel is unique and unique is good.'

'Well, I happen to have some peculiar pendants I received the other day.' He walks two steps backwards and picks up a pair of silver chains from which stylized, engraved animals hang. 'The Irish associated wolves with loyalty, strength and power.'

'My-my.' I hesitate a bit. 'I think I quite like wolves,' I say softly. A cool breeze envelopes my ankles, and I shiver a little.

'I thought you would be interested in them since you seem like one to appreciate the artistic qualities of a piece.'

'It's true.' I think of Samuel and I wearing them, but something about it feels off.

'Can you hold them for a moment?' he says, placing them in my hand. The chains slide over my fingers like serpents.

Graham scurries along the passage and heaves the window closed. I stare at his elongated shadow as he ambles back.

'They're beautiful, but I—' My hand quivers. 'I don't know if I'd be comfortable buying them.' I carefully return them to their place on the shelf. He looks confused. 'No reason for it,' I say and smile nervously.

He simply nods once more, luckily not questioning further.

I glance over various other items on the shelves, completely ungrouped. I pick up the same dagger I was considering the other day, and only now do I notice just how decorative the sheath is.

'Have you come to change your mind?' asks Graham.

The metal handle is engraved with fine patterns which are only visible when viewed at the right angle. When I take it out of its sheath, the spine is perfectly straight, and the cutting edge is in the shape of a shallow 'S', with a slight bulge near the upper part of the blade.

'It's a work of art,' I say.

'The attention to detail is superb,' says Graham. 'Certainly hand-crafted. And one can tell it was cast from a single piece of metal as well.'

I flick the blade into the air, catching it facing down. 'Perfectly balanced, too. How much did you say it was again?'

He walks over to the counter and finds the item quite quickly in his book. 'It's thirty-five,' says Graham.

'Seems a bargain. I'll take it.'

Once I've paid for it, he says, 'I shall see you anon.' I wave and walk out of the door with my textbooks under my arm, but at the same time, I can't help but ask myself: will he? I wonder if he is going to see me again at all. I can sense the pressure building; that something is going to happen.

On the way back, I examine one of the textbooks. It's jarring to be reminded of the events which led to the blurry ink I now see. It makes my head spin when I think about it for too long. I lie on the grass under the streaky shade of the trees at the park. The flowers are magnificent. Sitting among them, I inhale the breeze, catching their scent. There are now green leaves sprouting on the twisting branches of the trees. They are no longer bare.

After some time, I begin to hear the sound of the train becoming louder after each passing second. I sit up in anticipation. The ground trembles a little as it draws nearer. When it becomes visible behind the trees, I look at my watch: 09:17. I figure the train travels the same route every day. I walk up to the tracks and see an array of different cars, each carrying their own cargo, flicking past.

I wonder what it's like to be the conductor. It's a standard freight train made to carry heavy loads and can often function for decades under normal working conditions. It looks incredibly old, but judging by the smooth, metallic sounds, it still has years to go before being decommissioned.

I grin when an idea springs into my head.

SHARP

31 SAMUEL

'*Alkalophile, acidophile,* barophile, haloph—' My shoulder bumps into someone.

'Hey!' a female voice snaps. The corridor is entirely dark. There has been a power outage since about an hour ago.

'Charlotte?' I ask. 'Is that you?'

'Yes,' she says, a little excited. 'I... don't know who you are, though.'

'It's Samuel,' I say, giggling. 'I recognised your voice.'

'Thank goodness,' she says. 'All the passages look the same in the dark. I haven't a clue where I'm going.'

'I'm glad we're in the same boat for once, though. I'm afraid I can't be of much help in that department.'

'Hmmm?' She pauses. 'Men are supposed to have superior spatial intelligence.'

I cough. 'And every data set has its outliers.'

'Are you here for the test as well?' I ask.

'Yes,' she says, 'but I wouldn't know whether we write during power outages.'

'I don't know either, though I wasn't willing to take the chance.' She chuckles in agreement as we enter the hall.

Each desk has been supplied with an oil lantern. I would never have guessed this level of preparedness. I sit down at the nearest vacant seat and twiddle my thumbs. I recognise Mr Diara's voice but can just barely make out his face in the dim light. He instructs us to begin, and so I open the green booklet.

As soon as the questions appear before me, the magnitude of the task begins to settle in. A bubble of despondency wells up inside of me as I try to write down as much as I remember, but simultaneously realise that the sum of my knowledge just won't cut it. Who was I kidding? What was I trying to prove by studying so hard? I thought I could change, but I am who I am: nothing more than a fool. I don't think I even deserve to be in this hall. I don't deserve to be anywhere.

The session ends, and the test papers are collected. I walk out of the hall like a convict. I don't even need to wait for the results to deduce that I have done poorly.

I trip over something in the passage, and the side of my head strikes the ground when I fall. I hear a high-pitched ringing in my temples.

'What happened, loser? Failed again?' A menacing face leans over me, barely distinguishable in the gloomy passage.

'Most probably,' I say, not even trying to conceal my sorrow, yet feeling no malice either.

'Why not just die, you worthless creep?' he barks.

'Perhaps,' I feel a sense of sullen peace trickle through my skull, 'you may be right,' I murmur. 'You've always been right.' My vision trembles as I get to my knees. 'Have a nice day,' I say and push through the crowd, then pull myself up the railing of the stairs. My heart is pounding in my head. I open the fire escape, and my knees buckle as I take my first step up the spiral staircase.

The roof is dark and calm, and headlights below create intertwined, revolving shadows on the street. The sky above me is spinning as though I'm standing on a carousel. I bite my knuckles. It feels like my teeth are sinking into rubber.

People who don't contribute to anything don't deserve to live. I hear the crunching of the gravel, and the sound of my breathing makes me feel like I'm talking to spirits. My heart races as I stand on the edge.

A few months back, I thought that courage was simply speaking to someone you don't know, but I know now for certain that true courage is knowing you're alive but not fearing the alternative.

'Don't take this to heart, but it's time for me to go.'

'Wait there a moment, will you?' I suddenly feel the wind on my face, and my heart jumps. A hand reaches out from the shadows and rests on my shoulder. 'Wait for me, ok.' The figure steps onto the edge of the building, and her silhouette reflects no light. Only her face and hands are visible.

'Lucinda,' I say under my breath, 'what are you doing here?' Her fingers, cold as frost, gently wrap themselves around mine.

'Maybe if you decided to look up, you'd have seen the stars,' she says.

When I tilt my head upward, sure enough, the sky is sparkling with the most brilliant, white dust. The city is submerged in total darkness; no other light can wash out the constellations. Endless, glowing clusters stretch across the sky. I then feel awfully self-conscious: she knows. Lucinda knows that I wanted to end myself. Why is she not saying anything? The two of us just stand there, holding hands.

I step back, away from the edge. 'I'm sorry,' I tell her.

'Don't apologise. You can't apologise for the way that you're feeling. It can't be helped,' she sighs shakily. 'Though, please don't go just yet. I still need you here.'

I am filled with the strangest feeling— it's as though my past and future are crashing into one another, and there's no room for the present. At that point, I stumble backwards and snap back into my body. My head is spinning, and I'm forced to lie down.

Lucinda peers over me with an almost inquisitive expression. 'To be honest,' she says, 'I have no idea what's going through your head right now, but know that you're not what you think you are. If you feel lost— or worthless, realise that I found you, and you're worth more to me than you may ever know.' I feel like sinking into the ground, but find strength looking into her eyes, embraced by her gentle power and the delicate fortitude radiating from her palm.

'You know the last time I was here, you... intervened as well,' I say. 'In a metaphorical sense, I mean,' I mumble.

'The last time? How so?' Her hair flicks over one eye, and her other looks downward.

'I thought about you, and that's the reason I—' I keep silent for a moment. 'Do you ever feel like you're floating through life making little impact at all?'

'Samuel, you've had a bigger impact on me than anyone I know. We're living, and we're breathing, and no matter how you look at it, life is a gift. That's all there is to it.' She looks up at the stars. 'Thinking about it too much would drive anyone insane.'

She stands up and offers me a hand. When I take it, she spins me around like a dancer and then grabs hold of my shirt. I jolt when I realise I'm leaning over the edge of the building. The lights from below glow on her cheeks.

'Appreciate what you've been given,' she says with a childlike smile. 'It could disappear in an instant, my dear.'

'I promise,' I say, feeling the wind rushing past my ears, the adrenalin in my torso. She has the same scarlet glint in her eyes, and I remember that first evening so clearly. She pulls me up and closer; her fingers brush through my hair, and the same pain is on my lips. The kind of burning pain that feels so good. The pain that reminds me I'm still alive; that we're both still alive. Things could be worse, she said. Maybe I am a fool. But I think I'm ok with that.

She gestures for me to lie down on the roof next to her and she brings my head to her chest. I listen to her rhythmic breathing, and the only way I can think to describe her heartbeat is that it sounds like death because it excites me just the same. Though I'd never wish for her to be left alone.

The glinting stars surround us like a blanket. 'Th-there's Polaris,' I say, pointing. 'It actually consists of three different stars and... that's Aquila.' My hand moves just above the horizon. 'It's Latin for "eagle."'

She stirs. 'An eagle? I don't see it,' she says and giggles. 'Can you show me where it is?'

My hand traces an arrow-like shape. 'There are the wings. You have to use your imagination a bit, I know,' I say, chuckling for the first time. It feels slightly foreign.

'Ahh, I see it now,' she tells me.

'I can't remember the last time I've seen the stars like this,' I say.

I name many more stars and constellations for her. Then I point out the milky way.

'Beautiful,' she says and studies me for a second. 'What else can you tell me about stars?'

'Well, they're formed when molecular clouds become dense enough to collapse under their own gravity,' I say. 'For a long period of time, this gas remains around the star and adds matter to it. All the while, nuclear fusion takes place from the incredibly intense gravity and heat.'

'Then what happens?' She lies on arm to face me.

'Well, one of two things can take place. The process could become unstable, which would result in a supernova if the mass is great enough. If, however, it remains stable for long enough, the molecular clouds will be blown away by radiation and, one is left with... well, a star.'

'That's amazing, Samuel,' she says and lies back down, nuzzling her face in my neck. I take her shoulder and pull her nearer, studying the way her body rises and falls with each breath. Her eyes are closed now. Everything around me feels serene, as though the world has come to a standstill for her to rest.

Even she feels scared sometimes, scared of her own soul. Yet, she's entirely unafraid of sharing it with others, which is courageous in its own way. When I'm with someone so comfortable in their own skin, it makes me want to be just that.

I pass my fingers through her hair and tell her, 'I would read your letter. I would wear your heart around my neck. And, from a field of white, I would pick you: the black rose.'

ADORATION

32 SAMUEL

Lucinda's eyes peer over the top of the book. 'What are DNA strands made out of?' she asks.

'Nucleotides,' I say.

'Name the four DNA bases.'

'Adenine, Thymine, Cytosine and Guanine,' I say. She nods and reads a little more.

'What's the difference between ssDNA and dsDNA?'

'The former has one strand of nucleotides, whereas the latter has two, complementary strands, which have hydrogen bonds between them.' She nods.

'Can DNA move in the cytoplasm?' she asks.

'I know RNA can, so I assume so.'

'Uh-uh,' says Lucinda. 'It can only be present in the nucleus.'

'Oh,' I say.

'It's alright,' she says compassionately. She looks like she belongs out here, in the lush park. It's a bright summer day, though her matte black dress swallows the light like a black hole.

'I can't help but feel like an impediment,' I mutter.

Lucinda shakes her head. 'You're illogical,' she says, 'about yourself at least.'

'Well, if I don't get better at this, then I'm not going to do well, and I'd feel awful.'

'Why?' she asks.

'Because that's how it works. You only succeed if you put in the hard yards.'

'Though, why will you feel awful?'

'Why!' I say in dismay. 'It's obvious,' I mutter.

'It isn't,' she says. 'Do share.'

'When I succeed, then I'm useful and worth something. When I don't, then I'm not,' I mumble. 'I don't want to feel useless. In fact, I'm tired of it.'

'That's the most illogical thing I've ever heard in my life,' she says. 'So, you base your self-worth on your accomplishments? That's a recipe for disaster.'

'Well, it makes sense. It's the only thing I can use to judge if I'm a good person.'

'You're a fool,' she says.

'No need to tell me twice,' I say.

'That's not what I meant,' she says quietly.

I realise I must have said something to hurt her feelings because she looks like she's about to burst into tears. She puts the book down and embraces me. At that point, I can't even make sense of the conversation. All I can think about is how close her heart is to mine. I feel remorse, but I can't think of anything to tell her that would make her feel better.

'I think we should just get on with it,' she says. I nod.

After some time, the two of us decide we've studied enough, and we lie down on the grass. Being so close to the ground, I notice a ladybug crawling up the shoot of a dandelion. I grab hold of the bottom of the shoot and gently sever the stem to lift it. Lucinda is looking at the sky, seemingly distracted. I study her fingers resting on the grass, then allow the spotted critter to crawl onto her hand.

'Oh,' she says. 'What's this?' After lifting her hand to inspect it, a twinkle forms in her eye. 'Thank you.'

'For the ladybug?' I ask.

'For existing too,' she says.

'You don't have to do this for me,' I say.

'I *want* to do this,' she says. 'I'd like to be here to help you out,' she says. Soon after, she mutters, 'Besides, I can't use my textbooks in any case.'

'Pardo—'

'Never mind that,' she says. 'It's a lot less lonely to study like this. The air's much cleaner here as well.'

She flops onto her back, and her chest expands, drawing in a deep breath. My gaze is drawn to the white ribbon in her hair. Only now do I see the freckles on her face, so faint, it seems she could sneeze, and they'd be gone. I continue perusing the material and periodically close my eyes to recall snippets of information.

Just as the sun is nearing the end of its arc, Lucinda says, 'Samuel, would you like to see something far out?'

'For sure,' I say excitedly.

Lucinda gets up and walks past the roundabout, moving into the forest. She walks up a piece of inclined turf and stands on top with her arms outstretched.

'Look,' she says.

I join her and find a train track underfoot, then peer left and right, observing that it starts and ends within the darkness of the forest. The wooden sleepers look terribly old; grass shoots up between them.

'Do you trust me?' she asks with a fair amount of intensity. She then breaks into a grin. 'Or are you too scared?'

'No,' I say with a gulp. I cross my arms. 'I'm not scared of anything. Of course, I trust you.'

She feels the track with her hand for a brief moment. 'Then do as I do,' she says, lying down on the track, lengthwise, with her hands tucked up against her sides.

I kneel and feel the track as well... the tiny vibrations... 'No-no-no, hang on a second!' I begin with wide eyes. 'This is—'

'Anything...' she cuts me off in a playful tone.

'Dammit!' I curse, remembering the promise, and I don't think there's any convincing her otherwise. Besides, I wouldn't want to go back on my word, so I'm forced to follow suit. I tilt my eyes down to see that she's looking at her watch. She then giggles excitedly.

'Don't move, ok?' she says.

'Of course, I won't!' I exclaim. 'I want my fingers… and my head, thank you very much.'

'Never thought I'd hear that coming from you…' she says and giggles. All the while, the distinctive sound of the locomotive becomes more apparent every second.

The train suddenly appears after turning a corner within the forest. I yelp and begin hyperventilating. She's right: if I move, I'm toast. Though, I can't say that I'm not at least a little excited.

I squeeze my eyes shut, and the train horn blares, but it's far too late to stop. The track is rattling my bones by the time the locomotive passes just inches from my nose. Hissing pistons and crankshafts fly over our heads, and the thunderous sound of metal-on-metal makes my teeth chatter. I shout out, but nothing can be heard besides wheels on steel. With my senses dialled up to eleven, it's as though the feelings within suddenly have room to breathe; it's the catharsis of being inches from death. I wonder if that's why she did this in the first place.

Then, just like that, it's over, and it's as though the words in my mouth had hopped onto the train and disappeared into the forest.

Lucinda gets up and flicks her hair back. I get up but immediately stumble over the track and roll onto the grass. Adrenaline pulses behind my eyes, and I feel disconnected from everything. She takes my hand and pulls me to my feet, giggling like a child. And the coolness of her touch makes me snap back into my body.

'My God, Lucinda,' I rasp. 'That was… incredible!'

'I love the thrill of it,' she says in a shaky voice. She stands up and flicks her hair back before twirling around.

'When first did you attempt this?'

Her eyes are crescent moons. 'Just a few days ago.' She brushes her hair behind her ears, though it's still all over the place.

'How did you know you'd fit under the train?'

'I never knew for certain but had no doubt it would be fun,' she says and chuckles.

I laugh and study my shaking hand. 'I bet some of these trains have guard rails,' I tell her. 'Underneath, I mean.'

'Mmm,' she says. 'Though I've rarely seen those kinds of trains here.'

I gaze upwards, and the trees above me wobble about. I drop into a sitting position. 'Lucinda,' I say, 'do you know the concept of compound probability?'

'Are you alluding to the fact that the more frequently an event takes place, the higher the chances of the undesired outcome occurring?'

'Exactly,' I say.

'That just makes it all the more fun, don't you think?' Her two-tone laughter makes me feel ecstatic.

I look up at her. 'Ok, I admit. It sure does.'

'I'm just glad you don't prioritise safety. It's a very dangerous thing to do.'

'Umm, avoiding danger is dangerous?'

'Remember this, Samuel. People who prioritise safety don't realise they are damaging themselves. One day you're going to be falling off a cliff, and you won't know how to fly because you've never left the nest. Safety is the most commonly accepted fallacy to exist.'

'You think it's a fallacy?'

'I know it is. People preach to us to take the road less travelled, and those same people are putting up signs to enforce rules whose purpose is beyond them. They prefer to live comfortably, shackled by their unconscious patterns, not realizing that the lines they draw on the floor for themselves create nothing more than a cell.' She sighs. 'The only way to know one's limits is to test them. Though I know you don't really care much for safety, and I respect you for that.'

'It's true,' he says, 'I guess I'm just not scared of much.'

'But I know what you *are* scared of.' She giggles.

I cross my arms. 'Take your shot.'

'Not living up to your potential.'

'I surrender!' I say with a gulp, holding up my hands. She takes it as an opportunity to launch a tickle attack, and I'm left breathless from laughter.

'My goodness,' she says, 'this has been the best day.' I gleam and feel like a candle is burning inside me.

The setting sun illuminates the one side of her face with a golden glow. At that point, I notice the scar once more: a thin white line running from her neck down over her collarbone. I've wanted to ask her about it for a while now, but I'm afraid it's a soft spot for her. My lips tremble.

'Do you sometimes feel like your life is going too well, and it's only a matter of time before something bad happens?' I say.

'Does this count as going *too well* in your eyes?'

'Well…' I rub my hand over my wrist, 'I mean, the past few weeks: they've been like a dream with you here.'

'Oh please,' she says. 'Really? I'm flattered. Though just you wait until—' Lucinda shudders, and she flicks her head around to look at something behind her. She turns back to face me and smiles, but I can see her hands oscillating in the fading light. 'Must have tempted fate,' she mutters.

'What's the matter,' I say, enclosing her hands with mine. I wonder whether it's because I mentioned—

'It's nothing,' she says, scrunching her eyes. 'I swear.'

'No need to convince me,' I say.

'I'm convincing myself!' she groans.

'You don't have to be afraid. I'm here, alright.'

She sighs and closes her eyes. 'I know,' she says. 'I trust you.' Her hands seem to calm down a bit. 'I'm not afraid,' she says, 'because I know that I'm just seeing things, and they don't scare me as much with you here.'

'What is it you're seeing?' I ask.

'It's ridiculous if you think about it. Absurd, really. Just completely illogical. It's not really... *tangible*. It's in my head. I know it.' I look over my shoulder to find nothing but trees masked in shadow.

'Just look at me,' I say. 'Look right at me.'

Her eyes jitter a bit, and her lashes flutter for a moment as she shifts to sit on my legs and wrap hers around me. Her cheekbones appear to shimmer in the gloom surrounding us. I find myself getting a little shy because of the way she's clinging to me. I guess I don't mind being so close to her, but I sure hope she doesn't notice the butterflies in my stomach.

'What's the matter now?' she asks. 'Are you feeling self-conscious?' I brush my hand through my hair. She bursts out laughing. 'Thank you! I'm no longer frightened.'

'Gee,' I say with a simper. 'It's my pleasure, I guess.'

She looks over to the books nestled in the dimly lit grass. 'It's far too dark to work,' she says. 'Let us head home.'

I nod and give her my hand to stand up. She skips towards the road and stops by the sidewalk. I hobble along to catch up. We watch our shadows arc across the pavement as the streetlamps pass us by.

'This is nice,' she says. 'I prefer it to walking alone.' I squeeze her hand affectionately.

'My gosh!' she pipes after just moments. 'There it is! It's the bloody wolf. I knew I saw it. That cunning beast!'

I spin around and freeze the moment it comes into view, then lean sideways and whisper in her ear, 'Let's try to make a break for it.' I strain to mask the agitation in my voice.

She jerks forward and tugs my arm behind her. Both of our feet echo with eerie synchronicity. I catch a glimpse over my shoulder to find it's rapidly closing the gap. We can't outrun it. With that, I slow to a stop and turn around to face it, keeping Lucinda behind me. I keep my hands in front of me, which jitter in anticipation.

However, as soon as it gets close enough to get a good look, it veers off to one side and disappears into a row of black bushes beside the road.

'Well, that was rather odd,' I remark.

She grabs my wrist. 'We're going to my house. No way are we staying out here with a wolf on the loose. That'd be madness.'

'Madness?' I laugh at the irony of it all. 'Lucinda, that was no wolf,' I say. 'It was a dog, as a matter of fact; quite a large breed, but far from a wolf.'

She stops, not looking back. 'Well, I guess that makes a little more sense,' she mumbles. 'I was wondering why a wolf would run around in a neighbourhood. They're very shy and usually seen only in packs.'

'Here I was thinking *I* was round the bend,' I say, laughing. Her eyes are thin, but her lips are smiling.

She punches me with surprising power. 'Oh, shut up,' she says. 'Sometimes you talk too much.' She continues walking, and I tiptoe to catch up. Just then, she stops in the middle of the road and closes her eyes. Her fists are clenched as if concentrating intently. 'This can't be who I am, Samuel,' she whispers. 'This is not what I want to be.'

'Well, what *do* you want to be?' I say softly.

'How can I live at the mercy of my fears? How can I see things which I know are not real and be so afraid? It's cowardly.'

I hold her at arm's length. 'A person without fears has no compassion either. Your positivity is a miracle in itself, and the confidence you have in your abilities is astounding. No, it's more than that— it's inspiring. You're an inspiring person, and I want to be someone like you. Believe in yourself, for goodness' sake! I believe in you.'

Her head dips with her hair covering her face, but as she turns, a smile is revealed on her lips. 'Come along now,' she says, flicking her hair. She tugs my arm once more. 'All this praise is far too embarrassing for my liking. Besides, you should be no one other than you.'

'This *has* been the best day,' I say.

CONFRONTATION

33 LUCINDA

'**I** *just opted for a salad* on impulse. N-no reason for it,' I stutter, spearing a cherry tomato with my fork.

Father shoots me a suspicious look. 'I know how much you fancy a good steak or anything a bit more nutritious, for that matter. Where has your usual craving for meat gone?'

'I wanted a bit of a change, that's all. It's lunch anyway, and I don't need something too filling.' I'm in no mood for a rich meal, but it's difficult to tell why.

'Are you feeling alright?' he asks. 'You've been awfully spaced out lately. Are you despondent about Mother?'

My lips tremble at the thought. 'Well, it's part of the reason, I guess...' I begin, at that point, pondering the notion of spilling the beans on Samuel's predicament.

Father's face is lit by the flickering candle, and his jawline casts a shadow over his cheeks. 'Though, something else has been troubling me for some time,' I say, deciding to just go ahead with it. 'It's just that... Samuel's family doesn't have the funding for his final year of studies.' At that point, I wonder whether it's even my place to put forward such a complication.

Father keeps quiet for quite a while, and I handle the situation by staring at the wine goblet in front of me, studying the golden reflections on the patterns etched in the glass. I bite the inside of my lip.

'I had a hunch that something was brewing under the surface. Are you sure you understand what you're getting involved with?'

I cheekily take a sip of wine, unperturbed by his response. 'We have more in common than one would think. He has a sound mind...' I say, and then mutter, 'during the times when his mind happens to be sound.'

'What was that?' he asks.

'He's full of potential if you ask me,' I say, placing my hands on my lap.

Father rubs his chin. 'Well, after talking to him, I can at least say he's not daft.'

I roll my eyes. As though I'd fall in love with someone who was. The constant chatter fills what would otherwise be a quiet environment with the clanging of cutlery and muffled words. I wonder whether father plans to intervene.

'Please, Father. Accommodate him, would you?' My speech speeds up unconsciously. 'I know him well enough to know that he means well. No doubt, he can be peculiar at times, but no one is without their faults, right?'

Father sighs. 'Well, he appears to make you happy, and I'm happy if you are. I know you usually think things through, though I'm just reminding you to be cautious, that's all.'

'I promise,' I say, at the same time admitting to myself that I have no intention to err on the side of caution. As with most things, I'm either fully committed or couldn't care less.

The conversation lingers for a little while, though the atmosphere in the restaurant remains warm and comforting. The deep orange candles aren't too intrusive. Each table is draped with a silky white cloth, upon which puta salt and pepper shakers lie.

'How is Samuel finding his course,' asks Father.

I spear a piece of lettuce with my fork. 'He understands the concepts very well.' I pause. 'All the detailed memorisation is not quite his forte, though I do help him out when he needs it.'

Over Father's shoulder, I catch sight of an approaching waiter with something concealed under a napkin. His slight smile makes me uneasy, and my knuckles become white, clamping the table's edge. Whatever he's scheming, I don't like it in the slightest. He whips away the napkin to reveal...

just a menu. I sigh, unimpressed by my knack for conjuring up false threats.

'Any dessert for you, Madam?' he asks. One hand is tucked behind his back; the other splays the menu pages in front of me.

'No, thank you. I'm all right,' I say.

Father says, 'I'm satisfied as well. May you bring us the bill, please?'

'Certainly,' he says and walks off.

I scrunch my eyes, and images of Father being stabbed to death flash through my mind. I was convinced he had some other agenda. My hands shudder, and I ball them into fists, trying to return to the present. It's simply my neurosis playing up again, that's all. Perhaps that's why I struggle to see things working out most of the time.

'Well, to be perfectly honest,' I say, 'Samuel struggles to see the bigger picture due to his circumstances preventing him from finishing his degree. He thinks himself a failure, for lack of a better word.' My voice quivers as I say this.

Father considers this. 'That is quite the dilemma,' he says. He remains silent for a while. 'What degree is he studying again?'

'The same as me, microbiology.'

'And you think that he will pass?'

I nod. 'If he puts his mind to it, I'm certain of it.'

Father looks a little sceptical but then says, 'Well, I do trust you wouldn't have gone after someone who lacked brains.'

I shoot him an unimpressed look. He glances past my shoulder and taps his index finger on the table. I study him, but his expression doesn't give away much.

After some time, we exit the restaurant, but Father still remains deep in thought. I glance his way periodically, eager to know what he's thinking.

Eventually, he stops on the sidewalk. 'I may be deciding on a whim, but I'll be happy to fund his studies. I think it's something your mother would have done if she had the means to. He seems to have potential, and education is the most valuable gift I could bestow upon the youth of today.'

My eyes light up. 'Really! That's fantastic,' I exclaim.

'I'll tell him he can work for my company for some time afterwards to pay off the debt,' he says. 'I think it would be tragic should he not finish his degree after making it thus far.'

'Thank you, Father.' I throw my arms around him.

'Though, he needs to pass, all right,' he says, patting me on the back.

'I'll make certain that he does,' I promise, with a slight smirk.

After we get home, I stand beside my dressing table, remove my necklace and hook it on its stand. Though, instead of getting ready for bed, I decide to go downstairs and paint, elated by the fact that things appear to be working out. I can't wait to tell him the news.

In that spirit, I find it apt to paint something for Samuel. I suppose he'd like something set at dusk, so I arrange a darker pallet with navy and maroon.

Long, flowing strokes leave the tip of my brush, and within no time, a mountain range materialises in the foreground. I dip my brush in white paint and pass my fingers over the bristles to throw light specks onto the canvas, creating stars which hang over the mountains.

The room is a little gloomy, and only the canvas is illuminated. The study mostly consists of all the clutter which slowly migrated through the house over the years. It'll soon be on its way out, I'd imagine. Though, I like the feeling it creates. I guess the atmosphere reminds me of Graham's store in a way, or perhaps it was the other way around. Something about the study reminds me of a place I used to know from my childhood. Of course, I can't quite grasp what it is.

I stare at the canvas, waiting for the base layer to dry. Though soon my sensible instincts kick in, realising it ought to take a while. So, I walk back along the still passages of the house, the rugs soft beneath my feet. I sit down at my desk and sigh, staring at the necklaces which used to belong to my mother.

My gaze then falls upon the unusual item I purchased the other day: the dagger. My fingers curl around the handle, and at that point, I realise it's a fair bit lighter than the average blad of its size, figuring it must be made from a titanium alloy rather than steel. Subconsciously, my thumb runs over the blade to test its sharpness, and it's at that point that I experience what feels like a jolt of electricity. I curse myself when I notice the cut. 'What am I, five?' I mutter, clenching my jaw.

Though, I don't get up to tend to it; instead, I study the thin, red stream trailing down my palm. It instils in me a strange sense of calmness, as though I'm watching a tributary flowing through a shady orchard. The theory of blood structure and cells pops into my head: how the body heals itself on the fly. I notice the wound drying up as the platelets in my bloodstream collect around the cut. Moments later, there's nothing more than a dry streak of red on my hand.

At that point, I take out a notepad and place it in front of me, proceeding to write down a structured summary of the day's work, organising my thoughts. I've always found that accumulating knowledge brings purpose into my life. Besides, what are we other than a culmination of our memories; even intuition is drawn from past experiences. Perhaps that's why I still act like a child on occasion.

After some time, a sense of déjà vu starts to set in. The information is just too predictable to be engaging, and my own thoughts are boring me. At that point, it occurs to me that the marks for the last test should be out by this stage. If I don't go and check, it ought to keep me up anyway.

My footsteps are silent along the passage, and so is the night air outside, devoid of sound or movement.

The black tarmac resembles a meandering trench, swallowing orange beams from the streetlamps above. I stare at my feet as I walk, and the thought crosses my mind that Father had told me just hours before not to walk alone at night. I shrug. He'd never know anyway.

I cross the bridge and the river beneath sparkles in the moonlight. Soon enough, the sounds of restaurants and pubs saturate the air. Though their lights, burning like dull fires, are stripped away as I am met with the spotless halls of the science faculty. It's eerily quiet.

For the first time since I can remember, I felt unsure about what I wrote down. My mind was clouded for some reason. Though, who am I kidding? I can't be worse off than Samuel. Doing well is so important to him, yet he struggles so much.

I get to the board and run my finger down. I'm nowhere near the top this time. It must have been worse than I thought. Squinting my eyes, I'm a little aghast to find sixty-two per cent next to my name. I curse under my breath. How can I expect to do well with that waterlogged book?

After scanning the rest of the list, I find that Samuel did a little better than he has previously, though his average still leaves something to be desired.

It seems we both have our work set out for use, especially if I want to get Samuel on Father's good side.

BOTCH

---

34 SAMUEL

By the time I notice the heaviness in my arms, I had already been carrying my genetics and molecular biology textbooks for quite some time. Since we'll only be working with the latter for the next few weeks, I decide to leave the other in my locker. This time, I scan the top of the metal compartment before opening the latch. I swing the door open, half expecting another prank to be lurking. No, nothing this time around. I swap the books and quickly close the latch again. I then take the first few steps down the passage.

'There he is,' I hear a gruff voice say.

He must have meant for it to be audible because when I turn to see who it is, he's looking straight at me. I look away, but the appearance of his triangulated face is burned into my mind. His spikey, brown hair stands above the rest— what a mop-top. I don't say a word; just continue to walk away.

'You should have seen the look on your little girlfriend's face,' he says, half shouting. 'It's hard to believe a freak like you even has one.'

I stop dead in my tracks. 'My *what*?'

'Your pathetic companion,' he says. I face him. His folded, veiny arms conform to his stocky exterior. 'Most fun I've had in weeks.'

It was *them*. I don't believe the audacity.

'He's totally gonna snap,' says one of his friends. His expression is both anticipation and amusement.

'Hell yeah, I am!' With that, the traffic in the corridor slows to a halt. Everyone's attention is on us.

He smiles with one side of his jaw. 'What's this? Could it be the hero is out to save his beloved damsel?' he says, fluttering his hands sarcastically.

My eyes twitch with disbelief. The fact that he is openly admitting to such atrocities— how could he possibly be so arrogant?

On the other hand, he is a fair bit bulkier than I am, and I notice two others by his side, each trying to get the better of me with their meanest stares. I walk straight up to them on impulse, determined not to be intimidated by these brats. The instant I see the malevolence in his eyes, I can't help but think I may have gotten a bit ahead of myself. I don't know his limits, nor am I aware of my own. I mean, I could never take this guy on. But for him to be so arrogant... he's asking for it. There has to be something seriously wrong there. Then again, I think as my fist sails through the air, there's something wrong with me too.

It hits him square in the gut, though his retaliation is astonishingly quick, as he grabs my wrist while his other set of white knuckles hooks around and connects with my jaw.

A shudder is sent down my spine, and my teeth gnash. He must have thrown me after that because my back hits the lockers with tremendous force. I sit there with my neck craned up, staring at him, grimacing from the metallic taste of blood in my mouth. This is what I get for being such an idiot. He takes off his backpack and rolls up his sleeves. It's too late to turn back now. He lunges forward, and my hands instinctively cover my face, but I'm knocked sideways.

With my face pressed against the floor, I see a row of shoes: the students have formed a ring around us, but they seem too scared to make a move. They just mutter as though they're watching a film.

'You had enough yet?' he asks. I run my tongue over my teeth and feel a chip in my molar. Had enough? There's no way I could stop now, not after all this commotion. 'Are you kidding? I'm just starting to enjoy myself.' To be perfectly honest, the surge of adrenalin that I'm experiencing is more exhilarating than scary. I stand up and press one foot against the lockers. A wave of dizziness trickles through my head. I can feel the floor pulsing under my feet as though it were alive.

'Now you're starting to get on my nerves,' he spits.

I look him in the eye. 'Oh, but won't be an issue? Fortunately for you, processing nerve impulses can't be done with an empty head.'

His eyebrows form triangles. I can almost see steam rising from his head as he seethes in rage. He charges at me, utterly possessed by anger. He sees nothing but me, and he feels nothing but fury. Yet, I know he is entirely blind to my intent. At the last moment, I stoop low and kick off the locker door, with my elbow covering my head. His upper body soars over me, and my elbow knocks the air from his gut. He crumples to the floor, choking.

'How's that for a demonstration of karma?' I smirk.

He appears immobilised. I can't see too clearly, but I take the opportunity to stagger across the hallway. Luckily, the other two don't intervene. I need to get hold of his textbooks so that Lucinda will at least have something decent to work with. As I reach for his bag, he lashes out and kicks me in the stomach. I slide across the floor. I wheeze, and my vision distorts for a moment. I hear the crowd muttering. For a drawn-out second, we look at one another but do nothing, each waiting for the other to attack.

A girl with a blue bow in her hair pushes through the crowd and stands between him and his backpack. He seems to want to move but instead groans as she takes out one of the books. She scans it and places it on the floor next to her. She takes out a thicker one and looks at it for a second. He seems unable to decide what to make of the situation. She turns around and faces me. It's Charlotte. Is she helping me out? Her expression is almost scorn.

My question is answered when she faces the brute. 'You're a bloody fool,' she tells him. She averts her eyes as if passive, though she then swings the book through the air with full force. It sounds like a gunshot when it hits his face. I blink slowly, hardly believing my eyes. His body slumps to the floor, his eyelids slightly ajar.

'You just knocked him out with a book!' I gasp and start laughing from my stomach. Soon after, I splutter from the splitting pain in my abdomen.

'And you're no better, Samuel,' she says. I flinch, half expecting her to do a number on me too. The bloke's friends step in to intervene. 'Now, you wouldn't lay your hands on a girl, would you?' she says fiercely. 'Thought as much, you imbeciles.'

The book she's holding…. it's the exact one I was after: the genetics book.

'Please… give that book to Lucinda. This lot ruined hers.' The crowd is now quite substantial. I should probably leave before the authorities gather word of this.

'I shall give them to her on the condition that you promise to stay out of trouble.' She clutches the books.

I nod. 'From this day forth.' I must look a sight. I lick my bloody lips and watch her slink off into the crowd.

RESOLUTENESS

35 LUCINDA

I*'m just in desperate need* of a break from all of this nonsense. University has had me burning the candle at both ends. I suppose the holidays are drawing nearer, but it doesn't help motivate me a great deal.

I'm up far too early this morning. Nevertheless, during the hour of twilight, the yellow glow radiating from the sky instils in me the sort of euphoria that only natural beauty can bring. I tiptoe along the sidewalk and stare at the fields of whitish-gold grass dotted with pale pink flowers, and it makes me feel so fulfilled. Even small butterflies, some white and others blue, teeter above the riverbanks.

As I get to the university entrance, I come across Charlotte swinging around one of the flagpoles. She seems preoccupied by her thoughts, so I simply wave. When she notices, however, she blinks, confused, but then bounds up to me.

'How do you do?' she asks, and before waiting for a response, she says, 'These are for you.'

The gesture seems suspicious to me. 'Is that so?' She holds out a couple of books. I take them and am astonished to find that they're the genetics and molecular biology textbooks. 'How?' I ask. 'How could you have come to own these?' They look to be completely intact.

'It was Samuel,' she says. 'I guess he… tugged a few strings.' She smiles nervously.

'I guess I'd better not ask.'

'I'd prefer that,' she tells me.

I sigh. 'How have you been lately?' The two of us walk into the building.

'Quite well, actually,' she says. 'The anticipation for the holidays is getting to me at this point, though.'

'Seconded,' I reply. 'Have anything planned?'

'I suppose I'd just relax, for the most part, that is, if I don't happen to be doing something fun.'

'Ditto,' I say. 'I thought I might go on a bit of a trip.' At that point, we cross the grassy patch in-between the buildings belonging to their respective faculties.

'Where to?'

'Not anywhere too far, I'd imagine. Just some place that's not the city.' I grin. 'It's quite magical out there if you know where to go.'

She laughs. 'Whatever floats your boat.'

A lull follows, and we peer up at the massive building looming overhead. It is split in two by the shadow of the adjacent law building. Rows of rectangular windows line its side, their vertical frames looking like the bars of a prison cell running across each floor. I quickly dismiss the thought: it's not as though I'm trapped here. I come here by choice. For the most part, in any case.

'I hope to see my aunt,' she says, 'as well as my cousins; they're a fun bunch. Are you planning to visit family as well?'

'Family?' I shudder and feel a sudden emptiness. 'I'm not all that close with my relatives,' I say, 'aside from my father, of course.' I pause. 'They live in the Amazon, you see. It's not all that convenient to have them visit.'

'My goodness. That sure is miles from here.'

'Mmm. I can't say I really know who they are anymore.' I glance her way without turning my head. Perhaps she doesn't know how to react to that. 'But who knows what the future holds? I'm sure I'd see them somewhere along the line, presumably,' I mutter.

'Presumably?' she repeats.

'Never mind that,' I say, laughing a bit.

The two of us stand there for some time. Charlotte doesn't seem like the type to try and fill the silence.

'L-let's go in, shall we?' I offer.

As we turn to face the door, I see Samuel standing at the entrance. He's facing the other way, but I've come to recognise him from a mile away. I walk up and brush my fingers through his musky grey hair. He jolts in surprise.

'Oh dear,' I say. 'I never meant to startle you. Have you been waiting here for—'

As he turns around, I shudder. He has a vertical gash over his eyebrow, and his bottom lip seems to be cut just off-centre, not to mention his bruised jaw. I wonder what else is hiding under his clothes. When he sees my piercing stare, he swallows hard.

'Sorry?' He shrugs.

'Idiot,' I whisper. 'Look at the state you're in.'

'I thought women found scars attractive.' I give him a fierce look.

'Please, may you take better care of yourself, dear?' I plead.

'Do I not even get so much as a thank you?' he asks.

'You scare me,' I reply, 'but I do thank you.' I look up at his face once more, seeing the cut on his lip. 'So, what exactly happened?'

'I... tugged a few strings,' he says.

'That's what Charlotte said.' I say. Charlotte shrugs. 'How did you even find that bunch?'

'They made it quite obvious. Though, it seems they were overconfident.' He crosses his arms.

I roll my eyes. 'By the looks of you, it could have gone either way. I knew you'd get yourself into trouble.'

'Well, it appears Charlotte was in on it as well.'

Charlotte titters. 'I was seething when I saw them going at each other,' she says. 'I didn't stick around for that blockhead to regain consciousness.'

'She knocked the guy out!' Samuel exclaims.

'Gosh, Charlotte. I'm impressed.' I say. Charlotte laughs nervously. 'Though you two give me grey hairs.'

Charlotte glances at Samuel and struggles to keep a straight face. I ruffle Samuels' hair and afterwards hug his arm. 'They're the true idiots.'

He laughs. 'Perhaps you're right.'

'Naturally.' It makes me ponder the notion of inflicting harm for the sake of helping others.

Charlotte stops at a staircase along the passage. 'I think I'm off to the library now,' she says. 'Use the books wisely.'

'We sure will,' says Lucinda, and waves her off.

'Now that I actually have books,' I tell Samuel, 'would you like to go to the park again and study together?'

'For sure. Though, when's the next lecture?'

I roll my eyes. 'In a few hours. Don't you worry, I'll remind you when it's time to head back.'

The two of us walk along the street together and out of the city. When we cross the bridge, the park comes into view. The trees still appear to be relatively bare. I do wonder when spring will come. It ought to be here already at this time of year. Thinking this makes me remember something.

'Stay here for a moment, will you?' I tell Samuel, placing my books on the grass. I wander off, remembering that I had previously seen a specific type of flower nearby.

The sound of the stream draws me. I'm soon distracted by the meadow I find myself in. It must have popped up quite recently. I begin hopping over to the little patches of colour and gathering a flower from each. In no time at all, I have a small bouquet. I also make sure to pick up a specific type of purple flower. With that, I head back to where Samuel is sitting and hand him the bouquet.

'That's really sweet of you,' he tells me. 'I like them; they're pretty.'

I kiss him on the cheek and rub the purple flowers between my palms. I grit my teeth when I study his face. I wish he hadn't taken it this far. Maybe it was worse that he found out who it was on his own accord instead of me being there to talk some sense into him.

'This is Prunella Vulgaris. I've read about its antiseptic properties.' He closes his eyes while I dab it on his face. All the while, he's grinning at me.

'You're enjoying this far too much,' I say and chuckle.

'Perhaps,' he says, studying me. He pauses for a moment. 'I've been thinking... now that you know where my scars come from, it's only fair if... you know...'

'Oh, this? It's very faint,' I say. 'I'm surprised you noticed.' I pause for a moment. 'It was something that happened last year... I had an accident.' I fail to mention the fact that it was, indeed, a car accident. I don't look his way. I wonder what he will think of all this. 'It's quite funny, really,' I continue. 'I managed to hit my head rather hard. It caused retrograde amnesia.'

'Forgetting things?' he says. 'I get that all the time.'

'Well... it's not exactly like that. I didn't just forget some things, like being scatter-brained. I forgot almost all of it, I guess. If anything happened earlier than a year ago, the chances are I can't recall it,' I say and shrug. When I face him again, he's looking down with a distressed expression.

'That must be too awful to bear,' he says, looking back at me. His eyes echo despair, and he takes me in an embrace.

'It's not that bad,' I tell him. 'You can't miss something that you never even knew in the first place.'

He considers the notion. 'What was it like?' he asks. 'What did it feel like to have nothing to look back on?'

'I don't quite know what to make of it all,' I say. 'If anything, it was worse for my father than me. I remember regaining consciousness after the accident and having everything appear so foreign. I couldn't speak, nor could I think anything coherent at all. Everything I ever knew was just fragments of consciousness.

Certain things did begin to click into place over time. Though, for Father... he lost more than just memories. He lost the daughter he used to know. It's when my mother—' I trail off. 'We moved away from our family as well. We used to live in Brazil, believe it or not. It sounds crazy on his part: why move away when the very thing you need is support? Though, I don't question it.'

'I'm sure I'd have completely lost my mind if I were in either of your shoes,' he says.

I get a cold shiver thinking about all this, but I try to focus on the feeling of his embrace. His chest is warm, and his touch is like velvet.

'I think I may already have,' I say. 'I may be seeing things, Samuel. Things I know are not real. It's as though I'm living within a fantasy book. Inanimate objects sometimes come to life, or… or change their appearance.' My voice is quiet. It may be neurotic, but it's as though I'm scared of anyone else hearing.

'I noticed something to that effect,' he says.

'I— I need it to be a secret.' I bury my face in his chest. 'And… it's not that bad,' I reassure myself. 'Nothing to justify being sent to a psych ward. You know what they'd do to me. Shock treatment, or something worse…'

'Neither of us would want that,' he reassures me.

'I know I do things that are out of the ordinary. I just don't see it another way sometimes. I hope you don't mind.'

'To be honest, I barely even noticed,' he says, and moments after, the two of us burst out laughing. 'Though, that probably says more about me than you.' I take hold of him once more and ruffle his hair; it causes the pale streak to overlap the darker bits like running paint.

'Oh, you're a dear.' This time, I give him a peck on the cheek, and I feel his hands tighten around my waist. I like to think my gestures of affection still make his heart flutter.

SURRENDER

---

36 LUCINDA

The comb feels like spines passing over my scalp. Drenched locks cling to my shoulders. Every time a gust whistles through the window, the hairs on my arms prick up like seaweed in an ocean tide.

My dressing table is home to the collection of necklaces I own, most of which my mother and I purchased together. Their wooden stand resembles a miniature tree, with U-shaped hooks at the end of each branch. A circular mirror is also mounted above my desk, with mosaic tiles surrounding its centre. It belonged to her, and I can almost imagine her sitting where I am now, braiding her hair or using a curler. In most of the photos, she had styled her hazelnut hair to be curly. It makes me smile when I think about her, but at the same time, looking into the glass, my reflection makes me feel like an empty shell, washed up somewhere long forgotten. I'll never know whether I've become someone she would be proud of.

My textbooks lie strewn about the floor. I thought a shower would do me good, yet I still feel demotivated to study. I just turn off the desk light and stare at my stooped silhouette in the mirror. Something is weighing me down, and it's dragging my thoughts along with it. I begin tearing up for no reason at all. The energy seeps from my limbs, so I throw off the towel and jump into bed. Just as I tug the duvet over my body, I realise that I forgot to dry my hair. Though, I like the way I'm shivering because the sensation smothers my thoughts, albeit fleeting. I'll just skip dinner tonight, I guess. I'm too distressed to eat.

My father knocks on the door, but I don't respond. He opens it carefully, and a thin beam of light shines on my pillow. Luckily, he closes it once more, assuming that I'm just asleep; that's what I'd like him to think in any case.

When the light in the passage switches off, I slip into my nightgown and sneak through the door, ajar. After going downstairs, I unlock the front door and pull on the latch. The wind tugs it open, and the outside air burns my ears. I breathe a sigh of relief. Perhaps this was all I needed.

I cross the sidewalk and stand in the middle of the road. The wind muffles my breathing. I adore the wind. I listen to the way it resounds in my ears and gusts through the alleys which whisper all around me. I look at my feet in front of me as I make my way up the street. When I get to where

Samuel lives, I stop next to the white bench outside. There are two stories, and I see a light still burning on the second floor. That fool. He's still awake. I'm thankful for it, though. I needed for him to be awake. I even manage to smile a little.

I tiptoe along the top of a low wall and climb onto the tiled roof that his window overlooks. I jump when I see his face just behind the glass, though his eyes seem to stare past my head as if looking at something on the street. The white streak in his hair shines like a crescent moon. I wave, though his fixation remains. I wonder whether he even sees me; whether it's possible for him not to. I slowly slide the window open but accidentally trip when stepping over the windowsill. We both land on the floor with a thud. I hear my breath against the wooden planks, wondering what I'm even doing here.

He squeezes my triceps, and his hands are shaking a little. I'll just pretend I meant to fall through the window like that. 'Lucinda?' he whispers.

'Yes,' I say, still breathing fast.

'You look… ethereal,' he tells me.

I bite my lip, trying to suppress the quivering in my own hands. I realise he must be talking about my white nightgown.

'I never meant to bother you,' I whisper. 'It's just, I thought I'd—' I try to come up with a reason for me being here.

His chest oscillates in a silent laugh. 'You're no bother,' he says. 'You're always welcome.'

His warm embrace, like a miniature hearth, enraptures my senses. I feel no need to be fearful anymore. His heartbeat seems to dissipate through my body. After the nervous energy begins to wane, I become lethargic.

'I didn't quite realise what I was doing,' I say.

'What's going on? Why are you feeling this way?'

'The answer to that—' I breathe in quickly and look into his eyes. 'If only I knew.'

We stay silent for a moment. I roll over onto the wooden floor and look up at the ceiling rafters, riddled with dust. It's strange yet comforting to be inside his room. He stands up and tugs me to my feet. I notice his bed is equipped with just a single sheet. Does he not get cold at night? The walls are decorated with ancient-looking wallpaper. Opposite his bed is a desk strewn with papers and books. The floor, apart from a little dust, is spotless.

'Join me,' he says. 'Let us go on a walk. That usually does the trick.'

We exit into the passage, and I notice the room next to his is vacant. I follow him down the stairs, which almost seem alive as our two sets of footsteps cause them to creak precariously. On the lower floor, we pass a row of vertical windows through which soft moonlight passes, outlining the couch and oval dining room table.

'Where's your mum?' I ask.

'She's… out,' he says.

I wonder what he's thinking, though I figure I shouldn't prod. Having not met Samuel's mother, it'd be unfair to make assumptions. I grab hold of his hand impulsively.

'I was just feeling a little nervous, so I wanted to see you,' I inform him. Despite everything, he seems quite nonchalant about taking a midnight stroll.

'What's making you feel that way?'

'That's simple,' I begin but struggle to come up with something coherent. 'It just... descends upon me. I began feeling that every second I spend with you is like a grain of sand falling through an hourglass, and I just—' I trail off.

His eyes are black in the shadow of the moonlight. 'Why do you say that?' he asks calmly.

I gulp. 'I mean, obviously, there will come a time... when—'

'When we die?'

'No, not that. I mean— a time when we'll have to go our separate ways,' I mumble, 'or something to that extent.' I shiver, and, for a moment, we're back on the top of that tall building, though I try to get it out of my head. Samuel unlocks the front door in front of us and takes my hand.

'Is there a difference?' He pauses. 'Sorry, I'm just making matters worse, it seems.'

I grit my teeth. Usually, I would have something witty to say at this point to lighten the mood, but nothing comes to mind.

The hinge creaks open, engulfing us in the chilly night air. He still holds my hand, but I wonder if it's out of politeness. We begin ambling within the orange glow of the streetlamps.

'Would you answer me this honestly?' I then ask.

'What is it?'

'Do you find that I'm a hindrance some of the time?' I gulp, a little shocked at the directness of the statement.

The row of streetlamps abruptly ends. I can't see much anymore. We just continue meandering into the blackness.

I never thought about it before, but since the first time we met, it's not as though he had much control over it all. I simply imposed my will upon him from the very beginning. What's worse, is I have no reference point for proper human interaction.

He says nothing for some time. I dip my head. The ground transitions to soft grass. Perhaps I was too assertive, far too confident in thinking he was as fulfilled as I was. I clench my teeth at the thought.

He stops, and I wait, agitated for a response. My legs are swept from under me as I am spun around. The world surrounding us blurs. I can't help but let out a gasp, followed by a muffled giggle as my hands clutch his shirt.

The clouds above him glow softly. 'Don't doubt me like that,' he says, placing me back on my feet. 'And don't doubt yourself. It's not like you.' His other hand brushes through my hair, and my knees become weak. 'I'm certain there's something wrong with you.'

'I beg your pardon–'

'But that's part of the reason you have stolen my heart to the fullest extent,' he says. 'It takes so much courage to see life the way you do, to be the person you choose to be, in spite of it all. Just keep at it.'

'Huff-puff!' I say, pushing him playfully. Usually, after a fight with my shadow, I come out second-best, but he says the right things to reason with it. I think I prefer this kind of delusion.

We take a bendy road to loop around to where we started, and when the white bench comes into view, I skip up to it and sit down. I tap my hand on the space next to me, after which we sit adjacent to one another.

He tilts his head back. 'Do you remember—'

'Of course! There's not a chance I could forget.'

'Wait here a moment,' he says and disappears behind me. I turn back and watch him walk through the door of his house, noticing how archaic its exterior is. It has a black roof with narrow, vertical windows on both storeys. Two spherical lights rest on pillars which enclose a small walkway. It's distinct from the rest of the neighbourhood. I look forwards once more. About half a minute later, I hear a muffled tune that seems to emanate from the windows. As it progresses, I hear the source move closer.

His gaze is directed at the windowsill as he listens to the music box. He then brushes his hand over my cheek and kisses me on the forehead. I feel a warmth spread across my face. Just then, the rain starts. I trace my finger over the white streak in his hair. He takes my hand, and I skip along beside him.

I like the way the streaks of rain sparkle as they move through the beams of light along the side of the road. A blurry mist soon covers the roadside, and… a mass of tiny creatures flow within it like a living stream.

At first, they appear to be a teeming colony of ants, but when I stare a little longer, they take the form of scorpions. Most of them are no bigger than my thumb, but a couple are larger than my hand. Their exoskeletons snake along the road in pale ripples. As their numbers increase, the entire street becomes a living veil. A chill shoots up my leg, and I jump onto Samuel's back with my arms around his neck. I know he can't see them, so they can't hurt him. 'Carry me,' I tell him. My fringe is dripping.

'What's gotten into you?' he asks.

'I'm just a bit on edge,' I say, 'and quit being nervous already. I can practically see you blushing.' He faces the ground. The truth is, I'm also a bit uptight over it all, but the other half of me likes being carried.

'J-just take me to the sidewalk, and all will be fine.'

My torso feels like jelly. We cut across the road. I spring off his back when we reach the sidewalk and shuffle along the side of the pavement, staring at the critters.

'What are you seeing?' asks Samuel.

'Something I know I shouldn't be,' I whisper.

I stop and kneel beside the road, reaching out my hand; it trembles in anticipation. As my hand touches the swarm of scorpions, it is both fiery as a hearth and biting cold. They surround my fingers, and their stingers whip. Only it's different to what I expected. It's just a mild aching.

Samuel kneels beside me and does the same. 'You are peculiar sometimes,' he says. 'Something wrong with the rainwater?'

'No, it's just—' I pause, 'Never mind.' I figure he'd never understand. It makes no sense in any case.

I sigh and look to my right, tracking the road which falls out of view near the horizon. Mountains seem to float in the distance among the grey haze.

'Have you ever been there, Samuel?' I ask.

'What, you mean outside of the city? I have, indeed. We used to... well, as a family, we'd go there. My mum adored the place. It was lovely, actually, to get away from it all. We'd walk in the mountains and camp for days on end. But now—' he shrugs. 'I guess we just don't think about it anymore.'

'The two of us could go there,' I say. 'The summer break is drawing nearer, and... I think I've been there.' The faint, reddish-grey colours and the subtle contours in the mountains look like a distant memory somehow. 'Well, perhaps I have; I can't quite tell,' I mumble. 'Though would you accompany me?'

'Of course,' he says. 'It will be an adventure.'

GHOST

37 LUCINDA

B<i>y the evening, I feel</i> an apprehensive sort of excitement. I stare at the series of crossed-out days on my calendar. Tomorrow is October nineteen, the day I turn twenty-one. I am now in a precarious, transitive state. I will need to accept that I'll be a year older. Though, I don't really have anything to reference off of. What are birthdays like?

I study the contents of my room. All the things I've accumulated appear eerily out of place. There are fantasy books on the shelf, and lining the windowsills are mementoes from what seems like decades ago. Though, it all seems foreign to me now, as if I never knew a time I would have wanted any of it. I snatch the pocket watch from my desk, staring at the unmoving hands. I can't help but wonder whether my time is almost up.

My gaze settles on my window, tracking the swirls of light frost forming. I get up and open it to watch the white flakes drifting in the wind, a couple settling on my cheeks. They prick my skin and feel like embers emanating from an icy hearth when I close my eyes.

I am no longer a child. Tomorrow, I will be an adult. I giggle at the thought, but it sounds harsh. When I look around my room, I feel a sense of dread. All the posters and decorations, even the purple duvet cover… how am I to know whether an adult would consider owning those sorts of things? I don't feel like I belong here anymore. I run down the stairs, though I know I can't escape fate. I never thought I'd be a child forever, but the proposition that tomorrow I will come of age is far from comforting.

Perhaps a drink will help me forget about all of this. I'm compelled simply to take something from the cabinet, but then again, Father always notices when I've pinched some of the good gin. I'll have to just slip out for a while, but it's too far to walk all the way to the city at this time of night.

I slide open the glass door overlooking my garden and walk out into what feels like an obscure jungle. Mottled patches of frost glow in the moonlight. I hug the edge of the circular lawn and arrive at the shed, hidden among the bushes. It looks to be out of a fairy tale. Its shiny tin roof rests on dark, wooden walls. When I open the door, I see it: my two-wheeled friend, resting against the shed within a beam of white light.

I haven't ridden my bicycle in ages. I quite literally cannot remember the last time I did. My father says I knew how to ride it, so I'll just have to have a little faith and trust my instincts. Of course, both the tyres have deflated to the rim, but nothing a quick pump can't solve. I find a pump resting against the inside of the shed. Even after being neglected for years, the bearings remain smooth, and the clicking sound of the sprocket fills me with nostalgia.

For the first couple of meters, I teeter from side to side, but then, like clockwork, everything falls into place. I begin riding effortlessly, just like I used to. The tyres whirr after they transition from soft grass to open road. A pair of shadows revolve around me as the streetlamps pass me by, and the dark pavement ahead draws me in as I begin to gain momentum. The sensation is so familiar. I try to reach out and grab hold of a memory: when I learned to ride a bike or when I fell off it or anything— Even though they feel like a hairsbreadth away, nothing but incoherent echoes pass through my head.

I turn my head to the sky. Will the sleet feel the same tomorrow? What am I trying to run from? What could I possibly fear? Perhaps I dread facing up to the facts: what it means to be a year older. Am I now expected to contribute to society or be more mature? Wiser perhaps? It's all lies. Tomorrow, I will be no different. I'm sure I'm simply one year closer to death since my last birthday. I'd have placed another milestone on the road to my demise.

I freewheel down the sloped street, which splits, at the end, into a four-way intersection. Behind the traffic lights, nothing but darkness looms. The handlebars oscillate in my palms as I pick up a decent amount of speed, and projections in my head begin forming. I can see my breaks failing, and being unable to stop before the busy intersection, I'm torn to bits by a vehicle and strewn over the road.

I hit the brakes. No such case takes effect. The bicycle comes to a smooth halt. In fact, there are no cars on the road at all. I'm disappointed that it even crossed my mind.

Tears run down my cheeks, whisked away by the wind, as ephemeral as the echoes of my childhood passing through me. How can I even call myself an adult with nothing to look back on? It feels like I've lived for just a couple of years. Are adults even allowed to cry whenever they please? I should be feeling happy, yet the clouds distort with my tears. I can't tell why this is happening. It's almost as if I'm sensing the vast expanse of my empty past with the sort of bitter longing that new beginnings bring, and I can't let go.

It soon begins hailing, and the sky turns a darker shade. The falling ice hurts my skin. It makes my head spin, but a part of me craves it. My hair flicks in front of my face in a way that feels unfamiliar. My legs feel too long for my body. My white-knuckled hands, grasping onto the handlebars, feel as though they are no longer mine. I stop next to the road, now fully immersed in the city. A fusion of cold and warm lights bleeds out of every restaurant window, and the traffic streams past behind me.

A stream runs through my heart
I've been taken beyond the brink
No longer can I return to the source
A stream of honey and ink

I drift down the snakes and bends
And no matter how far I go
There's no way to know
Where it starts or where it ends

And I've now been given a gift
A story yet to be told
Still, it all flows through me now
A stream of black and gold

Muffled chatter reverberates from the door behind me. I take a moment to look at the signpost above. I remember it used to say, "Pub and Diner". During the day, it says that. But now, with most of the fluorescent letters burned out, it just says "Die" in unevenly spaced letters. I don't know if it was vandalism or pure coincidence that those particular lights stopped working. It makes me remember the fact that I promised Father never to come here alone. Though, I don't dwell on it for long. What's done is done. Besides, I'm only here for some good liqueur.

I push open the door, noticing a few panes missing from its grid-like frame. When it shuts behind me, an eerie draft remains around my ankles. It smells a little like the chemistry lab at the university. There are low tables with numerous, obscure figures hunched over them.

I walk up to the bar counter, situated further back. There is a hefty barman in an unzipped, black jacket and a stained shirt underneath.

'Give me anything over forty per cent, and I don't drink whiskey, or any sort of cider for that matter,' I tell the barman.

He considers me for a moment, then says, 'Are you lost, little lady? I think—'

'I can't quite tell,' I cut in, looking him dead in the eye. 'Do you consider me lost?'

I hear one of the other figures stir behind me. The door rattles in the wind, and a low moaning can be heard, the air moving through the missing windowpanes. I place three notes on the table, and he slides them under the counter, still maintaining eye contact. He removes a bottle of rum from the shelf, simultaneously scooping ice into a glass with the other hand. I then snatch the drink off the counter then take the change. The frosty surface of the glass is soothing against my palms.

My eyes are defocused; the bobbing ice blocks become amorphous clusters. With that, I down the drink. The taste of liquor on my tongue is rather sharp, but the way it burns my pallet scratches an itch inside me.

I stare over the counter, studying the bottles behind the barman. The question remains in my head: am I lost? I can't remember where I've come from, nor whether I'd ever feel as though I have a proper footing in the world, but is that the criteria? Does it make me lost?

My father says he sometimes feels as though he's gone astray without Emily by his side. They were married longer than I've been alive, and for it to be taken away in an instant… it most likely haunts him to this day. He'll never forgive himself for the accident.

At that time, we had been eager for a trip outside of the city, so we visited a forest area with a large lake, but I can't place my finger on exactly where it was. I recall nothing from the trip except for the moment our lives took a turn for the worse. There had been a fallen tree just over the top of a blind rise. Sleet was lining the tar at the time, so when my father hit the brakes, it was to no avail. The collision had me plummet through the windscreen. My head struck the ground. I broke my collarbone too. What happened after that, I cannot recall. But even worse: I can't remember what happened before it either. My childhood, my family, everything I ever knew… it had all been turned into a hazy mass of jumbled recollections that I can never manage to piece together.

And that's how my life started again, as if I was born on that very day. I had nothing because what does one have apart from their memories? All they would have is the present. And, in that present, I was a barely unconscious girl lying beside a wounded man and a dead woman, who I was destined never to know. I never even knew my own name.

For months after, I would be floating, unable to comprehend anything at all.

Over time, however, some things seemed to click into place. I came to speak and write just like I used to. Other things just never came back to me, though. When I try to remember events that occurred before then, I can never place anything in context. For a while, it was as if my emotions had switched off completely. I treated those close to me with indifference and drifted further away from who I once was. We moved here because Father had decided to start a new life for us. It was extremely difficult for him. He, too, had to let go of the life he had previously known, holding out for the passing of time to make things more bearable.

'Can I have another?' I ask. The bartender looks my way, apathetic. 'And what time do you close?'

'Bar never closes,' he says, pouring another round of what I realise is brandy.

I take the drink and stumble to one of the hardwood tables, less aware of the strangers surrounding me, less aware of anything for that matter. The dim strips of light blur into one another as time passes. I close my eyes, feeling into the detachment. 'I can't be lost,' I mutter to myself. 'I know exactly who I am, and anyone had better take my word for it.'

THRESHOLD

38 SAMUEL

With *Lucinda thinking* about taking a trip, I don't quite know what to expect. What are we to do, just saunter off into the mountains? Though, that sounds quite appealing now that I give it some thought.

She seems focused at the moment, flicking through the genetics book. 'Memory works in layers, Samuel,' she says. 'Information should be memorised in intervals that separate related topics.' I nod. 'Write down everything that you know about the metabolism.' She gives me a notepad and pen. 'It's necessary to form an outline of what you're going to learn by discovering gaps in your knowledge.'

I do as I'm told. In the meantime, Lucinda writes down the heading "Immune system" and jots down a couple of bullet points.

After about ten minutes, we swap pages and question each other on the topics, and then we each make detailed notes and diagrams. Lucinda also makes flashcards. The park is peaceful and still; an oddly suitable work environment.

'I appreciate having someone to study with,' she says.

'Me too. It's different, but I like it.' I chuckle.

After that, I go over the flashcards, and Lucinda takes a look at my notes, adding to hers every so often. Just having her around makes the process entirely different from before. The usual anxiety that my mind associates with studying has dulled completely. The grass beneath us and the subtle, surrounding sounds create such a tranquil feeling within.

I find myself wishing to remember exact moments like these; take a snapshot of time that will forever be etched in my mind. She rests her head on my lap.

'I was never lost,' she mutters, talking to herself.

I stare at her content expression for ages, and we needn't say a word, yet it feels like nothing is out of place.

After some time, I glance at her watch and notice the hour is near. Our literature class is just around the corner, though she sits up at that very moment. Could she sense it? I carry the books for her, and she takes my hand, strolling along with the usual skip in her step. She bumps her hip against mine and giggles. 'Honey,' she says. 'Where might we be off to?'

'Literature?' I say, grinning.

She looks shocked. 'I entirely forgot!'

'I've got to say, it's pretty great being the one on top of it for once.' I wink.

'Bask while you can,' she says, rolling her eyes.

This time, she bumps her shoulder into me, attempting to put me off balance, but instead bounces right off with little effect and gulps before landing on the grass.

'I'm sorry,' I say, lifting her to her feet. She has a black lace bolero over a white, knee-high dress with a navy cloth around her midriff. Despite her warm expression, she looks a tad tired. 'Has it been a long day?' I ask.

'Quite,' she says. 'I didn't get much sleep either.'

'Is something troubling you?'

'Yes,' she says. 'My birthday.'

'Is it today?' I ask in shock.

'It is.'

'I'm so sorry. It must have slipped my mind.' I twiddle my thumbs, feeling awkward.

'It couldn't have,' she says, ruffling my hair. 'I never told you, silly. Besides, I don't know when yours is.'

'It's true, I guess,' I say.

'So…' She gestures for me to elaborate. 'When is it?'

'November eleven,' I say.

'Ha!' she chimes in. 'I'm older than you.'

'So you are,' I say, trying to act nonchalant. Deep down, I'm a little embarrassed.

'I quite like the thought of that,' she says, looking pleased. I roll my eyes. 'I don't mind that you never knew.

It seems my birthday isn't a good day for me. I guess I just start thinking too much, and then…' she trails off.

'That's not at all ideal,' I say, squeezing her shoulder.

'Not to worry,' she says, putting on a smile. 'It's all better now.' She takes my hand and sways it as we walk.

When we enter the literature class, Mrs Clark is sitting in the front, reading to the students. Lucinda and I sit next to one another in the first row. I put the genetics book under her seat. After finishing the passage, Mrs Clark tells us about many of the good fictional writers who tie into the topics we are to explore next semester. This triggers a debate among the students as to which of these writers has been the most influential. I like to sit back and listen during these types of discussions. As the lesson draws to a close, my mind is saturated with names of writers and books.

'That was enough to put me off studying for the rest of the day,' says Lucinda, much to my shock. We walk side by side in the corridor. 'My head hurts, and I'm too tired to think any longer.'

'I think your headache is from lack of sleep,' I say, putting my books back into my locker.

'No, it's from drinking,' she admits. 'Unfortunately, there's only one cure for it.' She smiles mischievously at that point. 'More drinking!' she declares.

'Actually, there's scientific evidence quite contrary to that popular—'

'Tsk-tsk,' she says. 'I wish to go to a bar.'

I shake my head. 'Aye, all right,' I tell her with a grin, 'but I haven't a lot of money to spend on drinks.'

'That's no problem,' she says. 'I do.'

'Even so, I don't see it wise to get drunk straight after studying. We'd be reversing all of the work we put in.'

'Oh, you have much to learn. The only thing better than gaining knowledge is forgetting it all by morning.'

'You do have the strangest logic sometimes,' I say.

'Don't worry. I was only joking. I'll try to be careful.'

We walk past the flags and down the sidewalk, following the setting sun. Lucinda holds my hand in the city as we go deeper into chaos, light, and sound.

She stops at a place called Daisy's Bar and pushes open the doors. There are wooden tables scattered about. The only person inside is the bartender. Lucinda orders two drinks for each of us. I look at the bartender funny when he doesn't even ask for our IDs. Mine won't be of much help in any case.

I pretend to take sips of my brandy, though Lucinda is quick to finish hers. Soon, she's halfway through the second glass, lying on her arm with her hair strewn over the table.

'Lucinda,' I place my hand on her forehead, 'have you been affected so severely?' With my glass held to the light, I study the caramel-coloured liquid. 'You seem out of sorts.'

Lucinda looks inquisitively at me. She then giggles. 'Oh, that just can't be so. I'm far more accustomed to this sort of thing than—' She trails off.

'Than what?' I run my fingers through her hair.

'Oh, cursed turmoil! I cannot think as I usually do,' she says. 'I assure you I am by no means intoxicated!' her voice is oddly high pitched.

I pat her head, then scoot over to the bar and place a few pounds on the counter. 'Will that be sufficient?' I ask the bartender. He nods, cupping the coins in his hand. I hear a glass smash behind me. She is leaning over the table and breathing heavily. I reach for more coins in my pocket.

'And some extra for the glass. I apologise for this.' I look back. 'Do be careful, Dear.'

Her one eye is closed, and her other glares under a furrowed brow. 'Do not speak to me as if I were a child.'

'I have no such intent,' I tell her, laughing it off.

She picks up the other glass. 'I'll have another round— a double, might I add.'

'Oh goodness, no, Lucinda. Not on my watch,' I say.

She stands up with the glass in her hand. 'I said, I'd like another. Please be of assistance.'

Both the bartender and I stare at that point. After realising her request will not be fulfilled, she hurls the glass in my direction with hopeless accuracy. It glints in the gloomy air. The bar is entirely silent. It then collides with a lightbulb, and sparks shower the room. The bartender ducks behind the counter, and my body lurches when I see the next glass being flung straight at me. It smashes on the edge of the counter with an oddly satisfying ring. Perhaps I should have just obliged, I think.

'Why do you defy me?' she asks, almost too calmly.

I run towards the door and look back just in time to see the third glass being flung in my direction. My hands snap up to protect my face, but its trajectory is lower than I anticipated; it catches me in the gut. I crumple into a ball. She still has one glass left. But after a while, I realise that it will not come. I peer through the slits between my fingers and see her sitting on the floor, hugging her knees. The last glass is resting beside her. I approach her slowly. She seems meek at this point. 'I could not have,' she whimpers.

I kneel beside her. 'Lucinda, what happened?' I ask.

'I suppose I—' She rocks back and forth and sighs. 'This was not my intent,' she says softly.

The bartender walks up to us. 'How's the li'l lady doin'?' He twiddles his colossal thumbs.

'She'll get over it, I'm sure. I'll pay for all the damage.'

'You've covered all your expenses already,' he says, 'and thanks to you, the door is still intact.' My attention is brought back to my aching stomach.

'S-Sure,' I say.

Lucinda looks miserable. 'T-take me to the ladies,' she slurs. 'I don't feel at all well.' She falls over my shoulders. I figure she may be experiencing dizziness. I allow her to hold my hand for support. She picks up a steak knife from one of the tables on the way out.

'We won't be needing—' I begin, but she death stares me, gripping it firmly. I decide to leave it be.

'Trust no one, Samuel,' she says. 'Except for me, of course.' She winks.

'Aye, weren't you a little hasty, Lucinda.'

'What do you know of drinking?' she demands. I shrug.

'There-there,' I say and pat her back.

'It was just at the end of these storefronts,' she says. She pulls me into an alleyway. There are four, white doors suspended in darkness. 'Just wait out here, please,' she says, turning into the second last one.

'Sure,' I say, tapping my fingertips against the bricks.

I look up at the narrow strip of sky sandwiched between the walls. After a minute or so, Lucinda reappears in the passage. I turn around, wanting to return to the bar, but a shadow now covers the exit. I jolt, freezing in place.

'Let's go,' I say, snapping out of it.

I grab onto her. Just as I take the first step forward, the dark figure multiplies. Now, there are three of them. I squeeze Lucinda's arm in anticipation. She remains dead still, eyeing them out. Their silhouettes pulse like fire in front of the traffic. They'll just pass us by, I think. The one in the centre takes a step into the passage. I begin feeling claustrophobic with my hand pressed against the icy bricks. My eyes flick back, and I shudder at the sight of the end of the passage: an endless wall.

'Won't ya mind lending us your girl o'er 'ere, so none o' you get hurt?' the one says with a raspy voice. 'Looks like a pretty li'l un.' I shiver with a cold breath. 'Don't want any trouble,' he says. 'Just want some fun, that be all.'

At that point, I feel the freezing air from the street seeping into the passage, curling around my ankles.

'Go to hell!' I spit at them.

I watch the face of the man on the left scrunch up. 'That ain't a nice thing to say,' he mutters.

The left one approaches, and I push Lucinda behind me, trying to control my trembling stature. I charge forward, attempting to shove him out of the way. His flesh feels like iron against my shoulder. He grabs my scruff, and I'm tossed against the wall. My body strikes the bricks, and Lucinda yelps. But the pain I should be feeling is numbed by adrenaline. I know he is just toying with me. This isn't like the last fight. It's real this time. The man exhales down my neck, and I grimace at the stench of beer in his breath. He wrenches me to my feet, his arm around my throat, as the other two push their way past me. One of them is far taller than the rest.

'Don't touch her!' I yell. 'Don't you dare touch her!' They ignore me flatly.

Lucinda's head is turned down, and her hair covers her eyes. The largest man shoves her against the wall, holding a pocketknife to her chest. Her hands are tucked behind her back as though surrendering.

'You will make me feel unclean,' she says, her voice faltering. 'I will have to live with what you'd have done for the rest of my life.' Her stature is dwarfed by the man. The blade shimmers with the hues of lights bleeding into the alleyway.

I feel utterly powerless. A wave of nausea passes over me. I reach into my pocket and clasp the utility knife. The blade extends with a soft click-click-click-click. Yet, my wrists are bound: if I attack one of them, Lucinda's fate would be sealed. I long for some way out, trying to fight the overbearing sense of dread within me. With her stooping head, her hair masks her eyes, but behind that black veil is a broad smile on her lips. I stare, aghast. What could she possibly be thinking? She shouldn't do something rash. Then again, she has to if we're to make it out of this.

My longing is answered when both her hands shoot out from behind her back. A flash of silver bolts diagonally upwards, and the steak knife bursts through the man's wrist, pinning his arm to his own throat as she stands on one leg with her arm extended out in front of her. She brings her knee in and spins around; only at the end of her pirouette, the blade, in a reverse grip, finds the gut of her victim.

It's so surreal to watch that, for a split second, I don't know how to react. Then, my hand flies out from my pocket. It finds the face of the suspect breathing down my neck. I snap off the end of the blade and pivot around, escaping his grip; the newly extended edge follows, slashing open his stomach. I look away: I can't bear to see what I've done.

The third figure, standing behind Lucinda in the passageway, must have seen his odds of survival plummet. He tries to make a break for it. He manages to slip by her, but I stretch out my leg as he passes, and he trips, falling onto his stomach.

Lucinda immediately pounces onto her prey, embedding the knife into his spine. He rolls over, his entire body convulsing. She stands up, inspecting the victim. She then digs her heel right into his eye. He doesn't even make a sound; he just quivers until his body stops moving entirely.

She says nothing. After catching my breath, I am the first to speak. 'You just— We just— We killed them! We killed these people!' My voice shakes.

She wipes the knife handle clean, probably removing the fingerprints. 'They're not *people*,' she says. Her eyes are almost glazed over. 'They're something else, and I'm sorry that they had to die like that.'

'Well. I'm sorry they had to die as well.' I grimace. They were most probably completely blitzed.

She shakes her head. 'I meant they should have died in agony, each one of them. I've learned not to walk these streets empty-handed. I wasn't born that way. You were right, Samuel. Some things you just can't forgive.' I stare at her for a long time, wondering who she really is. All the while, she just looks back at me with the slightest hint of pity but says nothing more. The iridescent lights shimmering in her eyes are the only colour in her face.

I feel ill. We could have both gotten ourselves killed. Then again, I'd rather we were dead than have to witness what they would have done to her.

MALEVOLENCE

39 LUCINDA

Whose hands are here, with the capacity to show such kindness yet so swiftly resort to murder. At the time, it felt like my only option, but now I can't comprehend it. All I know is that one can only be taken so far before they reach the point of no return. Surely, Samuel realises that. He should understand. Though the way he walked home in silence, not giving a single hint that things would be alright... It makes me wonder whether he'd end his involvement with me. How can I expect him to love someone like me? He does not. He cannot.

I jump off my bed and run to my dresser, picking up the knife, and I direct it at my chest.

'Who are you, Lucinda?' I ask myself. 'You look like the innocent flower, yet you truly are the serpent under it.'

I stare at the shimmering blade, but after a few seconds, I scamper downstairs with it and enter the study. Before me stands the painting. How can I give it to him? He doesn't deserve to have a… a murderer in his life. I stab it. The blade punches through the canvas effortlessly. The surface becomes slashed and gouged, leaving it unrecognisable. Something about the feeling of it makes my hand turn limp and let go of the knife. I guess it touched a nerve.

He needn't even know about it. It's a shame he even knows me when I didn't even know who I really was.

The house is dead silent, with my father having gone to sleep quite a while ago. Samuel needs to know that I feel awful about what happened. I exit through the front door to find myself among levitating patches of mist, phasing in and out as they pass through moonlight shadows.

I only have to walk a couple of blocks before I see him sitting on the bench, staring forward, most probably tormented by his thoughts as well. He hasn't said a word since the incident. I study the white line of hair from his fringe to his neck and take precarious steps toward him.

'I don't expect you to forgive me,' I say, hearing my voice so clearly in the still air. 'And I don't expect you to forget. You need to write your own story, and if from here on out, I am no longer a part of that story, I will show you no hatred, nor will I hold it against you… I just needed you to know.' I begin to walk away. It doesn't take long before the tears well up in my eyes.

'Lucinda, stop,' he says and gets to his feet. When he comes my way, I bury my face in my hands. 'I was there as well,' he whispers. 'I killed as you did. The important thing is that you're alright. Of course, I forgive you.' He then takes my shoulders. 'Does your father know?' I shake my head. 'God, if this manages to come back to us. Even though it was technically self-defence, we'd still be convicted, and then we'll be—'

'It won't,' I say.

I'm sure the rain washed away our fingerprints; washed away the blood we spilt too. He studies me for a second, though he then nods.

He sits back down on the bench, and I snuggle up to him, hoping to calm my thoughts. I feel exceptionally guilty using him for support. It was my rash decision which pushed him into a corner. He runs his fingers through my hair, and I close my eyes and try to make it all disappear.

'If something had happened to you…' he says. 'I do not even wish to think that far.'

'I'm still here,' I say.

'And it had better remain that way,' he says. His arms envelop my torso in a warm embrace, and I could have sworn that I felt safe in that moment, albeit fleeting.

'I promise, dear,' I whisper. 'As long as there's blood in our veins, you won't be alone.'

PLAGUE

40 LUCINDA

'**P**ens down!' announces Mr Diaras. I stack up the papers in front of me, pleased with how I faired. This exam, medical terminology, was a lot easier than the others, as it's mostly just recalling information. Though, I felt a little distracted about midway through, when I had to explain Hypovolemic shock. It made me think of walking through all of that blood, feeling it on my hands, too.

A change of pace is long overdue. I turn back to see Samuel, sitting two rows behind me, and show him a thumbs up. I'm quite excited by the prospect of spending time with him during the holidays.

After the two of us begin to walk out, someone taps me on the shoulder. 'That was the last one,' she says. It's Charlotte. As usual, she has a bow in her hair but wears a shirt and skirt this time. She has white stockings and black shoes as well. It suits her. She'd probably already have a man if she'd just overcome her shyness.

'Indeed,' I say. 'It's about time too.'

'This semester has been far too long. Our grades should be released within the next couple of days.' She yawns. 'I'm all for a party at this point.'

'Hmm?' I'm marginally amused by the suggestion, which I never expected from someone like Charlotte. I was aware of social gatherings taking place in the past, but I figured they wouldn't be worth going to without friends. Now it's different, I guess. Also, there's the prospect of potentially making a move on Samuel... 'It does sound quite appealing,' I say.

'What does?' It's Samuel who speaks this time.

'Charlotte was just suggesting that we go to a party. I reckon it would do the three of us good.' Samuel nods, but his skewed smile makes it evident that he doesn't quite know what to make of it. 'Don't be such a worry-pot,' I say and ruffle his hair. He blushes. I then whisper in his ear, 'I'm sure it ought to be an eventful evening.' He looks down, his cheeks flushed, though he has a broad grin.

He binds his arm in mine. 'Aye, alright, dear.' The two of us wave Charlotte goodbye. 'We will see you anon, thank you for the invite.'

The two of us begin meandering home, and after we cross the bridge, I lead him into the forest near the end of the park. When our path meets the train track, I begin balancing along the metal railway. Samuel soon hops on the adjacent track, and before long, it's turned into some sort of race. I glance next to me to see Samuel beaming, struggling to maintain balance at this pace, though something about it comes naturally to me, and my feet glide along the track, never misstepping.

I jump off the track and look back at Samuel, giggling. 'I guess I won'.

'Well, what use am I if not to satisfy your childish desires.'

'At least you know your place,' I say snarkily, at that point, hearing the faint sound of the stream. I sashay away from the railway and into the forest, and before me appears a small rockpool, glistening in the dappled light shining between the branches above. It's so clear; pebbles, glistening like jewels, can be seen near the bottom. The water curls around my fingers when I dip my hand into the pool.

Samuel catches up behind me and kneels by the water's edge. The reflections off the water's surface dance on his face. 'It's pristine,' he remarks.

At that point, I decide there's only one possible course of action, unzipping the back of my dress. I quickly slip it off before he can turn around and run forward, leaping into the pool. It's deeper than I expected, and the cold instantly knocks the breath out of my lungs as I enter the macrocosm, materialising underneath the surface. Bright green tendrils descend from the water's surface, reaching down towards quartz pebbles lining the bottom, and shiny bubbles coat the leaves of these aqueous plants.

My hands reach behind me to feel the stone lining the edge of the rock pool. At that point my mind disappears from this place. Perhaps it's the thundering sound of rushing water, which reminds me too much of the blaring traffic. Or maybe the feeling of stone against my palms, paired with the forceful current, is too much like being shoved against that brick wall. And this time, there's nothing in my hand to save me. I feel like I can't breathe, that my muscles are losing their will to fight and becoming limp. I'm cold and warm at the same time. But in that moment, a sort of calmness washes over me, almost as if I'm just going to fall asleep. And I'm left watching the silvery meniscus, separating this reality from the real world. And in this macrocosm, time seems to stand still.

Breaking through the glistening surface, hands reach out and grab onto me, and my instincts kick in, thrashing about, trying break free. But this time, my body is wrenched around, and it causes my muscles to freeze in shock, but moments later, the space around me bursts into another dimension.

I'm surrounded by trees and flowers, lying on soft grass, with Samuel kneeling over me.

I try to say something, but my mind is blank.

His eyes are soft, jet voraciously prying for something from me. Yet I feel like I'm watching him and myself, pitying the both of us. I feel the wrath of my own lost innocence, the fact that I became an adult before I even knew what it was to be a child. And I feel for Samuel, who believes he can protect me from my own self-destruction. Then again, I guess I feel the same way about him.

'You should have told me you had trouble swimming,' says Samuel. The sound of his voice disrupts my inner dialogue.

'I don't,' I say.

He sighs and looks as though he wants to say something but holds his tongue. I sit up, though my muscles feel heavy. I felt like I was going to die... that there was nothing left to do, and the way I emerged from the water makes me feel like I snapped back from the realm of the living.

I stare at the ground, wondering if I'm imagining this very conversation. He puts his hand on my forehead, and then feels the pulse on my neck with his fingertips. 'Maybe it was some sort of cold shock response.'

At that moment, I notice I'm being held by him. And it's because he's shivering. I can almost tell where he was coming from: all those times he tried to push me away, because of his self-sabotaging mindset. It makes me remember what he told me... that parting ways was the same as death. I think I'm starting to understand what it means. I'm just not too sure where that puts me, whether I can bear that sort of responsibility.

'At least I could do something about it,' he says, his hands clutching my curled-up body like there's something incredibly precious about my existence. Perhaps I'm enjoying this a little too much; I feel very guilty about it. This whole thing was meant to be romantic, perhaps a little enticing, but there's a demon inside of me that has different plans it seems. I wish he would calm down. Though maybe I'm the one who shouldn't be so calm. It felt like I was going to die, yet I'm not very bothered by it all.

My right hand reaches out and plucks a Forget-me-not from the field next to me, then tentatively places it behind Samuel's ear. I want him to feel safe around me, but instead, it seems that he has to go out of his way to look after me. He kisses me on the forehead and takes a deep breath. I don't like having to rely on someone like this, it makes me quite uncomfortable, but I can't understand why. Perhaps a bunch of forgotten experiences led me to feel that way.

'I wish I could do more for you, that I could somehow help you with what you're going through,' he says.

I look at him sympathetically. 'I know you would like for that to be the case, but sometimes the demons I fight are those which only I can see.' My chest feels tight saying this. 'That much is beginning to become clear.' I sigh.

I think it's going to take a while before I'd be able to make peace with what happened in that alleyway. I should probably talk to Samuel about it at some point, but I think I'd lose my composure if I were to discuss it now. As far as I'm concerned, I'd be happy if I could just forget about it and move on.

Samuel runs his fingers through my hair. 'How about we go together this time,' he says.

'I'd be glad to,' he says, standing up and offering me a hand. The two of us approach the water's edge. He swings my arm back in anticipation before we both leap into the pool. It's still cold, no doubt, but I can't help but stare at the light scattering off the pale patches in his mottled hair.

The excitement in his eyes is contagious, and it makes me want to take this a step further. But part of me feels guilty. It would feel too much like I'm using him since his first instinct was to provide comfort. He wants me to me able to overcome my internal conflict.

The two of us burst through the surface of the water, and the sound of his laughter fills me with warmth. He and I drift with the current towards a nearby boulder, on which we stand. My skin is tingling from the cold.

'Really opens up the capillaries,' I say.

'Gosh, my head is spinning.'

'Hopefully I have something to do with that,' I declare, and I wrap my arms around his lower back and nuzzle my head in his chest, a tad frustrated by the fact that he's not taking to my advances.

He chuckles, 'You sure seem to have perked up a little.'

I look down, feeling a little smug. 'It appears so.' I bring my hands up to rest around his neck. I stand on my toes and lean in, taking in his musky scent, unable to fathom how he's able to hold back.

At that point, I break eye contact and dive back into the water, surfacing at the other end of the pool to climb out.

I then sit on the grass, hugging my knees, watching Samuel glide through the water towards me. I roll my eyes. 'You're unbelievable,' I murmur with a skew smile, rolling my eyes.

He attempts to give me a narrow-eyed stare, as he gets out, but isn't bold enough to maintain eye-contact.

I ruffle his hair and sigh. 'You'll figure it out someday.'

'Gosh, I can't read you sometimes,' he says.

'As is should be,' I gleam.

He grabs his shirt and uses it to soak up the excess water in my hair and then places it over my shoulders. I don't care that he can't take a hint. He's thoughtful and generous with his time. There ought to be plenty of opportunities to make advances in the future; besides, his supposedly inconspicuous glances didn't go unnoticed. Then again, he may have just been monitoring my behaviour to make sure I'm alright.

At that point, my eyes focus on a glistening thread before me. At its end hangs a tiny spider with subtle white and brown bars along its abdomen. I reach out and pluck the thread, letting it crawl along my hand. I take Samuel's hand to bridge the gap.

'Would you look at that,' he says.

'It's a Zebra-jumper,' I say. 'I'm pleased to see arachnids around again. I think it's because there's more prey to be had in spring.'

'What do they eat in any case?' he asks, staring at it crawling along his fingertips. 'It's tiny.'

'I think they go for mosquitoes and flies mostly. It's magnificent, isn't it? Look at its eyes,' I say, 'so big and curious.'

Samuel chuckles and nods. 'Anthropomorphising spiders... there's never a dull moment, huh?'

'Well, I consider them my friends. They're a vital part of the ecosystem, you know.'

'You're so sweet with even the tiniest of creatures.'

'Well, all life has value, I guess.'

Samuel grimaces.

'What is it?' I ask.

'Let me guess, we're all equally vital strands in the fabric of reality.'

'Don't you get sarcastic with me,' I snap.

'Besides, I'm not that presumptuous. So let us both just get on with our meaningless lives.'

At that point, the spider springs out of sight. Samuel bursts out laughing. 'Looks like it couldn't handle all this existential talk. Though, I can't say I'm not proud that I've had an effect on you.'

'A bad one at that!' I snap.

He looks away, masking a self-satisfied grin. 'I'd rather have that than nothing at all.'

FRAGMENTS

41 SAMUEL

'**M**um,' *I begin,* 'I'd like some advice regarding… woman.'

'Oh, my, I feared this day would never come,' says Mum. Soon after, she exhibits a wide smile.

'Heavens! Not that sort of advice, mum!' I cry. She looks conceited. 'I want to spoil her. I need an idea for a gift.'

'My-my, that is a tough one,' says mum. The two of us are well aware of the fact that we can't simply throw money at an extravagant gift. 'Special gifts always have some degree of emotional importance, you see.'

'So, something that means a lot to me as well?'

'Yes, exactly that,' says Mum.

I ponder this, trying to come up with something that meets the criteria. Just like that, it occurs to me... the stone. I've kept it for years, and I love its distinct sheen.

'Actually, I do have something in mind,' I say. 'It's a pebble which reminds me of when we used to live in Pennsylvania.'

Before mum can respond, I dash upstairs and snatch it from my desk. I return with it and drop it in her hand.

'Here,' I say. 'It glistens like the stars.'

She inspects it for a little while.

'This is all the way from Pennsylvania?' she asks. I nod. 'My goodness, I remember those times. You were such a curious young boy, always collecting things. Do you remember your room?' She grins. 'It was ever so cluttered.'

'I do,' I say, transported back for a moment. My problems used to be minute in comparison to now. Gosh, I used to worry over whether I'd have enough spare change at the end of the week to go and get ice cream.

'In any case,' I continue, 'I can't just give it to her like this...'

'Hold that thought,' says mum. She walks up the stairs and shuffles around in the rooms above. She then appears at the bottom of the staircase, holding a box with an entanglement of ribbons and fabric spilling over the edges. She places it on the table. Her hands part the colourful mess, removing a few dainty tools. 'I was thinking we could turn it into a necklace.' My eyes light up. 'Believe it or not,' she says, 'I used to make them.'

'I can actually imagine that.' I chuckle. 'I think it's a wonderful idea.'

She hands me a tool with a V-shaped blade at its tip. 'This can be used for engraving all sorts of things,' she says. 'We could use it to make a groove in the stone.'

'Yes, then we can wrap a chord around it.' I place the stone flat on the table and place the tool against its surface.

'I doubt you'd make any progress like that.'

'I'm just marking a guide around the circumference of the stone so the chord will be properly seated once I've cut out the groove.' Mum nods and, judging by her expression, seems quite impressed. I rotate the stone, making a thin line. 'I'm guessing the engraving may take some time.'

'I can help you if you like,' says Mum as I switch my grip to how I would hold a pen.

'That won't be necessary,' I say. 'Though… I wouldn't mind if you watch over me just a little.'

Mum smiles. 'Of course.'

I begin using the tool. The stone proves to be moderately tough, requiring a few rounds of engraving to make an impression. Once it's deep enough, Mum and I choose a nylon cord for it. Although thin, I have no doubt it is strong. I'm surprised by how snugly she wraps and ties the cord around the stone. Once we fix a hook to each end of the string, I find myself unable to hide my content.

'I can't believe *we* made this!'

'I've got to say, it wouldn't be out of place lying on the shelves of a jewellery store,' she tells me.

'Certainly,' I say.

The stone slowly rotates when you hold it up by the chord, and the way it glistens is magical. It's as though it were lit up with constellations.

'Thank you, Mum,' I say and give her a hug. At that point, I wonder whether the glow on my face is too obvious, not that I care all that much anyway.

When we walk past the flags that evening, the night air flows through the corridors like the current of an icy river. It's now time to find out how I fared this semester. Lucinda and Charlotte are with me, as they had decided that we all go together. I'm not too sure how I feel about them seeing my grades, but it can't be helped at this point.

We get to the notice board. Seeing the infamous column of surnames makes me incredibly nervous. Moments later, when I see the grade next to my name, it seems surreal. I'm compelled to draw a line with my finger along the row to ensure I'm looking at the correct one. I managed to get eighty-two per cent for the test. I know I should feel happy about it, but it's a sort of hollow sense of pride rather than joy. If my other two tests were forty-three and forty-seven per cent, that makes my aggregate... fifty-seven for molecular biology. My eyes smile in vain. That's how it feels somehow, even though I know that it defies logic. Passing is by no means futile.

'This is precisely what I wanted,' I say under my breath. A strange, tingling sensation rushes through my head. I already managed to pass genetics and chemistry. I guess I'm just not all that used to what it feels like to succeed at these sorts of things.

'For sure!' exclaims Lucinda. 'Don't look distressed. You did better than *me* in the last one, for heaven's sake! Let us celebrate!'

Her expression changes when she looks into my eyes. I figure it must be difficult for her to understand how I feel. I can barely comprehend it myself. She takes hold of my hand, and I try to just focus on the coolness of her touch.

'Celebrate?' says Charlotte, who seems to have caught up with us. 'That's what *I* was going to suggest!'

'Did you pass?' Lucinda asks Charlotte. She lets go of me at that point. I am a little shocked by her insensitivity. Did she even consider the possibility that Charlotte didn't?

'Yes,' says Charlotte. I feel relieved to hear this. 'It most definitely calls for a celebration.'

Lucinda beams. 'What do you have in mind?'

'There are all sorts of fun events taking place at this time,' says Charlotte.

'Yes, the end of term is usually bustling with parties,' says Lucinda.

The three of us exit the building at that point. The sun is setting, and the streets feel emptier than usual.

'Let's get stoned!' shrieks Charlotte. Lucinda gasps and smiles awkwardly.

I take hold of Lucinda's shoulder. 'Trust me, your imagination alone already does wonders,' I murmur to her.

She shoots me a narrow-eyed stare but soon breaks into a skew smile.

'We'd love to go,' says Lucinda.

'Tonight then?' asks Charlotte.

'Tonight?' asks Lucinda, taken aback.

'Works for me,' I say.

Lucinda nods slowly. 'You are aware we still have university tomorrow.'

'It's just for checking your papers,' says Charlotte. 'We don't have to go if we don't feel it to be necessary.'

'Oh, all right. In that case, count us in.'

'52 Rodrigue Street. Nine o'clock.'

'Fantastic,' I say, checking my watch. That leaves us with two hours to get ready.

'Let's go to your place first,' says Lucinda.

'Sure thing,' I say.

The three of us continue through the neighbourhood while Charlotte tells us how long it's been since last she went to a party. I fail to mention that I can barely remember the last time I was at a celebration.

We walk over the bridge, and after we pass the park, Charlotte veers off our street to get to where she lives. She waves to us. 'I'll see you two later!' she calls out.

When we get to my house, Lucinda kneels to pick up the newspaper. 'I would suggest we steer clear of news for the time being.' I nod in agreement as she tosses it away. I unlock the front door to my house. The two of us climb the stairs and enter my room.

'In the shower you go,' she says and sits on my bed.

I give myself a quick rinse and scurry back to find her gazing out the window. I take the opportunity to quickly slip my bottom half on and proceed to fumble when clasping the belt buckle shut.

'You needn't be self-conscious,' she says, starting to button up my shirt. She leaves the last two undone.

Next, we go to her house so she can get ready. She goes to shower, and I am left alone in her room. I look around and am astounded by all that she's collected. There are plenty of books about all sorts of topics, and her desk is stacked with the strangest of things: some old, some new and everything in between as well.

'What do you propose I wear?' she asks, appearing with a towel wrapped around her. She opens her wardrobe, and I stare at her feet, feeling a little flushed.

'You'll be lovely in anything you put on,' I say.

'You flatter me,' she says and giggles. I scrunch my eyes shut while she slips on one of her dresses. After a few moments, she asks, 'Am I *that* hideous?'

I gasp. 'You never looked at me.'

'Says who?'

I open my eyes, irked and wanting to retaliate, but the moment I see her, my mind goes blank.

'How's this?' she asks. She spins in a deep violet dress. It's made of velvety fabric and has a frill across her neckline, which drapes over her shoulders. The back is an open V that extends down to her hips. I practically melt on the spot, and she must have been able to tell because her eyes sparkle.

'My word, you're magnificent!' I am genuinely enthralled. 'There's just one more thing to top it off.' I reach into my pocket to reveal the necklace. The stone, suspended by the thin chord, swivels around and glistens.

'Oh my,' she says, captivated. Her palms rest on her cheeks momentarily before she throws herself onto me and squeezes the breath from my chest. She holds me at arms-length, and her eyes become shiny. 'It's exquisite.'

'I found the stone when I was younger.'

'My goodness, Samuel. It's too special for words. Oh, put it on, will you?' I fasten the chord at the back of her neck and kiss her on the cheek. It looks like a miniature galaxy resting on her chest. 'I'll hold it dear for as long as I live. I love it,' she says with her lashes cast downward.

I help her choose a matching pair of shoes. We decide on white slides whose heels are slightly raised. They contrast the deep shade of purple in her dress.

'Stay here a moment,' she says and disappears into the passage. She reappears after some time with a dark tie. 'Would you mind wearing this?' she asks.

'Not at all,' I say.

She tiptoes towards me and wraps the tie around my neck. She braids it in a knot, which I haven't seen before, and pulls the other end for a loose fit, allowing the top of my shirt to remain open. 'Why, thank you,' I say, wondering why she knows how to do that.

'You look spiffy!'

I dust off my sides. 'Thanks, Dear.' I do a playful bow. 'Well then, do you know how to get to the party?'

'Yes, we go north-west. Then, if we walk for long enough— That reminds me,' she says, snapping her fingers. She goes to her desk and picks up a little, black book. 'We'll need a compass if we stand any chance of navigating those mountains.' She then picks up a pencil and scribbles in the book. I figure it's a checklist.

'That mind of yours never rests.' I beam. 'Though, I should be keeping one of those myself.'

She winks. 'I think it'd come in handy.' She puts the book on her desk. 'Shall we go, my prince?' she asks, holding out her hand for me to take. I giggle, and the two of us retreat along the passage. I push open the door for her. She steps outside, and her hair moves like a charcoal sea in the wind. I follow her out and close the door for her to lock.

As we walk along the street with bound arms, I find myself wondering how I managed to become so tranquil and fulfilled; whether I even deserve to feel this way. I know Lucinda would tell me that we all deserve happiness, no matter our past circumstances or shortcomings.

The wind has whisked away the haziness, revealing a moonlit sky. Not long after, we hear the sound of music drawing nearer.

BITTERSWEET

42 LUCINDA

'*Stay by my side, Lucinda,*' he says.

I wish he were more relaxed, but I do know he can be anxious at times.

'I won't leave it,' I assure him. 'What on earth are you pent up about, in any case?' I ask, noticing his firm grip.

'This place is bound to be a total sensory overload,' he moans.

'Perhaps it's precisely what you need,' I say. 'If the music is loud enough, it ought to rattle some sense into you. And you had better dance. I have standards, you know.'

'In that case, the only thing lower than your standards is my self-esteem.'

'Total hogwash,' I say, a little shocked but equally amused. I jab his ribs playfully. He doesn't budge but grins sheepishly. His tie shines in the light, and so does his hair. I nudge him, a cue for him to put his arm around me.

I see vibrant lights escaping through windows, dotted about the house's dark façade like islands. As soon as we walk through the door, the music becomes clear in tone. We mix with the masses. I see wigs, scarves, and extravagant hats. Many wear bootlegs varying from navy to silver. They seem about our age, some a little older. Most have coagulated in groups with similar attire. Tuxedoes with silky suits and shirts, buttoned half down, seem to be in vogue as well. I love eyeing out the clothing the girls wear. Many are in plain dresses with decorative buttons and white collars. Others sport turtlenecks or shirts with cardigans. I find it oddly liberating to take note of trends like these yet feel not an ounce of an urge to conform to them. Samuel and I are most certainly on the same page regarding that.

I wonder how Charlotte came to know of this. She seems the secluded type. I can't imagine this to be her scene. Then again, I suppose I haven't known her for all that long.

The venue opens up to reveal a dance floor, seemingly the porch of the house, and behind it lies a vast garden with mounds of grass and trees at its border. The lawn alone is probably large enough to hold all the guests simultaneously. A live band is playing rock-and-roll; to this, various couples are dancing. The atmosphere is festive, with constant bustling and laughter. I wonder how Samuel is dealing with the elaborate lighting. I hook my arm in his, but his shoulders are tense.

'For heaven's sake, relax,' I say. His eyes dart around as though he's being stalked or something.

'I'm simply surveying the site,' he says, now staring at the bar counter.

'For what, exactly?' I ask.

'Imminent threats,' he whispers.

'God, you're neurotic,' I say. 'Besides, I'm right here.' I rest my head on his neck.

He closes his eyes for a moment. 'You're right.'

'I'm always right,' I say and huff. 'When it comes to what's best for you, anyway.'

We observe some of the other couples in the room. Well, I do. Samuel mostly just looks at me. He's probably not used to seeing me dressed this way.

'Darling?' I say. 'Would you dance with me?'

'Perhaps if I were to be drunk enough,' he mutters.

'But it is my wish,' I say, squeezing his knuckles.

'Anything for you,' he obliges. 'Though, I'm afraid you will have to lead me. I'm hopeless at dancing.'

'Naturally,' I say. He growls. 'Naturally... I will lead you.' I beam.

To be honest, I'm also a tad nervous about dancing in front of others.

'Though having said that, I'd never turn down an offer for refreshments. May we sit briefly?' I ask.

He pulls out a chair for me at the granite bar counter, after which he takes a seat himself. A young man is working as the bartender.

'We'll have two... Manhattans,' says Samuel.

Before the bartender makes for the rows of liquors, I say, 'Make them doubles.' I turn to Samuel. 'I just remembered you told my father you don't drink.'

'Well, I don't think I have much choice when I'm around you. I seldom do, though,' he clarifies.

'No wonder there's so much wrong with you,' I say.

'Excuse me?' he asks, alarmed.

'I said, no wonder you don't like parties.'

His eyes narrow, but I just pat his head and grin sheepishly. After the bartender slides the drinks over, Samuel takes precarious sips from his glass.

We soak up the scene for some time, and before long, I'm lapping up the remaining dregs. I peer to the side to see Samuel staring into space, his foot tapping the ground. What started off as mellow excitement is now on a steady incline.

I get up and tug his hand to the dancefloor. Surprisingly, he follows willingly and looks animated too. The lights trace circles on the floor beneath us like luminous brushstrokes. At that point, another song begins, this one sounding more like a tango, and the lights now turn deep shades of orange and red.

'Am I not meant to ask *you* for a dance?' he says.

'I suppose I took the liberty,' I say but feel a little shy that he pointed it out.

'I'm all for that,' he says.

His hand is quite a bit larger than mine, and my fingers contract around his. His other hand finds its place on my lower back. We start off with a simple box step, quickly migrating to a waltz. All the while, I can't wipe the smile off my face. He is actually quite the dancer.

'Who taught you this?' I ask.

'To dance?' He pauses. 'It is more of an intuition really, and some observation.'

Remarkable, I think. 'I could have learnt to dance. Formally, I mean. I was offered the opportunity.'

'What made you decide against it?'

'I was young and foolish and have regretted it ever since.' My eyes are turned towards his neck.

'How do you remember it if you were young?' he asks.

'Father told me,' I say. 'I figure I lacked the foresight I needed at the time, or perhaps I saw it in a different light back then. I was a different person after all.'

I spin around and sink down, keeping my knees bent. He holds my waist on either side. With outstretched arms, I fan-kick as I am lifted into the air, after which I twirl back into his embrace, giggling.

'Why, you need no lessons. You have it in you already; I know it.'

'Hmmm? Well, it takes two to tango.' I giggle.

'Quite literally,' he says.

I lean over his hand, arching my back and splaying my arms. His mottled grey hair assumes whatever colour the spinning lights lay on it. Every so often, the beams make his face flash white. We are each offered a glass of what looks like spirit shots and take them without hesitation. This time, he downs it with me.

'Those were rather potent.' I hold onto his shoulders to support myself.

'You aren't going to go crazy on me again, are you?' he asks. I glare at him. 'I was only joking,' he says. 'I like your fiery side.'

At that point, I begin feeling calm. My breathing slows. The music cascades from the floor and surges through me, but more detached than sharp sounding.

Just then, I catch a glimpse of Charlotte's face in the strobing lights. She's pressed against a fellow with dark hair, and they're kissing in the midst of everything. This seems to give Samuel an idea because he takes my hand and leads me to a porch on the farther side of the house. We walk onto the lawn. At its edge, the wall casts a shadow over the grass, forming an invisible patch. Samuel sits down on the grass. I soon push him onto his back and straddle my legs around his waist. I then lie down on top of him. His chest is incredibly warm; the music seems to have dulled.

'Samuel,' I say, 'I'm feeling thirsty.' He shudders, and I look up at him, confused, but can't make out his expression in the dark.

'Thirsty?' he asks.

'Yes, thirsty,' I repeat. I rest my head again, feeling dazed. Everything around me is spinning. I'd imagine water will help, but I don't know whether I'd be able to walk back on my own.

'Why me?' he asks.

I giggle. 'Don't be daft. Who else shall I ask?'

'I don't know if I'd fulfil your request to satisfaction,' he says. I roll my eyes but realise that he couldn't have seen me do so.

'I'm sure you will,' I say, a little confused.

He gulps, and I feel his hand move into the open back of my dress. I giggle again. 'Samuel,' I say, 'what on earth are you doing? We're in public.'

'What? You changed your mind?'

'No, dear.' I roll my eyes again. 'Water will do.'

'Water!' he exclaims. 'Oh god,' he whispers.

I roll over and sit cross-legged. 'Yes, water. What did you think I meant?'

He sighs deeply. 'Never mind that.' He gets to his feet. 'One moment.' I watch him disappear. When I sway my head, everything appears temporarily out of focus. He reappears and places an icy glass in my hand.'

'Thanks, dear,' I say, taking a sip. 'It's ever so refreshing. I reckon it ought to do the trick.'

He sits down and places an arm around me. I see a shirtless bloke hopping about on one leg to the sound of the music. His dreadlocks are flying about eccentrically. 'Look!' I say, pointing. Samuel bursts out laughing, and I can't help but join in.

'He must be entirely blasted!' he bawls.

'Oh my,' I say, catching my breath. Just then, a firework shoots off into the sky, followed by a series of "oohs" and "aahs". 'What a scene.' A second one whizzes sideways, ricochets off of the house and lands on the grass. People disperse crazily. A second later, it ignites in a blue and yellow half-sphere. Some of the sparks even land on my skin but are instantly blotted out. Samuel finds the whole thing highly amusing. I jab him. The next set, thankfully aimed with a little more care, lights up the entire sky.

When the fireworks come to an end, I go back to lying on him, but this time, I stare into his eyes. We kiss passionately, and I feel so tingly and warm, yet so safe where I am. He runs his fingers through my hair and down my back, and I curl my legs around him.

'My god!' he manages in between his breaths. 'We should do this more often.'

'I think so too.' His eyes shine. I twirl his hair in my fingertips. 'I've noticed that you've become more muscular lately.' My hands follow the contours of his torso.

'I guess I've been working on that.'

'I can certainly tell,' I say. 'You're quite enchanting, to say the least.'

He closes his eyes. 'If you say so. Though, I suppose I need not mention your flawless figure.'

'You're exaggerating.'

'Not in the slightest,' he says. We touch noses like cats, and I can feel the sparks flying within the space between us.

ELATION

43 LUCINDA

I *sigh with satisfaction,* throwing myself onto the sofa. I could barely tell up from down by the time we left. Samuel had to help me get home. Though, the walk back must have done a world of good because I feel almost normal now, apart from the remnants of dizziness.

I just knew he'd appreciate going to a party in the end. Along with that, I found him to be unusually affectionate, which I quite enjoyed.

I get to my feet and make my way along the passage, turning into the study. I stare at the mess resting on the easel: a gouged, scratched-up canvas. I hope Father hasn't discovered this; otherwise, he may begin asking questions I won't be able to answer. He seems to be still sleeping, though. I remove the canvas and stack it among the other forgotten works scattered around the study.

I think I ought to give it another go. It always makes me excited to put a new canvas on the easel. The paints are dispersed around the room from when last I used them, so I line them up neatly and prepare a jar of water to rinse my brushes.

I'm sure Samuel would appreciate anything I'd have to offer; he's sweet in that way. I figure he'd want something set at night since he fancies dull hues.

I begin sketching the outlines of features in the environment: sharp dunes in the background, rocks scattered over a bare desert, and trees which hold no leaves. A single crow hovers above the barren terrain, scouring the ground for a potential scavenge. I can feel what it must be like to be there. Nothing moves apart from the desert dust, and the harsh cold is inescapable during the time of night it depicts. With only outlines on the page and before even a single drop of paint stains the canvas, my vision of the final product is clear.

I can't quite tell why this particular image came to mind. Perhaps it's because when things are going a little too well, I tend to wonder when fate will take a turn.

I wish Samuel were here to talk some sense into me. Why is it so hard to have faith? I find that my thoughts tend to spiral out of control when everything goes quiet. Unfortunately, the holidays might involve exactly that, but at least I won't be alone.

The dizziness returns at that moment. My vision blurs, and I feel my hands catch my fall on the carpet floor. The room feels like an ocean: the way it ebbs and flows. My drawn-out breaths become slower and slower. I try to concentrate on what's happening to me. Perhaps I've become dehydrated. But the more I listen to the sound of my breath, the more I drift away from reality.

I wake up with sharp sunlight on my cheek. I gasp and abruptly sit up. Dust is perceivable within the rays streaming through the window. My back joints feel tender.

'You fainted, Lucinda,' I say. 'How did you manage to do that?'

Perhaps I had a tad too much fun yesterday evening. I put my fingers over my eyelids and reminisce over the fireworks display and the way we danced together. I then hug my knees and grin. I usually feel terrible after a night out like that, but the only trace of it now is my stiff back. I scrunch my eyebrows. Why am I in the study again? There is a blank canvas on the easel. But only, it isn't. I drew some outlines on it, but everything feels hazy, and I can't for the life of me remember what it was.

'You'd better clean up,' I mutter to myself, 'before Father sees the state you're in. He wouldn't like this one bit.'

I tiptoe upstairs and fling my shoes into my room, then hop into the shower. The warm water soothes my muscles almost instantly.

Thankfully, when Father wakes, he doesn't notice anything off. He had made breakfast for the two of us in the meantime: flapjacks and syrup. He only remarks, 'You returned quite late last night, Lucinda.'

'I did,' I say. 'I don't feel tired, though.' This, funnily enough, is not even a fib. Perhaps the exhaustion will hit me a little later on. I go to the fridge and remove a cheddar block to grate over the flapjacks.

'At least you had fun,' he says, then pauses for a moment. 'Have I ever told you of your aunt, Adeline, and your uncle, Ulric?'

'I think you may have mentioned them before, yes. Why do you ask?'

'Well, I think it's important that we maintain contact with family members, you see.' I nod.

'Where do they live?' I ask.

'In the Amazon,' he says. 'They're quite cultured too. I'm sure you'll love their company.'

I smile and say, 'I think I just might. We'll have to see when I meet them, I guess.'

Father nods and seems as though he wants to say something else. Instead, he just finishes his food. 'I'd better go and stock up for the week,' he says at last.

'I'll see you later, in that case.' I tell him.

When I'm finished eating breakfast myself, I immediately return to the painting. Now, the outlines I've drawn seem to make sense to me: it's a mountainous landscape with an eagle flying high and proud. I'm certain that's what it was. I colour the mountains with a deep blue hue and sprinkle white specks over the dusky sky to form stars because it reminds me of Samuel's hair. He'd never know this, and the thought makes me grin. I add a hint of light just above the mountains like the sun is about to peak over them. They still seem rather bare. I must have just begun adding the finer elements.

At that point, I breathe life into the image by detailing the mountain's edge and adding form to the rocks scattered about the landscape. I dip my brush in a heterogeneous mixture of dark and light green paint to populate the trees with leaves, also dotting shrubs over the foreground of the image. I paint long blades of grass in the bottom corners as well.

Some say they find it difficult to decide when an artwork is finished; that it's common just to keep adding detail indefinitely. I've never experienced this. I can always recognise the point at which I finish a painting.

Just then, I hear the clanging of the door knocker. I am a little surprised since I doubt it'd be Father, unless, of course, he forgot his keys again. I scamper down the hallway, thankful that I had changed into new clothes. When I open the door, I am greeted with a bouquet of wildflowers. Samuel holds them out for me to take in their aroma.

'I love them!' I declare. 'I'll go get a vase,' I say and hop over to the dining room. I walk around the table and open the cupboard. Samuel follows me inside and places the flowers in the vase after I set it on the table. 'Magnificent.'

'There are many more at the park,' he says. 'Come along. I'll show you.' I take his hand, and the two of us make our way there.

'My goodness, there most certainly are!' I exclaim as we walk onto the grass. I kneel and see hundreds of minuscule blossoms. The swings and merry-go-round have become partially hidden by all the sprouting vegetation.

I can't hide my excitement. Seeing all this new life makes me feel revitalised. There are many different types of beetles scurrying amongst the flowers. I don't yet know how to identify all of them. Perhaps I should have brought an entomology book along. I kneel on the grass, inspecting them more carefully. They're the shiny, green variety. Samuel kneels next to me, this time knowing precisely what I'm looking at. 'Sweet,' he says. I smile, a bit embarrassed, but I can't take my eyes off them.

Something black and white darts past us in a blur, and I nearly topple over backwards. I hear the bark of Tracy's dog. Sure enough, she is here as well.

When I see the adorable face of the collie, I can't help but bound up to the animal with excitement. I kneel beside it and stroke its back. I wonder why. How could I exhibit no fear at all, even after it scared me to death when I first saw it? It felt entirely different last time. I was so blinded back then. Though I know it's the same animal. Something about the way it moves when it runs around...

'Mrs Clark,' says Samuel. He walks up to the two of us. I realise I've been focusing so much on the dog that I never even greeted Tracy.

'Now-now,' she says. 'Remember, I wish to be called "Tracy" when we're not in a formal setting.' Samuel and I nod.

'I'm glad our paths have crossed outside of class,' I tell Tracy.

'Likewise,' she says. 'I think Charlie is pleased too.'

'Hmm,' I remark, 'He actually seems very friendly.' Samuel winks, probably remembering the last encounter.

'Of course,' says Tracy. 'He wouldn't hurt a fly, though he's learned to jump the fence, so you may see him taking a leisurely stroll all by himself.' The three of us chuckle. 'In any case, how were the last few months of university?'

'Great,' says Samuel.

'Now-now, there were a few ups and downs,' I say. 'I think I speak on Samuel's behalf as well.' I giggle.

'You two are still studying next year, if I'm not mistaken,' says Tracy. I nod.

'I don't know what's going to happen next year, really,' says Samuel.

'Oh, just you wait and see, Dear,' I tell him. 'There's most certainly a reason to look forward to it.'

DISPELLING

---

44 LUCINDA

'*Sleeping bags, tents,* mattresses, water bottles… Hmmm, what else?' I peer at Samuel, who's on the couch, looking a little dazed. I jab him, and he jerks upright, startled. I simply continue the list. 'Oh, mosquito repellent.'

'You clearly know more about this than I do,' he says.

'Can't deny that,' I say unapologetically. 'May you switch on a light for us?' I ask him. His house is awfully dark. He springs to his feet and flips a switch. A chandelier fixed with six bulbs lights up the room.

'I'm surprised you're not turning your nose up at this place,' he says. 'It's a total eyesore at the moment.'

'I'd never do that.' I chuckle. 'Though, I'd be happy to help out with a spring clean if you'd like.'

'I could never ask that of—'

'Nonsense,' I interject. 'It'll be fun, I know it.'

'Perhaps,' he says, pausing for a bit. 'Though, I do doubt it.' I laugh and tap the pencil on his nose.

'I suppose I'll be supplying all the camping gear,' I say.

He nods. 'I'll do all the food. I'm guessing we'd need items that don't easily perish if they are to last a multi-day hike.'

'Yes,' I say. 'Preferably canned food; something that we don't need to cook as well.' I pause for a second. 'How much experience do you have with the outdoors?'

He shrugs. 'The bare minimum, I'm guessing. What exactly is there to know?'

'I suppose there isn't all that much. Most of it is common sense: finding level camping ground, remaining near a water source, avoiding sunstroke, and such.'

'I doubt we'd get sunstroke here,' Samuel remarks.

'Mmm, I think you may be right.'

'Perhaps we ought to take a walk outside to better understand what it'd be like on the hike.'

'Excellent idea,' I say. As we're about to step out the door, it opens, and a woman enters.

'Mum,' says Samuel.

'Evening,' she says. She appears friendly and has greyish, curly hair with a tinge of ginger in the mix. A pale blue, button-up shirt is covered by a green blouse, which she wears over her shoulders.

'Nice to meet you, Ms Onyx,' I say. She takes my hand and shakes it energetically.

'My my!' she enthuses. 'You must be the one Samuel can't stop going on about.'

Samuel buries his face in his hands. 'How did I know this was going to happen?' he mumbles.

I gleam, very much amused.

'Mum,' says Samuel, 'Lucinda and I plan to go off into the mountains for a hike.'

'That's lovely,' says his mother. 'Just as long as you don't steal him forever.' She winks.

'I promise,' I say with a coy smile.

'I believe it would be to your benefit to get out a bit,' she continues. 'It's important to feel some sunshine once in a while and take one's mind off things for a while.' I nod. 'So, are these mountains the ones just south Xys?'

'Yes,' I say. 'Some look a little steep, but we should find a good enough path through them. We may even scale one if we feel up to it. I'm sure the view would be nothing short of spectacular.' Samuel looks excited when I say this.

'Wales sure does have some beautiful territory. I do envy you, youngsters,' says Ms Onyx. 'It's as though nothing is insurmountable. Please look after Samuel, though. He's prone to becoming a little lost sometimes.'

'I've found that to be quite true.' He looks a tad frustrated by this. 'Don't worry, we'll orienteer as a team.' I tell him, ruffling his hair.

After we move out of the living room, Samuel and I get to work on finding the things we'll need. I ask him to lend me his second pair of old leather shoes. Because he owns few shirts, I tell him he can use one of my father's. Next, we throw together some tinned food and decide to pack some fresh fruit the day before we leave.

'Hmmm, I think we've got everything for the time being.' I glide down the stairs, passing through the orange glow of the sun diffusing through the frosted windows. This gives me an idea. I take Samuels' hand and lead him out the door, towards the oak tree which borders his property and the next. With that, I begin to scale its branches.

When I look down, I see Samuel at the bottom, staring up at me. 'You aren't going to join me?'

With this, he promptly follows. 'I was just quite impressed, that's all.'

When I look through the leaves, I can almost see over the tops of the houses, and it urges me to go a little higher. The branches are thinning out, to the point where I feel like an acrobat balancing on poles. He's quick to reach me at that point, the two of us ebbing and flowing in the wind.

'Look over there,' I tell Samuel. Over the top of the houses, the silvery river divides the neighbourhood and the city, and the mountains beyond carve out jagged lines in the skyline. I wonder what I would be like to be there, looking back to where we are currently.

'It seems like another world,' he says.

'It is,' I say, 'from the whispering grasslands to the still lakes.'

'So, you've walked in the wilderness before then?'

'I suppose I have.' I pause. 'What else could explain this insatiable desire?' The sound of the moaning branches is thrilling.

'So, you don't fear heights then?'

I shake my head. 'I fear falling, but not heights. Though I trust myself not to fall. Trust is incompatible with fear.'

'You tend to use logic to rationalise your beliefs.'

'Better to choose good delusions, don't you think?'

'Definitely,' he says, his eyes gleaming at the sight of the setting sun.

'It'd be wise to pack torches in case we find that we haven't managed to set up camp before dark,' I suggest.

'For sure. There ought to be some torches in—' He trails off and swallows hard. 'Never mind.'

I frown. 'Where, Dear?'

'I was going to suggest the garage, though I then remembered that—' His voice is barely audible.

'Oh, come on then,' I say, and the two of us promptly return to the ground below. We walk around the side of his house. He doesn't resist, funnily enough, but the moment the two of us are standing in front of the door, I feel him shiver, though I wonder why.

'There should be torches somewhere on the shelves,' he mutters, 'because my family used to go camping after all, but mum prefers to use candles when the power goes out anyway, so I don't usually go in there except when mum needs a new record, but that's only when—'

'Hush-hush,' I say. 'It's alright. I'll fetch them.' I gesture for him to open the garage door, and he does so with a glum expression, holding it ajar at hip height. I duck under the door and brush my hand over the dusty wall behind me to find the switch. The light takes a while to flicker on. With a single source illuminating the room, all of the shadows diverge, forming radial lines. Something about this place gives me the chills. There are tools scattered on the floor and dust hanging in the air.

I run my finger along the shelves in the back and scan the row of boxes stacked up against the wall below. I do find a pair of torches in one of them, as Samuel proposed. To my surprise, they work too.

'You're still alive in there?' I hear him call. I chuckle and duck under the garage door once more to exit, rattling the torches in my hand with a grin.

'We'll see what else we can find at my house,' I say. We go back into the living room to find Ms Onyx reading a book on the couch, though she looks up as the two of us enter. 'Excuse me, ma'am. Do you mind if Samuel comes over for dinner?'

'Not at all,' she says. 'Please thank your father for me. I know this isn't the first time you've had him over.'

'I will,' I say. 'We have something important to discuss.'

HORIZON

45 LUCINDA

Lucinda *swings open the door to the shed,* situated near the opposite end of the lawn. At night, the garden is humming with insects. The white roses glow in the moonlight.

As she steps inside the gloomy, wooden structure, she becomes invisible, apart from her hands. Samuel jolts when a hefty, dark object flies at him, fumbling to catch it. He realises it's rather soft. She walks up to him. 'It's our tent. I don't know how I know, but somehow, I remember,' she says, grinning.

Samuel nods. 'I hope we'll manage to pitch it.'

'I'm certain of it,' she says.

'Can you ride that?' he asks. Lucinda's eyes are drawn to the other objects around the shed: a lawnmower, secateurs and a garden fork. Samuel grabs onto the handlebars of her bicycle.

'Sure,' she says.

'It's beyond me. I had no one to teach me,' he mutters.

'Is that so?' she says. They find themselves noticing just how prominent the surrounding sounds are, high-pitched trills that saturate the air. 'Spring Peepers,' she says.

'The toads?' asks Samuel.

'Frogs.' She pauses for a second. 'I'll show you how to ride if you like,' she adds.

'You sure?' says Samuel, already picking up the bike and sitting on the saddle, clearly eager. 'Why is there a big dip in the middle of the frame?'

'It's a lady's bike,' she tells him with quiet laughter. 'It allows one to ride it while wearing a dress.' He smiles at this and pushes it forward. 'I don't recommend hitting the front brake too hard,' she warns.

'Sure thing,' he says, rolling towards the lower edge of the lawn. 'Which side is the front brake?'

'Left,' she calls out to him. He seems very focused on his legs and doesn't look up very often. Despite this, he miraculously turns near the edge of the lawn and begins peddling back towards her, albeit awkwardly. His expression is slightly worried if anything. At least the bicycle is the right size for him, as the two of them are around the same height.

'Fantastic!' she acclaims, applauding when he stops the bike gracefully next to her. A skew smile forms on his face that she'd never seen before. He must be awfully pleased with himself. 'I never knew you'd get the hang of it so easily at your age.'

He looks smug. 'I do still have a fair amount of neuroplasticity left, thank you very much.'

'We'll see in a few years' time,' she says, almost nostalgically. She wonders whether he's thinking of growing old together, though finds it difficult to believe why people fantasise over such a thing. She wouldn't want to grow old at all if she had it her way. Instead, she'd choose to live in her prime and die before she's lost her lustre.

'Father should be home soon,' she tells him. 'Would you like to stay for dinner again?'

'I'd love to,' he says. 'I hope your father won't mind.'

'He won't. I think he may even be growing fond of you, actually. In the meantime, we can get some more things from the shed.'

He rests the bike against the inside of the structure and picks up the tent they found earlier. She finds a sort of tarpaulin that they can use as a groundsheet, as well as another bag smaller than that of the tent. She looks around. 'Can you help me find another?' she asks.

'Is it a sleeping bag?' asks Samuel. She nods. The shed is quite dark, and she finds it amusing to watch Samuel scour through the clutter.

'It's all right,' she says at last. 'One will be sufficient.'

Samuel spins around. The soft, outside light illuminates his face. 'One?' he asks as he deduces the implication of this. 'It'd sure be warmer.'

'Yes,' she says with a skew smile, 'amongst other things.' He's a little alarmed but marginally invigorated.

'Shall we go inside?' he asks timidly and nudges her out of the shed. 'Let's get the wilderness maps.'

'There isn't such a thing, Dear,' she says, tittering. 'Not for these parts, anyway. Though, we still haven't found a compass— or a collared shirt for myself. How about we take a look in my room?'

They go upstairs, and when Samuel steps into her room, takes in his surroundings. 'You can see the entire city from your window.'

'The mountains as well,' she says, the two of them looking out of the window. He walks up to her desk and brushes his hand along the sheath of the dagger. He then stares at the pocket watch. 'It doesn't work,' she tells him.

'I thought it was a compass at first,' he says. 'The way it shimmers is quite unusual. Surely it just needs to be wound up?'

She shakes her head. 'It's beyond repair. It's—' she considers sharing the reason for its sentimental value but decides otherwise. Instead, she removes a khaki shirt from her wardrobe. 'I almost forgot I had this,' she says. She lays out a few pairs of shorts for herself as well.

'Lucinda in shorts,' remarks Samuel, 'Now that's something I'd like to see.'

'Hmmm? I only wear dresses to appear more feminine; my personality betrays me.' Samuel chuckles. 'Though it is just a social construct, femininity, you do realise that.'

'I knew your opinion would be somewhere along those lines.'

'Indeed, you know me well, but there is much that I have yet to reveal. Do you know what I'm most excited for?'

'What?'

'The silence,' she says.

'I mean, it's pretty quiet now,' says Samuel.

She shakes her head and sits cross-legged on the floor. She gestures for him to sit in front of her and takes his hands. 'Just close your eyes and listen. We live enveloped within infrasounds.' She pauses for a while, hearing the sound of the distant traffic within the hum of the city. 'Now imagine only hearing a gentle stream or the song of a bird. It actually consumes a surprising amount of energy to live within the chaos we've brought upon ourselves. I can assure you, however, that we weren't designed for this lifestyle. We were made to embrace peace.'

Samuel huffs, 'Ah yes, we are but grains of sand floating in the wind.'

She giggles. 'I'm serious. We are children of moonlight shadows and solar flares, and whether we reach the summit of a mountain, or drown in a river, the wilderness does not care. I think there is something immensely freeing about that.'

Samuel takes hold of her hand but keeps his eyes closed. She studies his gentle face, thinking that, perhaps, in the silence, she will discover who she really is.

'Gosh,' she says. 'In any case, I think we ought to go down and wait for Father to come home.' The two of them go downstairs, and she gestures for him to sit next to her on the couch. He caresses her hair after she rests her head on his lap, and he occasionally places a gentle kiss on her ear. She secretly hopes that her father will be late. Her body feels like jelly, yet at the same time, her skin tingles.

The next thing, the door opens, and she blinks widely, realising that she had begun to fall asleep. 'Father!' She jumps to her feet, getting an enormous head rush in the process, but manages to stagger over to him for a hug.

'Are you alright, sweetie?' he asks. Lucinda smiles and nods.

Samuel stands up as well. 'Evening Jonathan,' he says. She knows Father asked Samuel to call him Jonathan, though can tell he finds it foreign to do so. 'I hope you don't mind me visiting.'

'You're just the person I'd like to see. Lucinda is welcome to have you over for dinner whenever she wishes.'

'Thank you,' says Samuel. 'I'll be sure to help out with the cooking to make it worthwhile.' Jonathan nods, knowing that Samuel wouldn't have it any other way.

BUZZING

46 SAMUEL

'I *was told that you passed* all of your subjects, Samuel,' says Lucinda's father.

The three of us are sitting at the opposite end of the table from when I last was here. We have each been given a glass of wine. I notice that Lucinda takes a sip of wine whenever I do but never reaches for the glass herself. Perhaps it's because of her father's watchful eye. Lucinda, up until this point, had managed to keep the conversation going quite nicely. 'I am aware that you are experiencing financial difficulties,' he continues. At first, I am surprised by him bringing this up, though I figure Lucinda spilt the beans.

'That is, unfortunately, the case,' I say hesitantly, not quite knowing what to add.

'Well then, what do you say to this proposal: I pay for your final year at university on the condition that you work off the bill at my firm. We can place you in a sector that involves biology so that you can gain some work experience as well.' My face lights up. 'I can't guarantee an interesting job, but it will allow you to finish your degree.'

'Mr Perdita, I cannot tell you how grateful I am. I don't know what to say.' Inside, I feel very guilty and perhaps unworthy. I just met him and he's being awfully generous.'

'You need not say a thing. I see it my duty to help capable people achieve their greatest potential.'

I feel like I'm on the verge of tears, though I daren't let myself cry. 'I will forever be indebted to you,' I say.

'It's no skin off my nose. Don't worry about it.' Jonathan looks pleased with his decision.

'Next year no longer feels so daunting.'

'I'm glad,' says Lucinda. 'I'm sure it ought to be a little more smooth sailing than this year was.' Her eyes smile over the top of the wine glass, cupped in her palms.

After dinner, Lucinda and I go up to her room and sit on the floor. She thinks that we need a compass if we are to find our way through the mountains, but I know that we'd get by just fine using the north star. 'It'd be more of an authentic wilderness experience,' I tell her.

'Well, I suppose that getting lost is the least of our concerns,' she says. I'm mildly surprised. 'There's dehydration, hyperthermia, snakes— '

'Snakes!'

'There ought to be, yes,' she says.

'I've always wanted to see a snake in the wild.' I can see it's not what she was expecting me to say.

'I'm sure we'll see one, in that case,' she tells me. 'If one looks in the right places, they do tend to show themselves.' She ruffles my hair. 'I guess if you're confident enough in your astronomy, then I'll be as well.'

By the time we step outside, it's dark and quite cold, though Lucinda doesn't seem to mind. We walk down the sidewalk for some time, heading back to my house. She's so engrossed by the list that she almost bumps right into the bench, though I nudge her out of its way. She takes my hand, and we sit down together.

'I think we've accounted for almost everything,' she says. She and I flick through the crossed-out items. At that point, we notice droplets falling on the page.

'Should we go?' I ask. The rain feels like tiny icicles on my skin. Lucinda's eyes are closed. The water trickles down her face, and her hair conjoins into thicker strands.

'Let's just stay here for a bit.' She squeezes my hand. I see a flash of lightning over the rooftops, and after a moment of silence, the thunder shakes the air. We both jolt simultaneously. 'It scares me,' she says, 'though I sometimes grow fond of the things which do.'

PROSPECT

47 LUCINDA

The following day, a deep, mechanical rumbling is what gets me to open my eyes. Something pricks my skin. I had fallen asleep with the notebook in my arms. I take it with me, tiptoeing towards the window. There is a truck parked outside of our house. I hop along the passage, tying the cincture of my robe on the way, curious to discover the rationale for it all.

Father is at the table, sipping at a cup of coffee and reading the newspaper.

'Morning, Father,' I say. 'I don't suppose you're going to work today.' It's already far past the time he's usually off to the office.

'No,' he says, eyeing me out for a few moments. 'I'm here to facilitate a few things, actually.'

'What sort of things?' I pull out a chair at the table.

'The two of us are to embark on a new chapter in our lives, Lucinda,' he says.

'The two of us?' I ask, inquisitive.

'Did I happen to mention our extended family in Brazil before?'

'Briefly,' I say.

He breaks eye contact for a moment. 'They will soon become quite significant to you and me. It was wrong not to have kept in touch.'

'I'm sure they'd understand,' I say, heartfelt. I know I'd understand if someone were to do something out of the blue after a loss.

'Even so,' he says, 'I see it fit for the two of us to make amends. We will reunite with them.' My fingers run over the corner of the notebook.

'You mean for a visit?' I ask.

'Not a visit, dear,' he says. 'We are to immigrate to Brazil. Your mother knew my family, and I would like that for you as well.'

'When?' I say, in fear that it came off cold.

'The first flight is scheduled for the day after tomorrow. It will take us from Wales to Spain. Then we're off to Rio, crossing the Atlantic Ocean. Soon after, we'll make the last connecting flight to Brazil. Most of our things will be shipped in due course to our new place of living, but I'd like you to choose only your necessary belongings.'

I stare ahead, entirely disconnected from my surroundings, subsequently finding small, rectangular papers on the table. The kind with a barcode and destination: flight tickets. Only two of them. Father goes on about something else, though I struggle to understand. '…is also a huge opportunity for eco-tourism. I'm going to find myself a job as a guide for nature enthusiasts and—'

'I'm glad, Father,' I say. 'It's what you've always, forever dreamed of.' What I said must have come across as peculiar; it'd have been better had I not spoken. I can't begin to grasp the implications of immigrating. It's too soon. It's the day after tomorrow. How many days does that leave me? Three? But only two if you don't count today. Not to mention that—'

'Are you ok?' he asks. I don't try to reason. 'Lucinda?'

'Sure,' I say, already drifting back to the feeling of loneliness, of hunger, of yearning for companionship. Yet, I never used to see it that way. I was living inside a feeling I could never pinpoint because I had never known the alternative. Though now I do— I have to let it all go.

'Now, I don't want you to take this the wrong way,' continues Father. He says something else about change sometimes being for the better, but I stare out of the window, not wanting to be here anymore. I feel sorry for him. He probably didn't know how I'd react to the news. I will myself to say something, yet no words leave my lips. I should be happy for my father, not sad for myself. Though, it's not only me. How will Samuel react? I don't want to know. How am I to break the news?

'Lucinda,' I hear, muffled. I didn't think I could hear something within my head so clearly. I hear my name again. It's father who's calling. I continue to say nothing. I can't say anything. There's nothing I could say that'd convince Father to leave me alone. I just stand up from my chair and turn my back on him. Even though it's not out of spite, I figure I'm an awful person for it. We have to go if Father is to pursue his dreams, yet all I can do is worry about leaving Samuel behind.

'Will we ever return?' I ask Father. I'm facing the empty passage. I can sense his eyes on me, and it feels like some sort of accusation. I wish for him not to look this way.

'To Xys?' he says. 'I doubt it, Dear. I don't think we'll be coming back here any time soon. We ought to start a new life in Brazil. Our family is in Brazil.'

'And what about Samuel?' I growl, looking over my shoulder.

'The promise still stands. I'll be working in the overseas branch from now on. He will be able to work off the debt here.' He pauses. 'We've been away from our family for long enough. It's time you meet them, Sweetie.'

Don't call me that. Only Samuel gets to use nicknames on me. God, I think I may be losing my mind. I knew this day would come. I knew that no matter what I did to prepare for what life would bring, there'd come a time I'd be lost. I stand there, knowing he is waiting for a response or at least some sort of reassurance from me. I want to say something to make it better. I should support the path Father chooses. Surely he knows what's best. But I just walk away; I step into the passage without looking back and without saying a word. I wish for him to know that I mean well but just can't tell him right now. The notebook, which I snatch from the table, feels foreign in my hands. I scamper outside, turning up the street. My palms rest on the bench. Samuel's house looms behind me, yet I can't decide whether I can face him.

I open the book and begin writing down more things for the trip. 'Torches, jackets, a first aid kit, for if anything happens to go wrong… which of course it won't… I'm sure that we won't even be needing that.' I scribble it out messily. 'How about a magnifying glass?' I ask myself. 'There're sure to be insects there… and I need… I need…' I breathe a few quick breaths tears stream down my cheeks. 'I need Samuel! None of it matters without him there.'

My eyes follow the streetlights down the sloping road, disappearing into the grey haze. I should be seeing him now, making the most of the last few days we have left. But how am I to tell him, after all we've been through, that we are simply not destined to be together?

I leave the book open beside me, curl up on the bench and begin to cry.

FRACTURE

48 LUCINDA

'Samuel. *I need to tell you* something important.' My voice cracks with uncertainty. The silence bears down on me, and so does the weight of the words I know I must say.

My hands cover his. They feel so warm, and I realise that mine are like ice, yet I know he doesn't mind; that he's come to love the way my hands feel, even though I may not. The persistent, meandering mist, curling around the legs of the white bench on which we sit, could not be further from the feeling of turmoil within.

'You can tell me anything,' he reassures me. I brush his hair aside, wondering whether he's mindful of my insides freezing over.

'My father and I…' It hurts to speak. The space around me feels so surreal. Perhaps it's just me wishing I could wake up from this nightmare.

'What is it?' he asks.

My gaze switches between each of his dark eyes continuously. Sensing his concern for me escalates my thoughts into worry. My vision floods and I bury my face in my hands. I can't bear the finality of it all. 'I may never see you again, my Love.' The words show themselves gracefully this time. It feels like I don't quite know what I'm saying.

'You may never see me again,' he repeats, as though in a trance. His eyes are closed now, but his lips tremble a little.

It begins drizzling ever so slightly, droplets beading on his hair like stellar dust. And now, the grey streak through the middle somehow gives me the feeling that a part of him had died long ago, as though he was made that way.

'We're leaving,' I say, as though I'm in a trance, 'flying to Rome, then Rio and ending up in the Amazon.'

I struggle to look him in the eye. His hands become fists, and he momentarily digs his nails into his palms. Anguish ripples through me at the sight of it. He then calmly holds me in his gentle arms, enveloping me in a wistful veil. I slowly take out the flight ticket and study it as though it's substantiating my own words.

'This is tomorrow,' he says. Flight number U347. 12 November 1975. Destination: Rome. 'You told me you wanted to travel to other parts of Europe,' he says, trying to sound positive. It's not enough to mask the disappointment in his voice.

'Not without you,' I sob, 'I would never have even considered that.' I wonder what he thinks of me leaving it to the last minute. Perhaps it's better that I only found out recently. I probably would not have been able to muster up the courage otherwise.

'Why do you have to go?' he says. 'What about your studies?'

'It's because my father wants me to get to know my family. They've lived in the Amazon for quite some time now.' I pause for a moment. 'If I had it my way, I'd say you and your mother should just move in with us. I'm going to have to transfer universities as well, I guess... I really haven't had much time to think it over.' I keep quiet for a while, trying to keep my composure. If this is to be the last time we are to see each other, he should remember me as I am. 'I don't know why it had to turn out this way.'

Samuel stares forward for a while. 'Who's going to take me to the mountains now?' he asks. 'I wanted to go with you.'

'I don't know,' I whisper.

'Are you certain I'll never see you again?'

'I don't know, Samuel,' I say. I grab hold of him, and he makes no sound, but I feel his tears on my neck.

'You've turned my entire being on its head,' he says.

'And you did the same for me. I'd never trade a single moment for anything in the world.' I whisper.

Even now, when he holds me tight, the drizzling sky doesn't stop my heart from fluttering in his faithful arms. His dead-loyal, adoring arms that I've come to grow so fond of. 'I made this for you to remember me by,' I say, reaching around the side of the bench to hand him the painting.

'It's beautiful,' he says. 'It's so lovely. I'll treasure it 'till my last breath. Your love for the natural world is so very evident here. I'm sure that you will visit beautiful places in the Amazon.'

'Promise you'll write letters?'

'Of course.'

I let out a sigh. 'Even though I may not remember my past, I'm certain you are the best companion I've ever had. I love you, and I'll never forget about you.' I give him one last kiss that momentarily takes me back to all the places we had been together, and every bone in my body is experiencing that very first moment: when I mustered up the courage to let him know I wanted to be his. Who knew that it was all destined to end so soon? 'Goodbye, Samuel.'

As I walk away, I feel as though I've betrayed my joy and forsaken his very existence, yet I know no other way. There isn't a way out of this. Love exists in a world that doesn't allow for it to last.

NIGHTFALL

49 LUCINDA

'Lucinda, we need to get going. It's nine o'clock already!' Comes a gruff voice. I rub my eyes, realising that it's Father standing at the door. I then spring out of bed in an instant, feeling a pang of guilt: I'm usually the one to wake Father up. He isn't all that good with those sorts of things.

'We had better make haste.' I say. Father dashes back along the passage. With that, I spring out of bed and proceed to slip on the dress I kept separate from everything else which had been packed up.

'Just take your carry-on luggage!' calls Father from the other room, 'We'll let the moving company handle the rest!'

'Alright!' I reply and grab my bag. We're both promptly in the foyer, with him dressed in a shirt and long pants but no tie. The two of us leave the house in shambles.

'Do you have the tickets?' I ask.

He waves them in his hand. 'The passports are in my bag as well.' I'm sceptical as to whether we'd make it to the airport and still check in before nine-thirty, though I don't tell Father this.

We half-run, and half-walk as the bridge approaches. I glance over my shoulder just to double-check I have the correct suitcase. Indeed, it's the one that contains my jewellery, Mother's photo, a few practical items and, of course, the necklace that Samuel gave me. It's surreal to think that the only place I've ever known will soon be nothing more than a memory.

Thankfully, we manage to wave down a cab within a block. We get in with our carry-on luggage. It's dark inside, but we can see the full extent of the city when we drive away. I can't even remember the last time I was in a car. I wonder if Father is thinking of the motor accident but I don't look his way. Instead, I stare out the window as we drive deeper and deeper into the expanse of the city.

Within a mile, however, all the buildings disappear and are replaced by open wilderness. The darkness is no more, with hazy light from above, and farther out lie the mountains. Their vast ridges look like waves; the rock is red and black. Patchy clouds above form areas of musky grey on the land below, but where the sun shines, so too do the rocks, their sparkling sheen like jewels… a treasure that I will never know.

Father seems agitated, frequently checking his watch.

'Do you think we're going to make it on time?' I ask. Father doesn't respond, seemingly preoccupied.

By the time we reach the airport, it's already nine-twenty-two. I barely manage to keep up with Father, who surges ahead. We go to the information desk to ask where the passengers for flight U347 need to wait. The lady directs us to another desk, where we stand behind a couple who are getting their passports stamped. Father still seems determined to get on the flight, even though I've long accepted it's impossible. We dash down another aisle and up an escalator, all the while incomprehensible announcements blare throughout the airport.

Despite our efforts, inevitably, the boarding gates had already closed. The two of us have to wait the rest of the day in our bare home. Father says that he's going to make a few phone calls to organise another flight as soon as possible and apologises for causing such a hassle. Naturally, I don't complain, figuring that it's tough enough for him as it is.

When I wake up the following day, I step outside and am greeted by a brisk breeze and a dishevelled newspaper on our doorstep. Upon seeing the front cover, I'm left paralyzed. It occurs to me that it may already be too late.

CRISIS

50 SAMUEL

I *find myself ruminating over recent occurrences,* unable to make sense of any of it. I never expected the holidays to be like this: alone in my thoughts. When will I accept the fact that everything has to come to an end? Nothing lasts forever; the passing of time defeats all. I was just being my naïve self, though Lucinda knew it. She could sense all of this coming. Perhaps that's why she was so calm about it, so prepared for our fate.

The work during the term was taxing, yet, somehow, this is worse: having nothing to do is far worse. I'm in my head constantly; there's no escape. I want to talk to someone, but I can't. What is there to say? To keep busy, Mum has given me all sorts of errands, upon my request, to keep my thoughts from spinning in circles. I look at the list, then at the assortment of vegetables in my arms. 'It seems this is everything,' I mumble and walk towards the tills, grabbing a newspaper on the way, after which I plan my route home. I've managed to avoid the park for the last couple of days. The memories are overwhelming, a stark reminder of what's missing. It's the same for all the places we had been together. They are no more; their essence drowned in longing, and each begs the question: will I ever see her again? She told me she didn't know the answer. There was a time I believed she had all the answers at her fingertips.

Just as I get called up to the tills, a newspaper article catches my eye: a plane appears on the front. Only it's a burning plane, and half of it is submerged in the sea. I read the headline: "TURBULENCE TRAGEDY IN THE ATLANTIC". My eyes skim over the article, stopping dead in the middle: "U347". I begin seeing the words in a blur. "South-bound flight ends in catastrophe... crash landing in the sea... heavy winds... communication failure... no survivors found". I look to the top of the article once more and feel faint, reading the four characters over and over: "U347". It can't be. It can't be that flight. I swallow hard. It is that flight: flight U347. She's dead. She and her father are both dead. And there I stand, pushed over the precipice of no return. I drop the newspaper; drop everything else in my arms too. The flour makes a mushroom cloud on the floor, and the jar of peppadews smashes over it, scattering triangular shards of glass among blotches of colour. At that moment, I could have mistaken it for a work of art.

A shop attendant storms up to me, starting to ramble away about damaged goods. This makes me take the wallet out of my pocket and throw all the money out. 'Have it!' I cry. 'Have it all! None of it matters. She's dead.' I turn on my heel, not even needing to push through the queue; they make way for me as I stumble out of the store and onto the road. I am the same person I was right at the beginning. I am Samuel, nothing more… I ceased to exist for myself. I existed for her. Now that she is dead, so too am I.

The ashen clouds are the absence of light. The wind chides me with its whispering howl, and I hate the air— the burning, sour air that scours my throat.

Across the road, I stagger, without looking, just like I used to, and before me stands the university building. It appears even more miserable than the day I arrived.

Upon entering, the snippets of chatter among groups instil nothing but emptiness, the same all-consuming void which was there before. I'm alone once more. I trip over something in the passage and fall flat on my face. It doesn't even hurt. I'm entirely numb. I rise to my feet, not looking back. It's all so dreamlike. Perhaps it's because what I'm feeling is far too real. I can't bear it. I simply can't.

All the lights and sounds surrounding me converge into incoherence. I float up the runs of stairs that seem to go on forever, ascending higher and higher and closer to heaven.

I exit through the fire escape and climb the second flight of spiralling metal stairs, and the way it echoes sounds like the remnants of her footsteps close behind. The heavens open as though weeping on my behalf, and the surface of the roof becomes glassy. My mind is taken back to when we lay here, gazing at the night sky. I had yet to realise that it would be both the first and last time. A second lightning bolt arcs across the sky with a crack that leaves my ears ringing. I thought I would be content; that I would find fulfilment. I was a fool.

Only now do I realise why she liked the rain so much. It's icy, and it's gentle, soothing even. It's like I'm holding her hands in mine. It occurs to me, the reason, that when drowned in the depths of her soul, I had found freedom. It was as though I never even existed; entirely liberated from the judgment I created, yet from which I could not escape. If she could visit the realm of the living for just a moment, I'd have her kiss my neck, and afterwards tear my throat out with her teeth, so I may never speak her name again.

My feet calmly take me backwards toward the edge, my heels suspended in the air. The upward draft makes me feel like I'm flying. My heart throbs in my chest, and my head is whirring with too many thoughts to comprehend. The horizon tips to one side, and the world starts spinning as I let myself fall backwards. The endless windowpanes rise above me. The passing of time slows with each consecutive heartbeat. Streaks of white and black fill my vision as the sky leaves me behind, and the ground rises to embrace me, to take me away to where I belong. Everything is going to be ok. I know it is. And then I feel it: the energy that surges through my chest, crushing me. The middle flagpole stands above me— through me with its crimson cloth still flying before the blackness beyond. I float inches from the ground, neither dead nor alive, neither still nor breathing; nothing more than a river of water and blood.

'I see you, Lucinda' I say. 'How is it so?' Her face is above mine, so close that I see the faintest of freckles, like constellations on her cheeks. Her hair drifts around her celestial gaze like a black sea. Droplets fall from the tip of her nose. Her gentle hands reach out and grasp my body.

'I am with you,' she says, looking at me with a warm expression. 'I said I'd never leave you,' she says, 'I promised.'

'I thought you were no more,' I say, with a certain detachment. 'I would have lived for you.'

'That you did,' she says, 'As I did live for you.' Her eyes shine grey, with a hint of sadness. 'Let me hold your hand,' she says, gently entwining her icy fingers in mine. 'Can't you see it? Why can you not see past this?' She reaches into my shirt pocket and removes my talisman. With a harrowing smile and a frigid voice as smooth as glass, she says, 'Don't worry, my love. Neither can I.'

Click-click-click-click-click...

DAWN

A desert engulfs a sun-bleached skull
An ocean sets ablaze an empty shell
In the warmth of winter, splintering winds burn
A fractured pocket watch with hands that never turn

I was once,
With childlike naivety
Oblivious to all that abolishes joy
Overseeing of that which I fear
Obstinate in my beliefs
And free

Yet now,
I see the rising sun behind a lightning flash
I smell fresh air clouded with ash
I hear nothing but a wistful moan
I feel nothing but alone

To you I plead, to you I pray
Fill my head with everlasting memories
Let the conch sing with the joy I once knew
Lead my heart to the warmth and light of day
And bring back the time I meant to spend with you

AUTHORS NOTE

'*If you can't love yourself,* you can't love someone else'— a very well-known proverb, and also, as Lucinda would put it, total hogwash! We will always have parts of ourselves we don't like, even despise. And this makes us unfit for love? I hope this book convinced you otherwise. If you wanted a "happily ever after" ending, this was probably not the right book for you. Such stories just never quite gelled with my personality. To be quite blunt, they piss me off; they're too open, too vague, and lack finality. For better or worse, my temperament is drawn to melancholy. It's sometimes difficult for others to understand how this can be so. I, myself, have little explanation for it, other than the fact that it just feels more real to me.

One thing that I learned in my Grade 12 year is that sadness, at its best, can be inspiring. I never chose to write this book. It was a need, an unquenchable thirst. Our shadow tends to surface one way or another.

Right thoughts, right words, right actions. Seems logical. Except it leads to the suppression of the shadow. It's amusing to watch people's expressions when you mention something real instead of affirming their flowery depiction of existence. The people who are closest to you, the ones you hold most dear, will most likely never understand even a fraction of who you are and the depth that encompasses your inner self. Why the need exists to have someone to walk hand in hand with your shadow remains a mystery. Perhaps it's because we, ourselves, struggle to accept the existence of these thoughts and understand their origin.

A great strength arises from harnessing the shadow. We lose irrational fears. What if that spider *actually* bit me? What if I *do* get robbed? What if I really slipped and fell off that cliff? What would it really mean? Is one's legacy something that's real, or a manifestation of primitive, irrational desires? You can feel into the shadow; become intimate with these possibilities. And suddenly their familiarity takes away their edge. We can accept the possibility of a black swan, giving it space to breathe instead of suppressing it.

When I was thinking about the two main characters, Samuel and Lucinda, my goal was for their characters to be non-conformists and plagued by, what they believe to be, their defects. They needed to be as flawed as they are admirable. I wanted one to feel their struggle and the impact the external world has on their psyches.

In some respects, Samuel and Lucinda can be regarded as two halves of the same person. While Lucinda has schizophrenia and anxiety, Samuel is living with depression and ADHD. More often than not, anxiety and depression occur together. Lucinda sees Samuel's identity as an outcast as a strength, and he admires her ability to achieve. Samuel sees his academic feedback as a measure of his intelligence but, even more than that, a measure of his self-worth. It creates an interesting dynamic in which Lucinda is his unattainable standard, causing him to act bitter towards her initially, but he grows to admire her for achieving what he could not. This may be true for many, especially if they tend to see the best qualities in others and wish for those attributes to be present in themselves.

It took me a long time to realise that neither intelligence, knowledge nor wisdom matter all that much. What would be a far fairer measure of a person's value is their capacity to show compassion, love and acceptance. Hopefully, the expression of love between these two characters has convinced you of this.